SILVER

STILETTO

CH00455501

OVER 100
GREAT NOVELS
OF
EROTIC DOMINATION

If you like one you will probably like the rest

NEW TITLES EVERY MONTH

All titles in print are now available from:

www.adultbookshops.com

If you want to be on our confidential mailing list for our Readers' Club Magazine (with extracts from past and forthcoming titles) write to:

SILVER MOON READER SERVICES

Shadowline Publishing Ltd
No 2 Granary House
Ropery Road
Gainsborough
DN21 2NS
United Kingdom

telephone: 01427 611697
Fax: 01427 611776

NEW AUTHORS WELCOME

Please send submissions to
Silver Moon Books
PO Box 5663
Nottingham
NG3 6PJ

Silver Moon is an imprint of Shadowline Publishing Ltd
Darker Dreams first published 2003 Silver Moon Books
ISBN 1-903687-31-4
© 2003, 2007 Tessa Valmur

DARKER DREAMS

BY

TESSA VALMUR

ALSO BY TESSA VALMUR
THE ART OF SUBMISSION
BOUGHT AND SOLD
DARKEST DREAMS
TANYA'S TORMENT

PROLOGUE

'It's all up to you. You may have told us how you want your dream to start, but how it ends, well... that's your choice.'

'You're absolutely certain?' Lara asked, dubiously.

The man nodded affirmatively, gave her a reassuring smile and leant back in his leather swivel armchair. Lara took a sip from the cup of coffee she held then placed it back on his mahogany desk. She re-crossed her slender legs, smoothed her short skirt over her thighs and looked thoughtfully at her hands resting in her lap.

'Would it help if you had another experimental session?' the man suggested, his tone was smooth and gently persuasive.

Lara had been soft sold plenty by professional gentlemen in the white jackets of consultant doctors. She had spent hundreds of thousands on keeping herself young and beautiful. At twenty six she had a body that any girl would envy. There had been an expression in the last century, something like 'money can't buy happiness'. But back then what could a girl buy? Breast implants, hair extensions, false nails. God how crude the beauty industry was then! Now, thanks to a few subtle genetic modifications to certain growth hormones, a little judicious laser surgery and a life of leisure and pampering, Lara at twenty six, looked like every man's dream eighteen year old girl. A perfect size ten, her narrow waist accentuated her generous breasts that were as firm and pert as a teenager's. Her legs and arms were slim and smooth; her skin a light chocolate brown with a coppery shine. Her hair fell in soft loose curls, the colour of burnished gold; the fashion colour of the moment, the summer of 2027. It fell almost to the swell of her firm and well rounded bottom.

Lara had, thanks to being a member of the super-wealthy, everything she materially wanted, everything she physically wanted... she had everything — except for the fulfilment of her deepest, most secret fantasies. Now, at a price, Doctor Patrick MacKennan of the Dreamscape Institute was offering her a chance to realise her most secret dreams.

'Alright then Doctor MacKennan, you've convinced me. I'm ready and willing.'

'Excellent. Shall we say tomorrow then at two in the afternoon?' the man smiled.

'I'll look forward to it.'

* * *

MacKennan read back through his case notes before bringing them up to date.

'Lara Lustral. DOB 2001, height 1.79m, weight 65.1 kg, social class Alpha 1. Dream test No.1 completed successfully. Client now wishes to experience full dreamscape. I will map and physically stimulate her autonomic nervous system with adrenal synapse focus and induce her desired dreamscape state. The client's first dream tests shows a deep physical and sexual frustration — in her dreams at level one she places herself in demanding physical situations where she is forced to struggle and defeat dominant forces. At level two however she is naturally sexually submissive but even in her dreams her social conditioning makes her reluctant to accept this. I will use electrode impulsing to stimulate her endocrine glands and the L2 computer will exaggerate her dreamscape by neurological messaging.'

MacKennan closed the folder of notes and slid it into a desk drawer. Call him old-fashioned but he found something deeply satisfying about old-fashioned pen and paper. And of course while any Delta class criminal or member of staff could hack into a computer that was programmed in Common Europa language, only a few Alpha class citizens could now write in English.

Lara Lustral was about to have the dream of a lifetime, he mused. Of course, in her dream she would experience whatever she wanted, controlling her dream with her subconscious aided by the computer. However, with her body wired up to the electrode impulser, MacKennan could interfere directly with her dream by stimulating or repressing specific glands of her endocrine system. He could also modify the computer programme to pull her dream in different directions. She would unwittingly be like a swimmer being dragged off course by a strong current of water.

* * *

How to spend the evening before the day of excitement? Lara mused, sipping some champagne and nibbling some delicacies she'd had her housekeeper make for her. She gazed around her apartment for inspiration but none came. She had planned to take a long, hot bath with some aromatic oils; relax then get a good night's sleep. But here she was at nearly midnight, too excited to sleep. She felt like a spoilt kid again, impatiently waiting for some presents to satisfy her. It was a feeling that she had frequently. She'd once overheard one of her servants describing her as a selfish and spoilt little bitch. Lara had to agree with the description but of course she still dismissed the girl.

After hours of daydreaming about what she might actually dream about the following afternoon when she returned to the Institute, she could stand it no longer. Her imagination crowded with delicious sexual fantasies, she rang her chauffeur and ordered him to be ready for her in ten minutes. Half an hour later he had dropped her outside a nightclub where she knew she would easily find some men to satisfy her needs.

'If the alarm goes off get your arse in here,' she warned, in her usual peremptory tone, glancing at the innocent looking ring she had slipped onto one of her perfectly manicured fingers. Her chauffeur nodded.

As was usually the case, the place was pulsing with barely contained sexual excitement and it took Lara no time to size up some men who looked just like what she was after. For the three men, the girl in the snakeskin, figure-hugging mini dress with the mane of golden hair was the answer to their dreams. Within an hour Lara had brought them back to another apartment she kept purely for such assignations. As she left her car in the basement parking zone, one man's arm firmly around her slender waist, she glanced back over her shoulder at her chauffeur.

'Wait for me,' she ordered, raising one cautioning finger to her servant. The smartly liveried young man noted it was the finger with her alarm ring and he nodded.

As he settled back to read a magazine and wait out the night in the car, he glanced in the rear view mirror in time to see the three men and his employer step inside the lift. As the lift doors glided shut he glimpsed a pair of impatient hands push the snakeskin dress upwards exposing more of his employer's shapely thighs.

Lara felt the heady, intoxicating mixture of excitement and sexual need rushing through her as she keyed her pass-code into the door lock and let the four of them into the apartment. It was not the first time she'd brought more than one man at a time back here. In her teenage days she'd been content with a string of boyfriends then as she moved into her twenties she'd sought more excitement. Of course as an Alpha One female, ordinary men treated her with respect and caution. One word of complaint from her and a Delta class man could face crushing fines or imprisonment. Her privileged position in society meant that she could happily play with Delta men then drop them once they'd satisfied her. Once in her domain they would always do as she commanded for fear of punishment at the hands of the élite-supporting, draconian authorities. Nevertheless as a precaution, she had the ring. If she pressed the gemstone three times in quick succession it sounded an alarm her chauffeur carried. Having an armed escort always at her summons gave her the confidence to play the sort of games that some people might describe as playing with fire.

The three men were all young, well built and mildly drunk. They told her that they worked in the construction industry. Lara liked manual labourers like these men; they were generally fit and pleasingly well muscled. Whilst one of the men began to strip off his clothes, his friends eagerly helped Lara shed her dress. In her skimpy underwear, she strutted across to the large circular bed, glancing back over her shoulder to see the effect her near naked body had produced on the three men. She dropped down onto the bed, turned onto her stomach and thrust her bottom up invitingly.

'Come on boys, what are you waiting for?' she taunted.

CHAPTER ONE

Lara settled herself back until she felt comfortable. The padded PVC was cool at first against her bare skin. The lights in the room gradually dimmed, the seat reclined, the young nurse smiled reassuringly as she began securing slender fibre optic wires to just above Lara's wrists. Lara watched as the wires were taped against her skin. Another nurse was brushing her hair clear of her nape and applying wires to her slender neck. There was the faintest hiss of gas as the door slid open and Lara glanced sideways to see Doctor MacKennan enter the room.

MacKennan moved across to the array of computer equipment that dominated the room. He settled himself into the chair that the visual display monitors ranged around. Lara saw him glance at her, his eyes sweeping down her prone body and she suddenly felt extremely conscious of the fact that under the white towelling robe she was quite naked, as instructed.

'Okay nurse, how long since the first sedative was administered?' MacKennan asked.

'Seven minutes Doctor.'

'Fine. Well Lara, everything is looking just perfect from where I'm sitting.' MacKennan glanced over the monitor screens and smiled at her. Lara saw his gaze lingering on where the towelling robe fell open just above the swell of her breasts. Lara looked at the two young nurses who were both watching her attentively.

Although both were doubtless social class Delta, they were well groomed and stunningly beautiful. Crisp starched white blouses, short white PVC skirts, flawless complexions and radiant blue eyes and blonde hair. Lara felt herself begin to feel sleepy but even as her mind became lethargic she found herself gazing more intently at the two young girls in nurses uniforms. Breast augmentation or genetic modification, Lara wondered dreamily, admiring the girls standing over her. They had no bras on but their generous breasts pressed firm and high against the material of their blouses, nipples and dark areolas just discernible.

'Now then Lara, time to sleep, time to dream...'

Lara closed her eyes and tried to focus her mind on what she wanted to dream. She knew from MacKennan's instructions and from the first test that it was crucial to slide into her dream without any outside distractions disturbing her last moments of consciousness. She had the start of her dream clearly mapped in her mind; it was based on an old film she'd watched on numerous occasions. The film had come out in the year that she'd been born. She'd bought it out of curiosity after discovering that she had the same name as the film's heroine. How she secretly envied the film's Lara and her action packed life!

'Are you ready to dream?'

'Yes...ready, doctor...' Lara answered sleepily.

Lara knew that MacKennan would now start to run the computer programme he had modelled on her dream wishes. Her brain would receive a series of impulses to kick-start her dream; from then on she would be in her own world. She knew just what she wanted from that world: the sort of adventure she craved but couldn't find in her own real life. Like last night, her little sexual adventure with those three men; that sort of thing but of course in real life it was so seldom perfect. But now, at last, she'd be able to have exactly what she wanted.

'Sweet dreams Lara.'

* * *

There was enough moonlight to see her way but it was dark enough to give her some feeling of reassurance. The night could hide dangers but it would also keep her hidden and since she was outnumbered she was content to slink through the shadows. Reaching the tunnel entrance Lara cautiously advanced. Under her boots the earth was soft and strewn with twigs which cracked ominously loudly in the stillness. The night air was cool against her bare arms and legs. In her black leather micro skirt and drab brown T-shirt she was dressed for efficiency not for warmth. From the belt around her waist hung two massive pistols in their holsters. She had a small backpack of equipment strapped across her shoulders and a second waist-belt strung with ammunition.

The tunnel was low and dark, the smooth stone walls cool and damp. Lara advanced with one pistol drawn, the fingers of her other hand trailing tentatively across the stone wall at her side.

* * *

MacKennan gave a malicious smile of satisfaction. On the two main screens facing him the two images now appeared identical in every detail. "Synchronisation Complete" flashed across the computer screens. MacKennan typed in "Control on instruction" and tapped the Enter button below screen two. "Control Off" flashed across the screens.

'Okay Lara, time for some fun...'

MacKennan lightly hit the Control button and leant back in his seat as "Control On" flashed over the screens.

Lara shifted slightly on the chair, her head turning and her lips parting fractionally.

'Let's get her prepared for stage two. Zara, slip her robe off. Suzi fetch the straps and restraints.'

* * *

The hall was eighty feet square, the high ceiling supported by a dozen giant stone pillars. A shaft of moonlight spilt pale light down into the centre of the hall, revealing a long wooden table set with high-backed ornate chairs and silver candelabra. A thick layer of dust lay across everything but the dusty floor was criss-crossed by numerous sets of footprints. Lara stood rock still in the open doorway, straining for any sound. She glanced at the faded tapestries hung on the walls and noted

12

that the double doors on the far wall stood ajar and that half way along the left hand wall there was another closed door. Very cautiously she stepped into the hall, her gun grasped with both hands, held before her at full reach.

Lara advanced down the left side of the hall, keeping her back close to the wall. When she reached the small door she paused, listening. Tentatively she tried the handle, which turned. At least that door was open, if she had to make a run for it that was one escape route, she thought. Letting the small door gently shut behind her, she moved on, keeping her back to the wall, her gun again held in a two handed grip at arms length before her.

She was two thirds of the way across the hall when the attack came and it was not in the way she had expected. She felt something sharp strike the bare skin of her right arm. Glancing down she saw a tiny, feathered dart protruding from her bicep. She flicked the dart out with one hand but already her vision was blurring. As she retreated towards the door behind her she felt her legs buckling under her. Another dart struck her thigh and a third caught between the shoulder blades. Stumbling and still holding her gun before her, she managed a few more steps before sinking to her knees. Out of the shadows on all sides figures emerged and closed in on her. Lara summoned the last reserve of strength she had and raised her gun with both hands, levelling it on the nearest figure. Her eyes closed and her finger went slack around the trigger. Her head lolled backwards, a dull pain in her neck making her eyes open. One of the figures stood over her and now held her own gun. She watched helplessly as leather cuffs were slipped around her wrists and fastened tightly.

'No, please...' she murmured weakly.

* * *

MacKennan watched with satisfaction as the two nurses carried out his instructions. Lara's arms had been slid out from the towelling robe, which now lay open, hanging redundantly

13

down the sides of the couch. Lara lay naked and asleep. He watched her arms slithering against the PVC as she tried to move them. Suzi had fitted supple rubber cuffs around both her wrists and these were now clipped to purpose made fastenings on the two top corners of the couch, holding her arms spread to either side above her head.

MacKennan turned his attention back to the screens. Maybe, he thought, Lara would like to dream that now, after suffering a little torment, she would break free. He watched Lara the adventurer on the screen regain consciousness then he glanced across to where his patient lay asleep. Well, with her neurons sending back messages to her brain that she couldn't free herself, her dreamself would be forced to remain bound and helpless. MacKennan smiled with satisfaction. He could now play with her for as long as it amused him, provided she didn't wake up, or course.

'Suzi, administer another ten milligrams of emothome.'

The young girl gave a dutiful nod and quickly prepared the syringe then administered the injection.

MacKennan felt his cock harden even more and press against his trousers. He glanced at the screen where the girl adventurer writhed and twisted helplessly as two young blonde girls tormented her. How amusing, MacKennan smiled to himself, she had incorporated Suzi and Zara into her dreams. Well, with a little judicious prompting it shouldn't be too long before I have the pleasure of her, he thought, tapping instructions into the computer then watching as a figure emerged from the shadows on the screen and advanced to stand before the bound Lara. The MacKennan of Lara's dreams was identical to himself in all but clothes and the Doctor gave a nod of approval.

'Now, Lara, what do you want to happen to you next?'

* * *

Lara looked forlornly up at her outstretched arms. The ropes were bound so tightly around her wrists they burnt and they were drawn so taut that her arms were held at full stretch, her feet barely able to touch the stone floor. The ropes were threaded through iron rings set in the ceiling and her arms were held outstretched.

The two blonde girls, who looked to be no more than teenagers, laughed as Lara groaned in discomfort, struggling to gain a purchase on the floor with her bare toes.

'Something wrong baby... feeling a little uncomfortable, are we?'

They each wore high black leather boots and short black leather skirts. Their generous cleavages were contained by tight black leather bustiers. One wore elbow length black gloves whilst the other wore delicate white lace mittens that left her long fingers exposed. Her nails, shaped like talons and painted blood red, trailed down Lara's arm. Her glinting blue eyes sparkled cold and cruel and her generous bow shaped lips were twisted into a sadistic smile as she stroked the end of a riding whip over Lara's bare skin.

'Poor little Lara has got herself in deep trouble, hasn't she?' the girl taunted.

Lara grunted with despair as the girl trailed the plaited leather of the whip over her bare back. She shook her head, hissing at the girl as the leather stroked from her collarbone down over her breasts.

They had stripped her completely naked and she could see her discarded clothes along with her guns laying in the far corner of the room.

'Keep your whip to yourself bitch or you'll be sorry when I get free from here!' Lara snarled defiantly.

The thought of the whip against her soft bare skin was too excruciating to seriously contemplate but Lara reassured herself she'd turn the table on her enemies soon enough!

'You'll wish you hadn't said that!' the girl warned, jabbing Lara in the ribs with the handle of the whip. Lara pulled and twisted frantically against the ropes but only succeeded in burning her wrists. The whip's tip trickled across her ribs and stroked up her back. Lara shook her head in frustration and gazed up desperately at her outstretched arms.

'Does this excite you? If I touch you like this...'

Lara shivered as the hard handle of the whip traced the line between the globes of her arse.

'Would you like to take it up your little pussy?'

Lara felt the handle rubbing her sex from behind, the warm leather teasing her vulva. She shook her head, clenching her teeth and shaking her head with despair, furious that she couldn't as yet free herself.

'Come on... relax... you'll learn to enjoy it, if you just let yourself go.'

'Go to hell!' hissed Lara, kicking back with all her strength. The girl behind her jumped aside just in time, giving a low curse as Lara's heel skimmed past her thigh. Immediately the other blonde girl stepped forwards, flicking a thin, short black rod from her belt. She grinned at Lara as she weighed the slender rod in her hand thoughtfully.

'Naughty girl...'

The girl's thumb slid across a button on the stick and it suddenly extended to about a metre in length. Instinctively Lara tried to back away but as the ropes became taut she knew with dismay that there was no escape from what was about to happen.

'I think we're going to have to punish you for that.'

The girl gave an insincere apologetic smile and stepped a little closer. Lara saw her give her wrist a sharp flick. The rod snapped across her ribs. A stinging blow that snatched the breath from her and sent stars shooting through her brain.

'See what happens to bad girls when they misbehave?'

Behind her the other gave a low throaty laugh. Lara glanced nervously over her shoulder and in the second her attention was turned from the girl in front of her the rod struck her again, its length slapping hard against her thigh. Lara gave a yelp of alarm and lunged forward, trying to kick out but the girl quickly stepped out of range. As Lara was dragged backwards by the ropes around her wrists, the rod flashed before her again.

'Oww!'

The pain washed through her body then quickly subsided leaving a stinging across her right thigh.

'Time to teach the bitch some manners!'

There came a sharp crack, pain like a jolt of electricity shooting from her rump to explode in her brain. She jerked herself against the ropes but there was no escape. The girl behind her flicked the whip again and it snaked through the air before licking like a tongue of fire across Lara's bare back. Howling with pain Lara struggled to turn to face the girl with the whip.

'Look out behind you darling,' the girl with the whip laughed as she retreated a pace and whilst she had Lara's attention diverted, her accomplice struck from behind.

Thwack!

'Oww!'

Lara stumbled and twisted, caught like a puppet by the ropes which held her arms outstretched above her head. The rod had sliced down across her bottom, a stinging blow that brought tears to her eyes. Desperately Lara turned back to face the attack.

'Which tastes sweeter Lara?'

As the girl with the rod smiled innocently at Lara and stepped back clear of the kicking range of her slender legs, the other girl darted forward. The whip hissed and bit across Lara's bare back, making her lurch forward and cry out in anguish. As she stumbled and struggled to recover her feet the whip thwacked again across her rump and she gave a howl of protest. Turning to defend herself against the whip, Lara suffered a muscle-numbing blow to the back of one leg from the rod. With a cry of despair as her leg buckled under her, she blinked back the tears and struggled to keep her footing.

Watching the spectacle from a short distance was the man,

his face impassive apart from the suggestion of a smile in his eyes.

'That pert little arse is of yours is just crying out for some tenderising!' One of the girls laughed. Lara struggled to turn aside from the blow but the whip came down with a sharp crack, the cruel leather burning a line across both globes of her rear and tearing a howl of protest from her lips.

'Damn you! Just wait until...Uhh!'

The rod struck against her belly, knocking the wind from her. For a second she hung her head forwards, gasping for breath, her eyes closed. A couple more blows from both rod and whip left her dangling from her outstretched arms, too dazed to do anything but hang helplessly as more punishment was meted out to her. After yet more strokes, the torment seemed to be concluded and Lara was left, suspended, dazed and sobbing, her young body throbbing from the succession of stinging blows that had rained down on her.

A hand caught hold of her hair and drew her head back. One of the blonde girls stood close before her, appraising her condition, smiling with satisfaction as she saw the tears streaking Lara's cheeks.

'Beginning to feel sorry for yourself? Want to co-operate or are you still feeling rebellious?' the girl taunted, lifting Lara's chin with the handle of the whip. Before she could answer the rod struck against the inside of her right thigh making her cry out in distress.

'Please... don't whip me any more, I'll do anything you want, just don't whip me!'

Lara looked around the room, frantically trying to work out how she could escape. She had to persuade them to untie her hands! Then she'd have a chance...

'Shall we untie her master?'

'Can we stretch her over the bench and torment her?'

The two girls stroked and caressed Lara's bare and trembling body as they spoke.

'Collar her then,' the man ordered.

Lara shook her head in protest.

'No... please...'

'Hush now baby, you'll like the feel of it once it's on.'

The blonde girl smiled mischievously and Lara felt a shiver run down her naked body as she stroked her face with one hand, the fingernails of her other hand furrowing deeply into Lara's mane of golden hair.

'Now, keep still.'

The soft fingers twisted and clenched in her hair, forcing her head still as the other girl sidled up behind Lara and slipped a broad leather collar around her throat.

'No...'

Lara tried to shake her head in objection but the girl tightened her hold and with her other hand she placed one cautioning fingertip against Lara's trembling lips.

'Hush now darling, there's nothing you can do to stop us, so don't even try.'

'Please... too tight...'

The leather was snug around her neck and buckled fast. The girl who had fastened the collar remained standing behind her, her breath warm against Lara's neck.

'Doesn't that feel nice?'

Lara trembled nervously as the girl's hands caressed her bare shoulders then skimmed over her skin until she could feel her hands lightly brushing her breasts.

'Get your hands off me!' Lara hissed, dragging her arms down against the ropes but unable to defend herself. The girl standing before her laughed softly and caressed her cheek. Her eyes sparkled, as hard and cold as ice.

'You've no idea Lara, what fun we're going to have with you.'

'Just wait until...'

Her defiant reply was never finished. A short, sharp pain stabbed into her stomach. Gasping for breath Lara felt the hands caressing her heaving breasts tighten their grasp and then squeeze progressively harder until she was whimpering

19

and writhing in an effort to extricate herself. The girl behind her pressed her body firmly against her back and the pressure on her breasts was increased. Gasping and shaking her head, Lara struggled helplessly for a moment then sighed with relief as the girl abruptly eased her grip and her hands travelled lower, the fingertips skimming over her bare skin until settling over the inside of Lara's thighs.

'Please don't hurt me...' Lara begged, blinking back tears and looking fearfully at the other girl who stood before her.

'Poor Lara, wishing you'd never embarked on this adventure?'

As she spoke, the girl reached up and stroked her fingernails firmly down Lara's outstretched arms. She groaned and twisted against the ropes that held her outstretched. The girl laughed throatily and stepped back to regard her. Lara shook her head despondently, sighing uncontrollably with shameful pleasure as the girl behind her stroked teasingly around her pussy with her fingertips. With a supreme effort of will Lara held herself in check from thrusting her hips back searching for more of the deliciously delicate touch that whispered around her sex

'Is that too nice? Would you like the feel of something else instead?'

Before Lara could respond the girl before her struck her across the belly with the rod and gasping with shock, Lara attempted to double over but her tethered arms prevented her.

'No! You can't do this to me!' she protested, weakly lifting her head and looking forlornly around her for help.

'Poor little Lara, has got herself in a lot of trouble of hasn't she? Come on baby, be a tough girl and take your punishment!'

Whack!

The rod hit her again and Lara groaned with agony. She twisted her hands, frantic to break free and defend herself but the ropes were tight around her wrists.

Whack! Whack!

Lara felt the rod against the inside of one thigh and then the other. Instinctively she tried to shy away but there was no escape and as if to reinforce the fact, the girl behind her brought the handle of the whip down cruelly against her bicep making her gasp in pain and her arm go numb.

'So, the hardened adventurer is already reduced to tears.'

The scornful statement was accompanied by another sharp blow against Lara's other arm.

'The bitch doesn't seem to have much fight left in her now.'

'Pity, it's always more fun to have them struggle when they're taken forcibly.'

'Never mind, let's get her onto the couch. She'll be more comfortable lying down!'

Lara lifted her head and through her tousled hair saw one of the girls loosening the rope around her left wrist. A moment later and she was on her knees, recovering her breath, the man standing over her.

'So Lara, you thought you could get the better of me?' the man laughed scornfully as he clipped a lead to the collar around her throat.

Lara looked up at him with anger and defiance blazing in her eyes. Her arms were both held outstretched to either side of her by the two blonde girls and when she tried to jerk herself free she was rewarded by the pain of a leather boot heel driving down against her right shoulder blade.

'Temper, temper... such a little vixen,' the man laughed.

'You won't get away with this!' Lara swore, struggling against the hands that held her.

'Teach her some manners girls.'

With the heel of a boot on both her shoulder blades now, Lara was driven face down onto the floor.

'Good. Now hold her still,' the man ordered.

Lara groaned as her arms were jerked backwards and upwards.

'Now then Lara, you've come looking for adventure, the question is are you enjoying what you've found?'

The man looked down scornfully at her, his arms folded across his chest, a smile of satisfaction across his face

'Well?' he prompted.

Lara gave him no answer but struggled against the hold the girls had her in. It was useless though. Apart from being able to slither her legs across the floor she could achieve nothing. When she tried to force herself up the pressure against her back was increased and when she threw all her effort into breaking free, the rod was lashed down across her prone body making her yelp then howl in distress.

'Lie still you silly thing or you'll get another taste of pain!'

'Maybe that's what she wants? Is that what you like?'

The rod struck her arse hard and Lara jerked against the hands and boots that held her.

'No! Please! Stop!'

'Let's take her across to the table. It's time for her to get a real taste of what she's been searching for.'

'No... damn you... let me go!'

Lara cursed the man as, with a wave of his hand, he signalled to the girls and they hauled Lara to her feet. Pulled by the leash she was dragged across the room.

'Get her over the table. It's what she wants.'

Lara swore and struggled as she was hauled backwards across a stout wooden table. The leash was slipped through a ring and drawn tight so her head was held down against the bench. With the girls still holding her arms the man then threw a waxed white rope around her slim waist and drew it tight with a slipknot.

'Uhh... damn you... no...'

Pulled down on her back with her legs dangling over either side of the table Lara kicked out at the man as the rope was drawn again around her waist then secured with a knot at her stomach.

'Now, now. Temper, temper!'

The man caught her ankle as she tried to kick him. Before Lara could jerk her leg free a rope was slipped around her ankle and drawn tight.

'If you're going to behave like some bad tempered filly,

we're going to have to hobble you!'

The rope was tossed under the table and retrieved from the other side. Struggle as she might Lara couldn't stop them from fastening the other end around her ankle. Her legs now held firmly against the sides of the table she knew it was only a matter of time before they had her completely bound and helpless. How the hell could this have happened? She was meant to have beaten her enemies and here they were humiliating her!

'So you thought you could stop me single handed?'

The man threw the question at her as a taunt as he knotted another waxed rope repeatedly around her right wrist.

'Do you know how many Alpha 1 class girls I've kidnapped and brought here? And do you know why?'

As he spoke the man fastened the rope around her wrist to the rope around her waist. Pulling the rope tight so that Lara's hand was drawn against her waist. She watched as he gave the rope's final knot a sharp tug to secure it.

'I'll tell you Lara. A dozen girls including yourself. You're going to help satisfy the barbarian nations' insatiable appetite for enjoying our Alpha girls!'

'You can't sell us abroad as slaves!'

Lara shook her head in protest as she was forced to watch her other arm being bound in a similar fashion. She jerked her arms with frustration and anger but the ropes kept her wrists tight against her waist.

'Oh no, nothing so obvious. I'm going to breed from you. Your fertilised eggs will be injected into replicant generators. In six months I'll have a dozen twenty year-old Alpha females ready for export. And six months later, another dozen.'

'I'm not going to let you get away with this MacKennan!'

The man gave an apologetic shrug as if to say he would have his way with her, whether she agreed or not.

'Looking forward to your impregnation Lara?'

Even as she was digesting the fact of what lay in store for her, the two girls set to work.

Another rope was looped around her right arm midway between her elbow and shoulder. After being tightly bound half a dozen times around her bicep the rope was pulled under her back and then secured around her other arm in a similar fashion. Both arms were now drawn firmly back against her sides and held securely against her body below the shoulders as well as at the wrists.

'What a pretty sight, a delicate young Alpha girl being prepared for impregnation.'

'Damn you...' Lara hissed defiantly.

One of the blonde girls slipped another rope around the back of Lara's neck and fastened the two ends into a knot above her breasts. The collar was then removed from her and Lara watched helplessly as the girl pulled the rope down to the end of the table and secured it to a steel ring. As she drew the rope tighter Lara was forced up into a sitting position then the rope was tied off. The tautness of the rope prevented Lara from leaning back which didn't bother her until she felt the other girl gathering her long hair into a single ponytail.

'Please...don't...'

Lara shook her head in objection as she felt the tension increase as her hair was pulled down and her head was drawn back. Because of the rope around the back of her neck drawing her body forward, only her head was now dragged backwards. She felt them binding something around her hair and then the tension increased.

'No more... please...' she gasped as she was now forced to stare up at the ceiling.

'Not feeling too uncomfortable are we Lara?'

The touch of the man's hand on her bare skin made her shiver but there was absolutely nothing she could do to object as he stroked his fingers slowly across her bare skin.

'You have magnificent breasts, so perfectly shaped...'

Lara swallowed the lump in her throat as she felt his hand gently lift her left breast, testing its weight with his palm. With her head dragged forcibly backwards it was impossible

24

to see what he was doing.

'Your body is wasted Lara. You have no permanent partner, a few casual lovers, what a shame its full potential is not realised. Well, there's time to change that.'

'What are you going to do to me?' Lara asked, her heart hammering.

'Do to you?' the man bent over her now, almost whispering in her ear, his hand stroking her exposed neck just above the rope.

'My dear Lara, I'm going to impregnate you with my own sperm then whilst I wait for the fertilisation to take effect I shall play with you for our mutual amusement.'

'Yours maybe... my amusement will come when I see you on your hands and knees begging me to show you some mercy!'

The man gave a cold, hollow laugh that sent a chill down her spine.

'Since you doubt your true desires, perhaps I should give you some truth drug, to coax your deepest feelings to the surface?'

'Go to hell MacKennan!'

'Girls, fetch my things, it's time for Lara to be impregnated and at the same time we may as well teach her to tell lies.'

All Lara could do to object was to shake her head, but with the ropes pulling her at equal tautness in both directions, her movement was severely restricted. Her simple assumption that MacKennan would take delight in physically driving his cock into her defenceless body was abruptly proved wrong.

'Hold her head still.'

Her thrashing head immobilised by the hands of one girl, Lara gave a choked cry of alarm as a slender rod of rubber coated metal was inserted into her mouth.

'No...nuhh...'

With the rod holding her jaws apart a soft tube was slipped into her mouth and Lara felt cool liquid trickle down her throat. A moment later both tube and rod were withdrawn.

'Excellent, impregnation complete.'

'What do you mean?' 'Lara gasped.

'The sperm you've been impregnated with are modified. Enzyme resistant, they'll happily swim through your digestive system. When they reach your rectum they will go through the capillaries there and straight into your uterus.'

'No!'

'Fertilisation guaranteed.'

'Damn you...'

Now, a little jab here, a few seconds' wait and we can look forward to a more candid conversation.

Lara felt the faint prick just above her collarbone and her stomach churned in nervous anticipation of what she would now say. The hard fact was that truth drugs, in an attempt to combat crime and extract confessions, had become highly refined and utterly effective.

'There's no side effects Lara, you'll be pleased to know. Perhaps just the tiniest bit of drowsiness and after a while an increased thirst. The drug I've administered is quite harmless and takes effect in a mere thirty seconds.'

'Please let me go, this isn't fair...' Lara tried shaking her head pleadingly but the ropes bound into her hair and around the back of her neck held her helpless.

'So Lara, tell me what brought you here?'

'No...'

'You have to tell me the truth Lara: now, what brought you here?'

Lara sighed, wishing she could close her ears to the questioning that she knew would shame her if he probed her until she was made to confess to her darkest desires.

'I wanted an adventure,' Lara sighed despondently.

'Good girl. Now, have I done anything to you so far that has hurt you?'

'The whip, the beating... the ropes are too tight... why won't you let me go?' Lara begged.

'Because you deserve this. And didn't you expect this might

happen to you?'

'Yes...' Lara sighed.

'So you knew what would happen to you if you became my prisoner?'

'I knew you'd torment me, only...'

'Only?'

'Only I thought that I could escape. But I can't!'

'Well, now you're trapped here Lara, tell me, do you find your predicament sexually arousing?'

Lara shook her head, too ashamed to admit to the truth.

'You have to answer me Lara.'

'Yes...' she sighed.

'Good girl. So would you like it if we sexually stimulated you even more!'

'Yes, I would.'

Lara glanced sideways as best she could as she felt the man's fingers stroked through her hair. He smiled down at her reassuringly.

'Tell me Lara, if I do this, does it make you more aroused?'

Lara felt the man's hand slide down from her hair across her bare skin. His fingers stroked her breast. He then caught hold of her nipple between his thumb and forefinger.

'Yes...'

'And if I squeeze a little harder?'

'Uhh...yes...' Lara sighed, closing her eyes and focusing on the sensation.

'Good girl.'

The man turned his attention to the two girls who stood watching.

'Bring me two needled suction clamps. It's time for these lovely breasts to enjoy an extra dose of oestrogen just where it matters.'

'Please... what are you going to do to me?' Lara cried plaintively.

'There's nothing to worry about Lara,' the man soothed, 'I know how figure conscious you are. You won't object if your

27

cleavage is enhanced a little more, will you?'

'No... I think I'd like that...'

The man gave a laugh of satisfaction as one of the two young girls handed him a fine cord. Lara watched in dismay as he slipped the cord around one of her breasts. The two ends of the cords were fed through a single ring then pulled tight, drawing Lara's breast into a bulging cone of trapped flesh.

'Uhh...'

The man flicked a little catch on the ring that stopped the cord slipping back through it. By the time her other breast had been dealt with in a similar fashion the first had turned from tanned copper brown to a deep crimson.

'The constrictor will contain the oestrogen to the capillaries of the breast. You'll only need to wear them for a few minutes. You can bear that can't you Lara?'

'Yes...'

A few moments later and Lara felt suction caps tighten over her nipples. The pressure of the vacuums teased her nipples into firm erections and then she felt two tiny pricks as minuscule needles pierced each nipple.

'Release her breasts girls, that's enough, the injections are working perfectly.'

The cords were removed, Lara sighing feverishly as her breasts were allowed to pillow again into their natural shape across her chest.

'Please Doctor... will you let me go now?'

'What's the hurry Lara? Wouldn't you like me to satisfy that little ache that you must be feeling?'

A fingertip touched her vulva, making her moan. To her shame she was moist. The finger moved across her soft wetness. Lara groaned with fevered pleasure. Her clitoris was already swollen with arousal when the finger stroked her there. She sighed uncontrollably as the man played with her, stroking her at first then rubbing her.

'Doesn't that feel good Lara?'

'Mmm... yes...uhh...yes...'

'So would you like it if we carried on with this treatment?'

'Yes,' Lara answered, shamefully aware of what she was admitting but unable to stop herself.

'Excellent. Well now, look at how quickly her breasts have responded to the injections. Zara, untie her hair for a moment and let her see how good her breasts look now.'

With the rope around her ponytail slackened, Lara was able again to look down. Her cleavage, which had been generous enough for such a slim girl was now even larger. The breasts though remained firm and perfectly rounded. Lara gazed in stunned amazement at her body then gasped as one girl lightly brushed her thumb over one nipple.

'Please...so tender...don't...' Lara begged as her other nipple was given a light experimental flick with one fingertip.

'They'll be very sensitive for a little while,' the man announced, 'so perhaps now would be the perfect time you to enjoy a taste of clamping and weighting?'

'No, please don't...' Lara shook her head, begging the man but her imploring gaze was torn from him by a sharp pull on her hair as her head was drawn back again.

'Relax Lara, you'll learn to enjoy this. This and all the other games we're going to play together.'

CHAPTER TWO

Doctor MacKennan looked down with satisfaction at his sleeping patient. Her naked legs slithered across the black leather of the couch, but their movement was restricted. Broad rubber rings were locked around her ankles. From each ran a fine cord and these were clipped to the corners of the couch. In a similar way her arms were held back above her head, her wrists pinned to the top corners of the couch. The young woman sighed in her sleep and tossed her head from side to side. Her generous, glossy lips parted, showing her perfect white teeth as she sighed in her dreams.

'You know girls,' MacKennan glanced up at his two nurses, 'it gives me such pleasure to see a satisfied client.'

MacKennan lightly trapped one of Lara's nipples between finger and thumb and applied a modest pressure.

The sleeping Lara moaned softly, her back arching fractionally, her body tensing for a second then going slack. MacKennan glanced at the monitor screen. In the dungeon-like chamber, lit by flickering candlelight, Lara the adventurer writhed and twisted against the ropes that bound her. MacKennan smiled as he saw what was happening to her.

'This woman has such a fertile imagination. I feel pleased to be able to give her the dreams she so badly wants.'

Lara's naked body moved fractionally against the leather of the couch, her breathing quickening as he gently toyed with both her nipples.

'I trust you're enjoying yourself as much as I am, Miss Lustral?' MacKennan smiled.

The woman spread across the couch sighed feverishly in her sleep but didn't wake as he increased the pressure on each nipple, squeezing each little cone of soft flesh between thumb and forefinger until they were swollen erections of hard crimson flesh.

'Okay Suzi, peg her.'

MacKennan released his grip and immediately one of the

nurses slipped a small steel peg over each nipple. The tiny springs held the jaws of each peg tightly against the trapped nipples, whose shade quickly turned a deep purple.

MacKennan stroked his hand down the sleeping woman's body. Her skin was warm and in places moist from sweat. With her legs gently spread, her ankles fastened to the corners of the couch, he was afforded a good view of her sex. He wondered how it would feel to slide his cock into her. Should he do it without her knowing, whilst she lay sleeping? Or wait and take her later? He imagined her struggling and writhing against restraints as he slowly helped himself to her defenceless body. She would be forced to wait helplessly as he took his time. Then there would be the satisfaction of seeing her expression as he calmly drove his cock into her.

He glanced at the screen to see the effect on her dream that pegging her nipples had produced and he smiled when he saw what she was dreaming. Such a fertile imagination... and so keen to suffer, he mused.

He admired her vulva; the exposed lips swollen and shiny with arousal. As was the fashion, Lara Lustral had removed all her pubic hair and he was afforded a perfect view of her sex as she squirmed helplessly in her sleep on the couch. MacKennan gazed down at her for a moment longer, the sight of his client tied in her sleep and writhing unconsciously made his cock ache exquisitely. Her taut stomach and slim body held his gaze, her breasts rising and falling, the nipples, trapped by the tiny steel pegs, held forcibly erect.

'Suzi, I need milking please dear.'

'Yes, Doctor.'

MacKennan slumped down on a reclining chair and rested his hands behind his head while his nurse unfastened his white coat and then his trousers. With practised ease she slid his trousers and pants down his thighs, over his knees and down to his calves. MacKennan smiled as he saw the look of delight on the girl's face as she regarded his cock.

As an Alpha 1 Class member and in the medical profession,

31

MacKennan had been able to indulge himself in the costly business of genetic enhancement. He glanced down to watch the girl as she caressed his cock. Even with both her hands around his swollen shaft much of it was left exposed. The tumescent head thickened as the girl furled and squeezed her fingers around the shaft. He felt his balls tighten, rising and filling his scrotal sac as she coaxed him towards orgasm.

'Very sticky... and so warm...' she cooed appreciatively.

Her practised tongue flicked against the head of his cock, licking and teasing. MacKennan sighed.

'I think the Doctor is about ready to come. Would you like to come now Doctor or shall I make you wait?'

'Now...' MacKennan sighed.

The girl opened her mouth wide, just managing to slide his massive organ into her mouth. Furling her lips around his shaft, she sucked. The effect was immediate. MacKennan felt his cock jerking madly in her mouth as he shot three or four jets of semen against the back of the girl's throat.

Still holding his engorged shaft with one hand, the girl drew her head back, a little milky fluid trickling from her lips over her chin. Very slowly she drew the back of one hand over her chin and then licked her lips.

'Is that all Doctor? Surely not?' She raised one eyebrow with pretend surprise and with his shaft still held in her grasp, she gently teased the rim of his cock head with her thumbnail. MacKennan sighed as he watched the girl, mesmerised by her skilful performance. Her grasp around his cock had not slackened and now she tightened her grasp around his shaft, squeezing until the cock head swelled and the purple skin shone, tight and wet.

'Uhhh... God, Suzi...'

She knew just how control him. How to interrupt his ejaculation and how to keep him suspended, on the brink of spilling more semen, but just unable because of the pressure she knew how and when to apply.

'Now...' the girl sighed, licking her lips, 'I think you should give me a little more milk than that Doctor,' she gently admonished.

MacKennan groaned, biting down on his lip and gazing hypnotised by her control of his organ as with her other hand she fingered his scrotal sac, trapping his balls and rolling them between her fingertips. MacKennan sighed, another jet of semen erupting from the engorged cock head.

'Now, just a little more...' the girl smiled before slipping the tip of his shaft back into her mouth. MacKennan felt her teeth catch around the rim of the swollen head and then her tongue flicked firmly against the very tip.

'Uhh...'

More milky fluid spurted against the girl's tongue that lapped enthusiastically now over the tumescent head, until every last drop had been coaxed from him.

Standing up, the girl smiled down at him, wiping the back of her hand across her crimson cheek.

'Shall I lick you clean now Doctor?'

'Thank you Suzi,' MacKennan sighed, closing his eyes as the girl knelt back down between his legs and devotedly licked the spilt semen from his cock. The sensation was enough to keep his erection from subsiding and by the time she'd finished, MacKennan was feeling the urge to take his other nurse, who had the better arse, bend her across his table and to ram his cock into her tight little pussy. Maybe later... he persuaded himself. For now he'd content himself with watching some more dreamscape viewing. He turned his attention to the monitor showing the adventurer Lara bound helplessly and suffering from having her breasts clamped. Perhaps, mused MacKennan, glancing down at his erection, he would after all relieve himself again by shafting a tight little pussy...

* * *

'No more... please...stop...'

Lara couldn't see what they had done to her, but she could

33

feel and it was more than she could bear. She jerked her arms ineffectually against the ropes that bound her wrists against her waist. God, the sensation in her breasts was agonising! She tried to pull her legs free but the ropes around her ankles held them firmly against the sides of the table.

'Please... too much...'

With her shoulders drawn back by the rope around her arms she felt her breasts thrust forward and cruelly exposed. She had seen how they had made them larger, the injections swelling them substantially. And now, she realised with dismay, they'd clamped and weighted her nipples!

'Stop it! Please...' she begged.

The cord bound into her hair kept her head drawn back, tormenting her terribly while her body was kept held in a sitting position by the rope round her neck pulling her forward.

'Good girl Lara...you're doing well,'

Fingers stroked her vulva then slid into her pussy making her gasp.

'Very wet aren't we? You can't help it can you? This is just too exquisite and you want to come now don't you?'

'Yes... uhh...yes...'

She wanted to deny it but the drug they'd administered coaxed the truth from her and her eyes were wet with tears of shame and pain.

'Okay then, you've been a good girl. I'll let you come and then you can have a rest before we play another game.'

Lara felt some cool gel being rubbed over her clitoris and she sighed as the pleasurable sensation it created washed through her.

'Feeling warm yet?'

Even as the man posed the question Lara felt the sticky gel warming her clitoris and then she felt a hot tingling sensation spreading through her.

'Mmm...too hot... uhh...stop it...please...'

Whatever the gel was that he'd applied it was making her clitoris swell and ache like mad. A moment later and she felt

34

her hips bucking, her arse grinding against the table as she tried to reach her climax.

'Desperate for it now, aren't you?' MacKennan smiled with satisfaction.

'Yes, yes... please...'

'Please what? Do you need to come? Would you like it if I fucked you?'

'Yes...please... fuck me...fuck me...' Lara sighed breathlessly.

'Okay girls, take the nipple clamps off, leave her on her back and pull her arse down to the edge of the table.'

Lara offered no resistance as, first, the pain in her breasts was relieved and then the cord in her hair was released. A second later and the ropes that bound her were unfastened from where they'd been secured to the table. They dragged her down the table by her legs which were then spread and bound, her arse left thrust out over the edge. Her wrists remained fastened to the rope around her waist, her arms further secured by the rope bound around her biceps. A rope was threaded through the collar that had been replaced around her neck and tied so that she was prevented from lifting her head more than a few inches from the table.

'Very wet... ready and welcoming!'

'Look how's she panting, she's desperate for it,' one of the girls laughed.

'Eager little thing aren't you?'

Lara felt the man's hands stroking over her exposed rump but with the collar around her neck fastened close against the table she couldn't lift her head to see what was about to happen to her.

'Fetch a silencer Suzi, I think Lara may soon be needing one,' the man ordered.

'You don't need to gag me,' she protested.

'Oh, I know I don't need to. But I want to,' the man smiled, 'you're desperate for a cock up your hot little pussy aren't you?'

'Yes...' Lara sighed.

The man's hands stroked and caressed her arse, kneading her pert globes of flesh and sliding his fingers into the crevice between them until his fingers sank into her sex.

Lara groaned feverishly, tossing her head from side to side as best the collar allowed. The fingers stroking her sex slid deeper and a thumb brushed firmly against her clitoris making her cry out in pleasure.

'Time to have your silencer fitted Lara, there's a good girl.'

Opening her eyes, she saw the two girls stood over her, looking down, one on either side of her. They smiled and one rested her palm against Lara's cheek, her thumb brushing a line across her trembling lips.

'Open wide.'

Instinctively she clamped her jaws together and shook her head. The girls laughed, their eyes sparkling with delight at the prospect of their prisoner resisting their efforts.

'Come on Lara, open wide, there's a good girl.'

Hands caught hold of her chin. She thrashed her head. Fingers meshed into her hair and held her head down firmly to keep her still. There was rubber pressing against her mouth but she kept her jaws firmly closed. One of the girls pinched her nostrils shut and when Lara was forced to open her mouth to gulp air the rubber gag was insinuated between her teeth before she could react. She shook her head frantically but already the broad pad of rubber had muzzled her. Whilst one of the girls tilted and held her head forwards, the other fastened the muzzle strap behind her head.

'How does that feel Lara?'

'Now for the best bit.'

The rubber muzzle had a circular opening in the middle and with Lara thrashing her head in a frantic bid to thwart what was intended next, a soft ball of rubber was fed through the hole. Lara gurgled in nervous objection as she felt the rubber sphere behind her teeth. The ball was connected to a rubber pad that loosely rested against the hole in the muzzle. The pad itself had a strap and like the muzzle this was now swiftly fastened at her nape. With the strap drawn tight the pad now sealed the muzzle snugly and Lara realised that not only was she gagged but that she couldn't breathe at all through her mouth.

'Does that feel nice?'

'Nnnhh!' Lara groaned in objection.

'Be quiet darling... or else you'll regret it.'

Lara glanced from girl to girl.

'Time for Doctor MacKennan to look after you now. Would you like to see the treat that the Doctor has for you?'

Lara's response was irrelevant. The man moved around the table until he came into clear view of Lara. The sight made her want to shake her head in disbelief. The man's genital organs were massive beyond belief! If he tried to shove his cock up her pussy, she'd surely faint! Lara jerked urgently but ineffectually against her restraints.

'Nnnh!' she protested as loudly as she could.

One of the girls smiled apologetically and gave a small valve protruding from the mask a slight twist. Immediately the rubber ball in her mouth expanded, quickly filling her mouth, pressing her tongue down and silencing her.

'Something the matter Lara?'

Lara blinked back more tears in dismay at her plight as the two girls watched her with undisguised glee.

'Well Lara, I'm sure you'll enjoy this as much as I will.'

The man moved back down to the end of the bench. Lara tugged her legs against the straps but without effect. She felt the man's hands stroke between her thighs. She gazed pitifully at the girls looking down at her, trying to silently communicate with them and beg them to intervene.

'You're going to love this, Lara.'

'Just what you're little pussy is desperate for.'

The girls smiled with obvious relish at her plight. Their wide, expectant eyes betraying their blatant excitement and delight at what was about to happen. Lara groaned through the gag, her limbs pulling against the tethers as she felt the

37

man's cockhead push open the lips of her sex.

As his cock drove its way into her, Lara felt her sex being forced to accommodate something thicker than she'd ever experienced. She shook her head in objection, trying to cry out but the silencer reduced her protest to nothing more than a faint and incoherent murmur. As the cock was slid relentlessly deeper into her writhing, tethered body, Lara strained to free herself but the ropes held her helplessly bound.

She prayed that the man would come quickly and her ordeal would end. In no time the sensation of the monster cock driving in and out of her slim young body brought her to a climax and then, as he continued to use her, she came again. Too dazed to struggle any longer she lay passively as the ordeal dragged on. The sensation of the cock ramming into her aching body was too intense and another orgasm washed through her exhausted body. Her sex was now so sensitive it ached and throbbed at each thrust from the cock that penetrated her so deeply. Please, she thought, don't make me come again, I need to rest!

'What a deliciously tight little thing you are Lara! And so compliant!'

The man laughed and drove his cock into her again. Lara twisted her wrists against the ropes, jerking her arms desperately. She felt the cock ease out of her almost completely.

'Just enjoy it Lara...just lie back and revel in the delicious sensations I can give you!'

The man thrust his cock back into her as far as he could. Lara shook her head in objection and struggled frantically to break free from the ropes that bound her.

'Girls, she's getting herself far too excited. I think she needs soothing down.'

The two girls immediately moved to stand close beside her and one caressed her face with both hands. Lara felt soft fingers slide through her hair and draw her head down firmly, preventing her shaking it in objection. The second girl twisted the little valve on the mask again and the rubber ball that filled her mouth expanded even more. The girl then stroked her perspiration-beaded brow with the fingertips of one hand while with her other hand she caught hold of the collar around Lara's throat and held it firmly down.

The cock slid from her aching pussy then promptly sunk deeply back into her. Lara groaned through the gag but no sound emerged. The cock withdrew and again was quickly rammed back into her. The four soft hands subtly tightened their hold on her. Her head held quite still so that she couldn't express her objection in any way, she was left gazing up forlornly at the two beautiful girls who held her, their icy blue eyes sparkling with amusement and excitement.

* * *

MacKennan withdrew his cock from the unconscious girl who lay strapped down on the leather couch. She had remained docile and sleeping throughout the time he'd used her body. As a precaution, in case she might have cried out in her sleep and woken herself, they had applied tape across her mouth. His two nurses stood beside the couch watching, clearly excited and revelling in the spectacle.

'Should I administer more emothome to keep her asleep Doctor?'

'No, let's give her the chance to surface from her dream. If she stays under for too long it can become problematical. Release the rubber restraining cuffs; remove the tape from her mouth and slip her robe back on.'

MacKennan sorted his clothing back into some semblance of order, left the nurses and the Dreamscape Institute's "Dream Theatre" and quickly made his way to his own rooms.

He had taken a risk of course of... a big risk, but there was no way she could prove anything. The nurses were bribed well enough for them to support him and whilst Miss Lustral remained asleep they would slip a vacuum catheter into her and remove all the sperm. No trace of what had happened would remain. The rubber cuffs never left any marks. The only thing to suggest to his client that she'd actually been fucked would be the physical ache left in her pussy from what he'd done to her. This would be put down in her mind to the vividness of her Dreamscape experience. MacKennan was pleased that even in her sleep state her body had recognised the size of his organ and the fact had been incorporated into her dream.

And then there was the ironic twist in the tail of course. After she'd woken up and had gone home, Lara would be left feeling that her imagined sexual experience was so good it had physically affected her. It wouldn't be long before she was back on the phone booking in for her next appointment at The Dreamscape Institute. Proof positive that however much she gave a show of objecting, she had wanted to be treated the way she was in her dream.

* * *

Lara woke to find herself still tethered over the table. Lifting her head she looked about her as best she could. The collar chafed her neck and her body ached from her physical exertions. Of the Doctor there was no sign and of his two female servants only one was to be seen. When she saw Lara had regained consciousness she came across to where she lay bound and unfastened the leash from the clip on the bench.

'How are we feeling now then?'

The girl lifted Lara's head by pulling on the leash.

'Please... I need to drink...' Lara begged, relieved to find that the beastly silencer had been removed from her mouth.

'Well, my orders were to wait until you woke up then take you to your cell. There's plenty of water to drink there, you'll find it constantly trickling down the stone walls!'

Keeping her arms bound to her sides, the girl released the other ropes and helped Lara slide herself off the table. Her legs felt unsteady and her body felt stiff and numb.

She was led by the collar and leash from the room and down a narrow stone corridor. After a short way they came to a junction where the girl turned left and led Lara down a sloping tunnel which soon levelled out and continued to a dead end. On either side there were half a dozen heavy wood doors, set in narrow frames. The doors were studded with iron bolts and each had a small iron barred window. As Lara was led past the doors she strained to glance inside and to her horror in each cell she saw a young girl. All were naked and some were chained to the walls of their cells. Some lay curled asleep on stale straw, one was manacled directly to a wall, another lay helplessly on the floor, limbs tightly bound with rope, a gag in her mouth.

Reaching the sixth door on the right, Lara was led into the cell. Her heart was hammering, she knew that in a moment the cell door would be slammed shut and she would be as helpless as the other girls. But she might still have a chance to escape.

'Now, one of us will be back to feed you later on. In the meantime you can enjoy a well-earned rest.'

As the girl spoke she looped the end of the leash through an iron ring set in one wall. Before she could knot it though Lara twisted her body sideways and delivered a karate kick that sent the girl stumbling backwards. Out of the open door in a flash, Lara stumbled, turned and fled up the sloping corridor, not even glancing back to see if she was being pursued. From the collar around her neck the leash streamed behind her. Her arms were still bound, she was lost underground, naked and defenceless but she was for the moment free! At last she had chance to escape.

* * *

The buzzer to her apartment front door woke Lara from a sleep of fitful dreams. She stretched, rolled over onto her back and slid her right hand between her legs. Damp and hot with arousal, she swore when the buzzer went again. She fingered her swollen clitoris and sighed. Go away, just go away... she willed, but whoever was ringing at her door was insensitive to her need to masturbate.

Snatching a discarded camisole from the floor, she slipped it on. Her silk panties she retrieved from under the duvet and in nothing more than these skimpy red lace garments she went from her bedroom to the apartment front door. The security screen showed a message boy with a small box. Lara smiled to herself and quickly thought about whether she dare do what had flashed through her mind. Why not? If he didn't wanted to play her game and he blabbed, she'd simply deny it. A mere worker's word against an Alpha wouldn't have any credence.

She pressed the lock release button. With a soft hiss of escaping gas the door slid open. The youth immediately averted his eyes and proffered a scan-and-sign form for her signature.

'You woke me,' Lara announced, her tone peremptory and icy.

'Sorry Miss. It is nearly midday. Special deliver items have to be signed for...'

'Don't lecture me, you cheeky little Delta class brat! One word of complaint to your employer from me about your insolence and you'll be jobless!'

'But Miss, I only...'

'Come inside and stop whining!'

The young lad obeyed her without hesitation. Lara closed and locked the door and looked him over. Not a bad specimen, she thought. A bit skinny and not long out of school but he'd do...

Discarding the package without even bothering to see who it might be from Lara turned on her heel and beckoned the youth to follow her. He came quickly to her heel and once they were in her bedroom and he guessed what she wanted, he needed no encouraging. It took only a moment for her to get him undressed and order him to lie down on his back on her bed.

'Not bad...' she smiled as she knelt between his legs, stroking

42

his thighs and watching his cock as if came to full thickness and hardness without her even so much as having to touch him there. When he reached out to touch her, she slapped him down then promptly she straddled his slim waist, her back turned to him. Smiling to herself she took hold of his cock with one hand.

'Just keep still boy and let me do everything,' she ordered.

'Okay, just whatever you say miss.'

Lara rubbed herself against the length of his shaft then, when she knew she was close to coming, she slipped the cock into her pussy. The youth gasped appreciatively. Lara rose and fell against the cock repeatedly until her orgasm was triggered. Her sexual thirst satiated she slumped face down on the bed.

'Let yourself out now,' she ordered dreamily, already half way to sliding back to sleep.

'The hell I will! You can look after me first!'

Before she could react the youth was on top of her, forcing his knees between her legs.

'Get off me damn you!'

When she tried to clamber from under him the youth caught hold of her hair and used it to bring her to heel.

'Stop struggling now Miss or I'll have to play rough with you!'

Will you now, mused Lara, smiling to herself.

If it was in no way as exciting as her dream adventure there was still nothing to complain about in the next hour. Because she continued to struggle and the young man couldn't keep her still, he used his tie to bind her wrists together. Lara was careful to seem to try to resist but without actually putting up such a fight that he gave up trying to beat her. She swore and hissed at him enough to prompt him to gag her. To her satisfaction her own silk panties were forced into her mouth then he finished the gag with one of her stockings. When she continued to struggle he knotted the sash from her bathrobe around her bound wrists and tied it to her bed-head so her arms were held. Sufficiently restrained, he then took her from behind, pumping his cock into her sex urgently until he came.

Lara was left still tied and it took her ten minutes before with her long nails she managed to prise her wrists free from the stocking he'd bound her with. Rubbing her wrists with satisfaction she went back to the front door, checked it was shut after he'd hurriedly left then after pouring herself a glass of chilled white wine, she turned her attention to the package.

The enclosed videotape was from the Dreamscape Institute, sent with the compliments of Doctor MacKennan, along with his bill. Lara slid the tape into her player and slumped down on one of her sofas, along with the bottle of wine from her fridge. In the three days since she'd been to the Institute she'd found it almost impossible to get rid of snatches of her Dreamscape experience. It had been so vivid and so close to what she had imagined she'd wanted...and yet...

On the screen she saw herself stealthily advance down a stone tunnel, gun in hand, dressed just like her namesake adventurer from 2001.

She had come back from her dream session feeling like she had really physically gone through what she'd dreamt. Back in her apartment she'd taken a shower and had gingerly felt her sex. She felt deliciously tender there, her clitoris swollen and her pussy slick with arousal juice. It felt as if she'd really experienced what she had actually only dreamt. Rubbing cleansing lotion absentmindedly over her breasts, her nipples tingled and she had gingerly examined them. She remembered in the dream they had done something to her, what was it? For a moment she'd stood under the hot water that cascaded over her, willing herself to remember. Yes, she smiled to herself; they had fastened clamps around her nipples and hung weights from them. She looked at her nipples closely. They were acutely tender but looked unmarked. God, how could a dream be so real it made her body respond like this?

Lara watched the video, riveted by what she saw. Her dream persona advanced cautiously into a large, pillared hall. She'd forgotten that bit. How much more had she forgotten? When her dream persona was hit by the first of the darts in her arm, Lara nearly choked on a mouthful of wine. She felt her pulse quicken as she watched herself fall captive then wake to find herself suspended by her arms, naked and helpless. By the time the film had run through her whipping and then being tied down astride the table, Lara was hopelessly aroused again. She lifted her legs and stretched them the length of the sofa. As, on the screen, her alter ego was suffering her breasts being bound with cord; Lara had her hand between her legs and was stroking herself with practised ease and skill.

No sooner was the film over than she had her phone and was calling the Dreamscape Institute. Her call was quickly put through to Doctor MacKennan and within minutes she had the satisfaction of knowing that tomorrow she could return to the Institute and experience another session.

* * *

'Forgive me asking Doctor, but don't you find my dream rather embarrassing?'

'Miss Lustral, after so long in my profession very little surprises me. You have sexual fantasies. We all have sexual fantasies. My job is to help you to dream them. That I happen to be in them is interesting but not disconcerting. Your dream is not so dissimilar to those of some other female clients of mine.'

'That makes me feel more okay about all this,' Lara admitted.

'Good, now lie back and relax so my nurses can fit the neuron impulsers.'

'Will I resume my dream where I left off?'

'Not necessarily. Nurse, give the patient the standard dose of emothome.'

'Doctor, in the dream, when I, I mean Lara the adventurer, was given the truth drug... is that...'

'You admitting your deepest feelings? Yes, I'm certain of that. Classic guilt displacement formatting. Deep down, you want to be treated the way Lara the adventurer was. Is that so unnatural?'

'Unnatural! Being that submissive! Surely, I...'

'Miss Lustral, you must relax now or your dreamscape will be severely disrupted.'

'Sorry, Doctor.'

'Nurse, give the patient another five milligrams of emothome.'

Lara closed her eyes and tried to relax. She felt so different to the first time. Then it had been easy to drift into her dream with the two nurses standing over her. Now though she felt so self-conscious. What on earth did they think of her dream? And what did MacKennan really think? It had been almost too embarrassing to return but the intensity of her dream and the desire to submerge herself again in that world was irresistible. After she'd tasted the experience of Lara the adventurer, being Lara Lustral was just too bland!

Lara opened her eyes and saw the Doctor looking down at her. He gave her a faintly disapproving look then smiled as if to reassure her.

'Stop trying so hard Miss Lustral. Relax. Don't try to sleep, don't try to dream. Just lie there and think about smells and sounds from the last time.'

Lara took a deep breath, closed her eyes again and inhaled. Her nostrils took in the smell of perfume from one of the nurses. She pictured her face watching her but remembered her not in her nurse's uniform but in her high black leather boots, short skirt and bustier. She took another slower breath and the air was suddenly cool...

* * *

The air was moist and damp. There was not a sound except for her bare feet on the damp stone of the tunnel floor and the continuous dripping of water from the ceiling that was getting lower with every step that she advanced. Instead of finding her way out of the dungeon she seemed to be going deeper

46

underground. Damn, Lara muttered to herself and turned around. She had been stumbling around for what seemed like hours and had almost grown accustomed to the dim light. The walls in places were covered with a moss that seemed to shimmer with a faint green light and sometimes there were tiny cracks and shafts in the ceiling through which light seemed to filter.

Turning back, Lara retraced her steps until she reached a crossroads where she stopped to get her breath back. Her arms arched terribly from being rope bound. She had tried several times to rub the ropes against rough patches of the stone walls but soon gave up. The ropes were too thick and she became quickly despondent. Perhaps it would be better to be caught again, at least she wouldn't spend the rest of her life wondering around lost and doomed to starve to death!

As if in response to her thoughts a sound from the left corridor startled her. For a second she was rooted to the spot with fear but then she quickly came to her senses and slunk back around the corner and out of sight. If she ran she'd be heard and chased. Better to hide in the shadows and keep quiet, she told herself.

The two men were clad in kevlar body armour jackets, combat shorts, heavy boots and visored infrared combat helmets. One held a dart-firing handgun, the other a truncheon in one hand and a coiled rope in the other. Lara cringed back into the shadows as they approached the crossroads.

The men glanced in all directions, seemed not to notice her and Lara was slowly letting out the breath she'd held when the man with the handgun suddenly swung around, aimed and fired at her before she could react.

The dart hit her squarely in the stomach.

'Fancy trying to run for it, or are you going to be sensible?'

Lara looked down the corridor and told herself there wasn't even any point. She rested her back against the cold stone wall and waited for the tranquilliser to take effect. It was almost instantaneous.

'Please... I won't struggle... going to faint...'

She slumped to her knees and looked up imploringly at the two men.

'Wait till she's out of it, then bind her ankles.'

'What's the Doctor's orders?'

'Take her straight to him. He's got something planned for her.'

Lara felt her shoulder hit the floor, as she keeled over. She lay motionless, gazing sideways at the two men. One knelt down beside her, looped the rope around her ankles and drew it tight.

'You've been a naughty girl Lara, running away. So the Doctor is afraid that you're going to have to be punished.'

Lara sighed, her eyes closing against her will and she was hardly aware of being lifted from the cold stone floor.

CHAPTER THREE

The shock to her senses jolted her into awareness suddenly and left her coughing and spluttering. Her drenched hair plastered her face and her vision was totally obscured. The icy cold water she'd breathed in seemed to explode in the back of her head like a bag of needles. The freezing water ran down her naked skin making her shudder violently with cold.

'Again.'

A hand at the back of her head pushed her face down and again she was submerged in the steel cold water. Lara struggled to pull herself free but her arms were held. Hands pressed her shoulders down. Hands held her legs down. She thrashed frantically but ineffectually. A hand tightened its grip in her hair and dragged her head back. Air rushed into her lungs. She coughed and gulped air desperately, not knowing whether she had a second or a moment before she might be submerged again.

'Feeling more awake now are we Lara?'

The sarcastic tone of voice was unmistakable — her enemy the Doctor. Lara nodded, gulping air gratefully and shaking her head, trying to clear her hair from her eyes. She couldn't see a damn thing... then as her senses cleared and focused she realised that she had been blindfolded. Sure, her hair was plastered wetly across her face, but also they'd covered her eyes, although she couldn't feel any sort of blindfold wrapped around her head. Lara shook her head angrily and someone close in front of her laughed, mockingly.

'Again.'

'No...uhh...!'

Before she could raise any more of an objection, her head was pushed back down and submerged once more in the icy water. A few seconds later she was hauled back, gasping, lungs heaving, water pouring down her mane of hair and running in icy rivulets down her neck.

'Feeling awake now are we, Lara?'

'Yes...yes...'

'Good. Well now, where shall we start? Looking forward to playing some games, Lara?'

Lara knew from the sadistic tone that she was in trouble and she struggled to free herself. Numerous pairs of hands responded immediately, tightening their hold on her arms and legs. She was lying on a bench on her stomach, her head dangling over the edge. Even throwing all her effort into breaking free it was hopeless. Momentarily exhausted she lay slumped and despondent.

'Can't you see that escape is impossible?' taunted the Doctor.

'No, I can't see a damn thing!'

Lara tried to blink but found she couldn't seem to lift her eyelashes. She twisted her head, trying frantically to get a glimpse of light to reassure herself that she was blindfolded. For a second a horrible thought crossed her mind and such was her alarm, she blurted out -

'Damn you, why can't I see anything!'

'Because you're blindfolded Lara,' the Doctor laughed.

'But...'

'Nothing to worry about Lara, little padded eye patches. Peel them off if they're bothering you: they're not that sticky.'

Lara tried to lift her hands to touch her face but her arms, like her legs, were pinned down by powerful hands. She managed to twist and slither her limbs a bit across the bench they had her on but her efforts to extricate herself amounted to nothing. At a guess four men must be pinning her down. She didn't have a chance... she gave up struggling, panting hard and resigned to whatever lay in store.

'You bastard...' she sighed.

'Now, now... don't let your hot temper get the better of you or we may have to cool you down again.'

As a warning the hand behind her head nudged her face downwards a little and her nose was just pushed under the water for a second.

'Alright... alright...please... I've had enough,' Lara conceded urgently.

'Good. Now my dear girl, my men are all very aroused by the sight of your deliciously curvaceous body writhing naked and helplessly under their hands. I think they would all appreciate it if you used that lovely mouth of yours for something better than swearing at them.'

'Well, they can take a hike!'

'Oh dear...'

Lara never caught what the Doctor said next as her head was pushed back under the water. This time she was submerged for more than the customary few seconds. Hauled by her hair back up, air rushing into her lungs, she quickly gasped her assent to their demands.

'So glad you decided to oblige.'

'I didn't have much choice!'

The Doctor laughed. They were fastening straps around her ankles and securing them to the bench. A hand stroked down her bare back and caressed her arse. Someone else was gathering her hair into a ponytail and binding it with elastic bands.

'Fasten her arms to the bench as well.'

Her wrists were pulled down and her arms pressed against the length of the bench's sturdy wooden legs. Wristcuffs were buckled around her and these were then roped tightly against the bench legs. Hands stroked her hair and face, tilting her chin up and she caught the unmistakable smell of male arousal close before her.

'What if the bitch bites?' growled a voice beside her.

'She won't do that... not unless she's very stupid. Imagine what punishment that would merit. You won't bite will you Lara?' asked the Doctor.

'No...' Lara sighed, all too aware that if he chose the Doctor could submit her to anything. She wanted to get out of here intact. If she had to appease them and play their games for the time being, she would. Her chance would come to turn the table on them, she vowed to herself.

'Come on then angel, get your lovely lips around this!'

An engorged cock was brushed against her face and Lara dutifully gave it an experimental lick. The man sighed in appreciation.

Blindfolded, her sense of touch and taste were acutely heightened. It was strangely arousing being forced to do this, she reflected. Cautiously at first she licked the tumescent cock head that was offered to her. She'd done this plenty of times before and once, a guy she'd briefly gone with had blindfolded her for fun. She didn't mind experimenting... and now here she was tied down and faced with having to do this whether she liked it or not!

The man's hands held her head encouragingly and she furled her lips around the cock head and sucked. This was easily the biggest cock she'd taken and she realised that like the evil Doctor this man was unnaturally well endowed. She felt the man's organ jerk upwards in her mouth in response, his fingers tightening their hold on her head. She would have liked to be able to draw her head back and just give him a few teasing licks with the tip of her tongue to contrast, but she couldn't.

'That's it bitch, keep sucking...'

The cock was pushed deeper into her mouth, the shaft pressing against her throat, making her want to draw her head back. It was an enormous thing and the more she tried to shy from what was expected from her, the tighter the grasp on her hair became.

'Good girl, good girl... come on now, keep sucking.'

The shaft thickened, filling her mouth, the smell of male arousal pungent as she panted air through her nose. The urge to gag grew overpowering but the man held her head in place relentlessly and when she tried to shake her head in protest her reward was to have it jerked back and fingers pinch her nostrils closed for a second.

'Keep sucking or you'll regret it!'

With the cock shaft practically filling her mouth for a second she could hardly breath and she urgently tried to nod her assent.

The fingers released their grip over her nostrils. Lara resumed her sucking and licking keenly obedient now. To her relief she felt the shaft begin to twitch and throb.

'Swallow it all now or your pretty face'll be back under the water!'

The fingers meshed in her hair twisted and dug, then the organ in her mouth erupted, warm come splashing against the back of her mouth and running down her throat. Lara swallowed dutifully, gasping now for a moment's reprieve. The man's sperm slid thickly down her throat, hot and salty and in copious amounts. She sucked and swallowed desperate to feel it come to a dribbling end but to her disbelief the cock was still pulsing madly and spilling more of the milky fluid into the back of her mouth.

It was impossible to shake her head, impossible to cry out that she wanted him to stop: impossible too that a man could ejaculate so much spunk! She jerked her wrists against the leather cuffs that were bound around them but the cuffs and the ropes kept her arms stretched taut and hard against the bench legs.

'Had enough Lara?' the Doctor asked, his cruel tone of voice heavy with irony.

The hands grasping her head eased their grip; the cock stopped jerking in her mouth. Dizzy and gasping for air, Lara felt the organ slip out of her mouth. Her jaws parted slackly, her head hung loosely over the bench edge. Grateful that the ordeal was over, she gulped air, her breasts pressed against the bench, her chest heaving painfully.

'I expect you were surprised by my guard's virility?'

The voice of the Doctor circled the bench and a hand, which she guessed was his, trailed over her back, down one leg and then followed a similar course up her other side.

'Yes...' Lara gasped, still feeling breathless.

'Genetics my dear. Just as I make sure that my female servants are the most perfectly formed physical specimens, I have genetically reared my own personal guards.'

'You mean... that you've...' Lara's dazed mind stumbled back to what the Doctor had told her earlier. His plan to breed from her and his other captive girls. He'd said he had replicant generators; that in six months he could create a twenty year-old girl. So the guards...

'My bodyguards Lara, are all my own design. Bred from my captive girls and genetically modified with an increased dose of testosterone to create a more powerful fighting male. And of course, as a bi-product a more virile one.'

'You're crazy...' Lara shook her head in dismay.

'No my dear, I am brilliant and to think you fancied your chances of stopping me!' The Doctor gave a contemptuous laugh.

'Now you've kindly serviced Mk1, I think it's time for Mk2 to enjoy the service you are so generously giving.'

'So you haven't even given your guards names! Just numbers!' Lara responded scornfully.

'Indeed. Well, you might say that Mk1 was the prototype; he was my first new recruit. You'll appreciate that the others are somewhat more powerful.'

'You mean...' Lara shook her head as someone caught hold of her hair. Blindfolded she couldn't see what was about to happen but she could guess and what was more she could smell, this man's arousal was even more pungent than the first.

'I mean,' the Doctor explained, 'that the others have been further genetically enhanced. Still more powerful.'

Lara's head was lifted back and a cock was thrust into her mouth. With her jaws fully parted, she could barely take it in and the sensation was too much for her. She groaned in alarm.

'Oh and of course, you'll find the Mk2 version and his successors are somewhat better endowed!'

'Nuhhh!'

The cock filled her mouth, the head pushing down her throat, making her gag. Lara tried to thrash her head frantically.

'Perhaps it's time for a little precaution.'

Lara felt a metal rod inserted into the edge of her mouth. Tiny metal plates pressed down and up against her teeth, a spring was released and their pressure suddenly increased.

'Uuhhh!'

Now her jaws were held forcibly apart. A hand grasped hold of the ponytail and held her head back and the hands that had been meshed into her hair now stroked her face, wiping from her cheeks the tears that streaked them.

'Come on little girl... the more you lick and suck the sooner it'll be over.'

Lara obeyed as best she could. She was shivering with nerves now, fully aware that there must be at least four guards. The thought that the others might be even bigger than this one made her imagine what it might be like if they decided to use her body in another way. The thought of their monster cocks taking her pussy poured molten excitement through her and to her shame she suddenly felt madly aroused by the prospect of what might lie in store.

'Good girl... that's it... keep sucking.'

Her arousal was reflected now in her eager and devoted cock sucking. She had no choice, she told herself. These men had her at their mercy, she would have to do whatever they demanded of her.

Abruptly the cock erupted, a fountain of hot spunk filling her mouth. Lara gulped it down and kept swallowing until the pungent flow abated. Without needing to be encouraged she kept sucking then she eagerly licked the massive cock head until she couldn't taste any more salty come and the hot shaft in her mouth was clean.

'Our darling little sex-kitten is learning to enjoying the taste of her new cream,' laughed one of the guards.

'Just as well, it's all she'll be fed on from now on!'

'My turn.'

For a second, as the spent cock was withdrawn from her mouth, Lara had a chance to beg for a moment's respite. But when she tried to speak the steel rod prising her jaws apart made her pleading words incoherent. The men laughed and without any further preamble another massive cock was thrust into her mouth.

'Wonder what the bitch was saying?'

'Probably, "thank you for the cream, can I have more please".'

There was a rush of laughter. Someone placed their hand between the globes of her arse and stroked her sex.

'Our little sex-kitten is wet. She's obviously enjoying all this attention.'

'Perhaps she'd like to enjoy some cock up her tight little pussy?'

'Not yet!' The Doctor announced sternly. 'Not until her fertilisation is complete. Once I have removed her fertilised eggs, then you can all have her. Besides, with the modified sperm, fertilisation will be accomplished within twenty four hours. Lara is doubtless as keen as you are but you'll all have to wait patiently. Can you manage that, Lara?' the Doctor asked sarcastically.

Lara groaned; her mouth filled with hot, hard cockflesh, her jaws prised and pinned wide. More tears of discomfort and anguish ran down her dirt-stained cheeks. She was breathing hard and fast through her nose as the thickness of the cock in her mouth made breathing that way impossible.

'Good girl, yes... yes...'

The cock she was sucking on spilt come down her throat in a long, continuous stream. The man sighed contentedly and withdrew his organ.

'Right, just one more Lara, you can manage one more can't you?'

The man grasping her ponytail pulled her head back, three or four times in quick succession, prompting a ripple of laughter around the table.

'See how eagerly she nods her agreement?'

'Good girl.'

Another cock was forced into her mouth.

'That's it Lara, lick and suck. Good girl.'

* * *

Doctor MacKennan glanced at the information displayed on the computer monitor and noted with satisfaction how Lara Lustral had quickly, subconsciously incorporated it into her dreamscape. He felt very pleased with how smoothly this client was shaping up. He looked up over the monitor screens. In the centre of the room, under a pale green light, Lara lay on the fully reclined dream-couch. The thickly padded PVC was shiny with her perspiration. The young woman's long eyelashes fluttered as she dreamed. Her generous lips were faintly parted and occasionally her head tossed from side to side. Without the gentle tap tapping of him using the keyboard as he programmed the computer, the only noise that filled the otherwise silent room was the woman's soft, plaintive sighing.

MacKennan left the desk and walked across to where his new client lay sleeping. Her towelling robe was still loosely knotted at her slim waist but hung open exposing her slender legs. The thick, fluffy collar was parted enough to show the generous curves of her breasts and the deep shadow of her cleavage drew MacKennan's eye hypnotically. The woman was breathing deeply and quickly. Hardly surprising, MacKennan thought, given what she was dreaming. Her mouth was fully open now; her head tiled back fractionally, exposing her slim neck. He watched the pulsing of her carotid artery. Strands of her long, golden hair lay loosely around her face, the tips of a few just touching her sensual, curved mouth. He gazed at her lips, parted, wet and shiny. The deep crimson contrasted brilliantly with her perfect white teeth. His erect cock stiffened and throbbed, pressing urgently against the fabric of his pants which was already sticky and damp with arousal.

MacKennan glanced across to where Zara, one of his two trusted nurses sat, supposedly watching a separate monitor screen that kept a check on the sleeping patient's vital signs.

Zara was watching him however. She was perched on the high swivel stool, one long leg elegantly crossed over the other. Her short, white skirt rode up her thighs enough to reveal a glimpse of the lace at the top of her stockings. She smiled at the Doctor and MacKennan smiled back then turned his attention back to his client. Lara, his client. Zara, his servant. Close in the sound of their names but utterly different otherwise. Lara, twenty-six, Alpha 1 Class: wealthy, spoilt, a frustrated natural submissive. Zara, twenty two, Delta Class: a penniless, angry teenager who MacKennan had picked up off the streets.

She had worked for him for five years now. He had invested a lot in her and his investment had paid off. She wanted what he could offer; her appetite for advancement was voracious. He employed her, tutored her, groomed her and in return she demonstrated total loyalty. She had also, from the moment he'd picked her up, demonstrated a penchant for sadism. She was just what he had been looking for. He had given her laser surgery and some beauty treatments that would have ordinarily been completely beyond her financial reach. All in all, in five years he had turned her into a stunning and sadistic girl: his perfect servant.

A sigh from the sleeping young woman drew MacKennan's attention back to his client. Her body shifted on the couch, she seemed to try to turn into another position but this was impossible. Her ankles and wrists were bound with rubber cuffs. Those around her ankles were clipped to the bottom corners of the couch and those around her wrists were clipped to sides of the couch. Lara moaned softly, her head tossing from side to side. MacKennan walked back across to the monitor screens to see what was happening to her.

* * *

The two guards dragged her by the arms down the dank, gloomy passageway. Lara, weak and dazed after her ordeal on the bench, tried to make her legs work, stumbling as they dragged her. They had removed the blindfold patches but strands of her tangled hair were caught in the sticky marks left around her eyes. After her legs being strapped down for so long, her muscles were numb and aching. It was all she could manage to clumsily lift her bare feet to avoid them being trawled painfully across the rough stone of the tunnel floor.

She recognised the passageway with the cells when they reached it and a moment later she was hauled into the only cell whose door remained opened.

'Pity the Doctor wouldn't let us screw her, look at her, she's just crying out for a good shafting!'

Lara was tossed down across the straw strewn floor. She threw her arms up in front of her face to protect herself. Her forearms taking a grazing, she lifted her head and looked around in dismay.

'Just look at her arse!'

'Just like her tits, nice and big but good and firm!'

Lara glanced over her shoulder, a lump rising in her throat. The two guards stood in the open doorway looking down at her. Both men were well over six feet tall, probably nearer six and half feet. Now, she knew why. The evil Doctor had created them — human they might be, but refined for his dark purposes. They both wore sleeveless kevlar body jackets, that Lara knew would turn a knife thrust and absorb gunfire easily. Their bare arms were powerfully muscled, like their bare thighs. From their combat shorts hung side-arms, knives, and belt pouches of equipment. They both exuded an air of ruthless physical strength.

'What about if we took her now?'

'And risk mucking up the Doctor's impregnation programme? Don't be stupid.'

'Nah, you're right. Pity though. What about if we use the girl in cell number four? She'll not know we're not meant to. She'd never think to complain and the Doctor hardly ever checks on her, anyway.'

Lara crawled further into the shadows of the cell, glad that they seemed to be turning their attention elsewhere.

'There is another option...' said one of the guards thoughtfully.

'Yeah?'

'Take her up the arse.'

Lara felt her heart hammer in her chest as the men swung their gazes onto her. She stumbled to her feet and backed up against the far wall.

'Don't you think she'd be too small?'

'Yeah, probably, but I'm sure I could put up with the discomfort!'

Both men laughed and stepped inside the cell. Lara slid along the back wall, shaking her head as the cell door was pushed closed with a solid thud.

'Okay angel, there's two ways we can do this: the easier way or the hard way. Which is it going to be?'

As the men advanced upon her, Lara wondered what chance she had of fighting them off. They hadn't locked the door, if only she could dart past them...

'Come here little girl, don't be silly now.'

Lara ducked and sprang aside as one of the men made a grab at her. The door was agonisingly close but the other guard was still between her and it. She had to think and act quickly...

She made a feint to the man's right and as he lunged to grab her she swung to the left. Had her foot not slithered on the straw strewn floor, she might have made it.

'Got you!'

The man laughed, his hand catching hold of her long, tangled hair, Lara was spun off her feet.

She landed sprawled sideways across the mouldering straw and before she could pick herself up the man sank his weight astride her waist.

'So it's going to be the hard way is it?'

She was pushed down onto her chest and lifting her face she saw the other man now crouched before her. He was fumbling in one of the pouches strapped to his waist belt

'Now, we don't want you upsetting the other girls, so...'

Lara tried to twist her head aside as the man produced a gag. With one hand grasping her hair to keep her head still, he forced the gag into her protesting mouth. Lara struggled to lift herself up but she was pinned down too effectively. The man astride her had grasped both her wrists and her thrashing arms were abruptly subdued.

The gag was a rectangular pad of rubber with a small ball in the centre. The man was insinuating the pad past her lips and up against her teeth and gums. The ball of rubber, no bigger than a plum was already between her jaws.

'Come on now angel, stop making life difficult.'

Lara shook her head frantically but already the gag was in place and a thin rubber strap was being wrapped around her head.

'Yuhh carn do sish to me!'

Lara protested through the gag as the strap was fastened at her nape. The man grinned and pressed his thumb against a valve protruding from the outer side of the gag. Lara groaned as she felt the rubber ball in her mouth expand.

'Nurhh!'

She looked imploringly at man knelt before her. He smiled and kept his thumb held down over the air valve. The rubber ball kept filling, pressing her tongue relentlessly down, expanding upwards against the roof of her mouth. She shook her head as her mouth became completely filled. The man removed his thumb from the valve.

'Alright then darling, looking forward to this?'

Lara looked pleadingly at the man as she was forced to hear her attempt to object reduced to nothing more than a faint murmur by the ruthlessly effective gag.

'Right, let's get those lovely legs spread!'

The man stood up and unbuckled his shorts, kicking them off over his boots. Lara watched as he discarded his pants and his massive cock came into view. Already almost fully erect it reared up menacingly and the man grinned as he saw her

61

expression of dismay. No wonder when they'd come in her mouth she'd had to swallow so much come: these men were practically hung like bulls! She writhed desperately as her arms were twisted and forced behind her back.

'She wriggles like a hooked fish! I'll hold her, you rope her.'

With both her wrists held pressed together behind her back, a rope was wound in a figure of eight around her wrists. She felt it biting into her skin as it was tightened cruelly and she thrashed her head, trying to cry out but she couldn't make any sound other than a plaintive mewing. The rope, now tight around her wrists, was pulled around her shoulders and jerked tight. Lara groaned, her bare legs slithering across the stone floor as it was then wrapped again around her wrists. She tried dragging her arms away from her back, up or down, but she could only move them a few inches and already her straining arm muscles were aching from being forced back and tied.

'There's no point in struggling, it won't get you anywhere.'

'Right then, lift her arse up for me, I'll go first then you can have her next.'

The man astride Lara's back stood up, turned so that he was facing her legs and scooped his arms around her waist. Effortlessly Lara was lifted so only her face and feet remained brushing the ground. She closed her legs defensively but the other man parted them easily and jammed himself between them. Lara hung, panting hard with nervous expectation. The massive cock head nuzzled between her spread legs and then miraculously there came a reprieve. A sharp beeping noise brought a curse of rage from both men.

'Damn it! Christ, what a time to get a summons!'

'Bloody pager! Bloody Doctor!'

The men dropped Lara to the floor, where she lay panting and unable to believe her luck.

'Wonder what he wants?'

'Better go and see. We can come back for her. Leave her

like that.'

'You just lay there darlin', we'll be right back.'

Lara lifted her head and watched the guards leave the cell, slamming the door shut and locking her in.

* * *

'I think we'll bring her to the surface and make sure she's enjoying herself.'

MacKennan smiled at Zara who now stood next to him alongside the sleeping Lara Lustral. He had no sooner programmed into the computer for Lara to get a brief reprieve than the guard's pager had sounded. Curious how the imagination interprets neurological impulses, he mused.

In addition to the electrodes connected to Lara's prone body he had attached a triple needled fibre optic tube that trailed across to a portable stand from which three drip units were suspended. Through the tiny optic needles he could now drip-feed his client emothone, Pro-oxygen and votrimal in controlled amounts. The former a sleep drug, the second a counter balance — stimulating the oxygen to the brain and the votrimal to create muscular relaxation.

MacKennan had programmed into the dreamscape the option for drugging to see how she would respond and he'd been delighted to see the results. In her first session Lara the adventurer had been administered a truth drug which had made her confess her desires. Content that he now knew what he was fishing for, MacKennan decided it was time to coax the truth from the real Lara.

'Right then Zara, give her five percent Pro-oxygen.'

MacKennan gazed at the supine young woman. Her slender limbs slithered softly against the PVC, restrained by the rubber cuffs around her wrists and ankles. He fingered the knot that held the sash around her waist. The towelling material parted easily and the robe fell open to reveal a body of faultless beauty, its curves dominated by the breasts: so generous they covered perhaps half of her rib cage, yet so perfectly formed they kept an almost gently conical shape even as she lay fully reclined. The areoles were a dark, coppery orange, the nipples a deeper shade still. The tanned skin was smooth and flawless and her breasts cried out for attention. Well, they would receive plenty in time...

The dreaming woman stirred; her eyelashes fluttering more rapidly, her arms pulling sleepily against the restraining rubber wristcuffs.

'Give her ten percent votrimal please, Zara.'

The nurse responded, adjusting the third dial on the dispenser. Lara Lustral sighed and her eyes flickered open briefly.

'Can you hear me Lara?' MacKennan leaned close to her and spoke softly.

'Yes...' she responded dreamily.

'Are you enjoying your dream?'

'Mmmm...'

Slowly her head turned in his direction and she opened her eyes again. Her arms twisted and pulled weakly against the wristcuffs. He was confident that she was too sleepy to even recognise that she'd been restrained. Her eyes closed again but he knew she could still hear him.

'Do you want to wake up now?'

'No...dream...mmm...'

'You want to keep dreaming?'

'Yes...'

He smiled with satisfaction. He loved it when he coaxed an admission like this from one of his female patients. Just as he'd suspected, he had another sexually frustrated submissive Alpha class female on his couch. Well, he knew just how to treat her to give her the satisfaction she craved!

'Are you enjoying your dream Lara?'

'Yes...so real... so good...'

'Open your eyes Lara, I want to check that you're okay.'

The young woman dutifully opened her eyes and looked up dreamily at him.

'What's happening...Doctor? Where... am ...I...'

'She's a bit confused; caught between her dream and consciousness. She can't distinguish between the two in her present condition,' he explained to his nurse, who stood eagerly watching.

'Doctor MacKennan?' the woman gazed up at him, blinking back her lethargy.

'Are you enjoying your dream Lara? The cell, the guards... you remember? Would you like me to continue your dream?'

'Yes, please Doctor.'

'Excellent. Close your eyes then.'

MacKennan walked back across the room to the monitor screens.

Lara the adventurer lay on the straw of her cell floor, her arms bound behind her back. She gazed forlornly at the cell door. Little more than the valve of the gag was visible but the rubber straps pressed snugly across her soft cheeks that were smeared with tears. Such a merciless gag, MacKennan rubbed his jaw thoughtfully. This young woman was giving herself a hard time. Most Alpha 1 women imagined gags of soft silk scarves but this one... this one obviously had a passion for acute discomfort. Well, she'd put herself in the right hands, he'd happily make sure she got the dreams she wanted!

'Give her ten percent more emothome and stop the Pro-oxygen.'

MacKennan strolled back across to the couch. For a moment he contented himself just watching his patient as she drifted easily back into unconsciousness.

'Okay, let's unfasten her and turn her over.'

His nurse worked quickly and calmly, releasing each of the four rubber cuffs before releasing the fibre optic connector. When Lara was rolled onto her chest she sighed and her right arm moved weakly towards her head of its own volition.

'I'll strap her up. Get the connector back on her and increase the emothome by five more percent.'

MacKennan lifted Lara's right leg and slid the rubber cuff

around her ankle. For a second he realised he was fumbling and hurrying unnecessarily. Relax, he told himself. Nothing was going to go wrong, even if she did start to wake up, she'd be too dazed to be immediately aware of what was happening.

With both her ankles bound and the straps adjusted to a satisfying tautness, he relaxed again. Zara had the drug dispenser reconnected and anyway, Lara Lustral was dozing happily. He left his nurse to finish securing Lara's wristcuffs whilst he watched the monitor.

Lara the adventurer, asleep on her cell floor, woke with a nervous start and gazed wide eyed at the cell door as it rattled then swung open. MacKennan watched the screen as the two guards entered then shut the door behind them.

Well Lara, you had your chance to wake up, MacKennan, unfastening his long white coat, smiled to himself. Discarding his coat he pressed a button on the side of the couch. With the faintest mechanical hum, the bench gently split in the middle and the rear section swung slowly downwards until it came to rest in a vertical position. Lara Lustral stirred and sighed but she did not wake although she was now bent at the waist, her feet inches from the floor, her chest still horizontal to the ground and her arse conveniently displayed and exposed just as he wanted it.

'Such an obliging patient...'

MacKennan patted the girl's arse then gently grasped a buttock with each hand. Slowly he slid his thumbs down the crevice between the two firm and perfectly rounded mounds of flesh. The generous lips of her sex were already protruding clearly and with a little pressure he was able to draw apart the globes of her arse and expose her anus.

'Zara, if you'd be so kind as to unfasten my trousers.'

The young nurse quickly moved behind him; reached in front and deftly unzipped his flies. Without unbuckling his belt or lowering his trousers she slid her hand inside his trousers and with her long fingernails released the buttons at the front of his boxer shorts. A second later and she had drawn his cock out. With a little more effort she managed to extricate his balls.

'Thank you,' MacKennan muttered his appreciation.

His aching cock, freed now from its confines, swelled to its full length and thickness, coaxed by his nurse's stroking fingertips. He gazed at the motionless girl lying before him. The sight made his cock ache and twitch expectantly.

'Doctor MacKennan?'

'Yes nurse?'

'Won't the acute discomfort make her wake?'

'The pain? Oh, the pain would normally make her wake, yes,' MacKennan answered. He brushed one thumb tip across the closed crater of her anus and nodded thoughtfully.

'But of course, that's what she wants to feel. Fetch some lubricant jelly Zara, there's a good girl.'

Holding the globes of her arse apart with his hands he watched as his nurse rubbed a greasy gel against the sleeping girl's anus. With practised ease the nurse used her thumb to press thick smears of gel into the anus. She then insinuated her thumb and twisted it around back and forth repeatedly, softening the tight muscle until it allowed her thumb to be inserted and withdrawn with relative ease.

'That's enough Zara. Go and increase the emothome by another ten percent. Keep a watch on the dream depth monitor. Any time she starts to surface increase the emothome by increments of five percent.'

MacKennan stroked his thumbs between the globes of Lara's rump then let his cock slide between them until the head came to rest against the anus. With one relentless push the crater of the anus was forced to widen and he watched the head of his cock slide into the girl's body.

'Uhhh...'

His sleeping patient woke suddenly, gasping, her head lifting abruptly, her body tensing. MacKennan glanced quickly to his nurse but she'd already responded and nodded affirmatively. With a quick increase in emothome Lara Lustral sank back into unconsciousness as fast as her head sank down against the padded couch. MacKennan smiled, pushed his hips forwards and watched the thick shaft of cock disappear into Lara's body. The tightness was exquisite; too exquisite... his hands gripped her arse as his embedded cock erupted violently.

CHAPTER FOUR

Lara shook her head imploringly. The men kneeling either side of her grinned maliciously. One caught hold of her hair and stroked it idly with one hand while his other caressed her breast, lifting it so he could appreciate its generous weight. The other guard was crouched over her, his legs resting against her hip as he searched through one of his combat jacket pockets. Lara knew there was no point in trying to evade them anymore.

For a few seconds, her arms bound behind her, she'd darted around the cell like a trapped wild animal before they'd caught her. With their combined strength, they had swiftly overpowered her. Now she lay on her back, her arms trapped under her, breathing hard and feeling like a hunted creature brought down by a pair of hungry predators.

'Here it is.'

The man kneeling at her waist produced a small silver foil-wrapped package from his pocket and gave a satisfied smile. Lara looked apprehensively at what the man held, swallowing nervously as he unwrapped the foil. She was breathing hard, still struggling to recover after trying to escape them. The gag made breathing through her mouth impossible and only able to inhale through her nose; she'd quickly felt out of breath. Seeing her watching him, the man smiled smugly.

'Wondering what I've got here?'

Lara timidly nodded her head.

'A little present for you.'

Before she realised what was happening, while the other guard held her head still, the man inserted two little cylinders of wadding into her nostrils. Lara looked frantically at the man who grinned and stroked her cheek.

'Don't worry, they won't stop you breathing. But the chemical they're impregnated with will make you nice and docile.'

'Yeah, we'd hate it if you hurt yourself, struggling

unnecessarily.'

'Alright then, darlin'? Starting to feel more relaxed are we?'

Lara glanced from one man to the next; she could already feel her arms and legs relaxing as they spoke.

'Okay then little girl, time to roll over.'

Lara sighed through the gag as the men lifted her easily and turned her face down.

Both men now stood up and discarded their combat shorts. The cocks were still thickening and lengthening as she watched. Their balls hung heavily in their scrotal sacs, at least twice normal size. The men gazed down at her and feasted their eyes, their cocks engorging in response to the sight of Lara's naked and helpless body. She tried to struggle to her feet but her legs wouldn't respond. She shook her head in disbelief and looked up as the men circled her. She glimpsed one man's cock as he moved past her field of view. It was hard now, the massive head glistening with pre-come fluid. It reared up, thick and dark red against his stomach. The brief glance she was afforded made her whole body shiver with nervous sexual expectation. These men's cocks were for certain too large to be natural. The evil Doctor MacKennan, hadn't been lying. He had created these brutish creatures for his own sadistic designs — and now they had designs of their own on her! Lara shook her head, moaning through the gag as a pair of powerful hands caught hold of her ankles and drew her legs widely apart.

'This'll make you nice and welcoming for us.'

A slippery gel was dribbled between the globes of her arse and then a pair of hands massaged and kneaded her buttocks, encouraging the lubricating gel to spread. Lara panted harder as her nervousness increased. She pulled feebly with her arms but they were securely bound against her back and her efforts quickly exhausted her. She felt she was inhaling through a filter, a filter soaked with some subtle drug that drained her strength and left her muscles feeling like jelly. This was so unfair... damn them...she sighed as thumbs now rubbed the sticky gel over her anus. She remembered the sight of the massive cock from a moment ago and she shook her head in protest at what she knew was about to befall her.

'There now... feels nice doesn't it?'

A thumb had insinuated itself into her anus and was rubbing more gel around her sphincter muscle.

'That's it, you just lie there and enjoy this...'

'Just what a horny little girl secretly wants, isn't it?'

Enough gel had been soaked into her anus now to soften the sphincter muscle sufficiently to allow two thumbs admission at the same time. Lara sighed through the gag, tossing her head from side to side. To her shame the sensation was deeply arousing and she was growing more excited by the minute.

'Feels good doesn't it?'

Lara groaned as both thumbs were pushed deeply into her rectum, making her squirm and try to arch her back. The men laughed with satisfaction.

'Reckon, she's desperate for it.'

'Well, give it to her then.'

The thumbs withdrew and without pause Lara felt the broad softness of a cock head push against her anus. With an easy thrust the cock drove into her, making Lara want to buck under the sensation. God, it was so big!

'How much do you reckon she can take?'

Lara was panting hard, her body quivering with fevered anticipation. The man had paused, just the thick head of his cock embedded in her and his broad hands grasped around her slender waist as, she guessed, he readied himself to thrust inside her.

'I reckon half and she'll be fully stuffed.'

'How does she look so far then?'

A hand caught hold of her hair and drew her head back so she met the gaze of one man. With his other hand he flicked loose strands of her tousled, golden hair clear from her perspiration-soaked face. Lara was forced to watch, unable to utter a word, thanks to the ruthlessly effective gag, as he stroked her face with his other hand.

'She looks like she's loving it.'

The man traced the line of the rubber pad inside her lips that pressed against her teeth and gums. He then gave the valve protruding from the gag a slight twist and with a hiss of escaping air, Lara felt the rubber ball in her mouth contracting.

'Let's see what's she got to say for herself.'

The ball quickly shrank and to her relief Lara was at last able again to lift her tongue that had been pressed down so mercilessly into the floor of her mouth. She gratefully swallowed some saliva and flexed her aching jaw muscles.

'Now then angel, you don't mind us playing with you as long as we're gentle do you?'

'Uhhh...'

It was an effort to clear her throat and speak with the soft ball dangling in her mouth, the rubber pad still jammed against her jaws. Lara groaned as the cock that was just penetrating her arse was nudged a little further into her.

'Mmmm...'

Lara couldn't prevent a groan of pleasure escape her. The cock pushed deeper. It was unbelievably exquisite, the sensation of her back passage being forced to widen so much, she'd never felt anything like it before. She sighed dreamily, her body was deliciously weak and the sensation of the man penetrating her arse was so good!

'You're enjoying this you randy little thing, aren't you?'

Lara sighed, nodded her head affirmatively.

'Good, 'cause there's plenty more to come yet!'

The man pressed his thumb over the gag's valve and the soft rubber ball in Lara's mouth quickly expanded. The man grinned, Lara shaking her head in dismay as he held his thumb over the valve until her muffled protest faded then became inaudible.

'Give it to her then; she's gagging for it,' the man laughed.

The cock embedded in her arse sank deeper into her prone

body. The sensation of being forcibly stretched made her pussy ache in sympathy. She sighed contentedly, writhing as the cock easily filled her.

'God, that feels so good!'

'She's loving it, the randy bitch, aren't you?'

Lara gazed dreamily at the man grinning at her as he lifted her head by her hair. The cock sank deeper into her and she groaned as she felt her back passage now acutely stuffed and stretched uncomfortably. She glanced up urgently at the man watching her and he smiled with grim satisfaction seeing her expression now change.

'She's game for more, give it to her.'

Deeper into her aching body the cock pushed and Lara twisted and struggled more urgently. Surely they could tell that she couldn't take any more of his shaft in her? She shook her head vigorously but the man didn't stop.

'God, she's good... so tight...'

The cock thrust even deeper into her and Lara imagined she was going to faint. Dizziness overtook her and her head went slack in the grasp of the man knelt before her. She was vaguely aware of the wadding being removed from her nostrils and then a sharp smell jerked her back into consciousness.

'Don't go to sleep now Lara, or you'll miss all the fun.'

The man held the little bottle of powerful smelling salts under her nose for a second longer then, satisfied she was fully awake, he slipped the tiny bottle back into his jacket pocket.

Lara shook her head as she felt the cock withdrawing from her body. She knew her ordeal had only just begun and to feel the cock pulling out of her aching body presaged only one thing... as it was rammed back into her she cried out frantically. Not a sound emerged. She gazed forlornly at the man watching her face. He knew just what she was thinking, just what she was wishing. Surely they'd show her some mercy...

'Good girl... feels good doesn't it?'

The cock withdrew almost completely then back it ploughed

into her. Lara looked abjectly at the man grasping her hair but he just grinned with amusement at her suffering. Rhythmically the shaft began pounding in and out of her, the man using her groaning and sighing with each thrust and each time he pushed a little deeper. It was too much: she couldn't take any more. Please...enough... Lara silently implored her assailants. Her prayer went unanswered though. The man had obviously recognised that his cock was far too big for her rectum and had tried to restrain himself to just thrusting half of the massive organ into her body. However, encouraged by his accomplice with each thrust he allowed his cock to push deeper into her. Lara would have tried to crawl away but she was pinned to the ground. She would have tried to push him off but her arms were tied behind her back. She wanted to tell him to stop now, that it really was too much for her but the gag was mercilessly effective. She shook her head urgently but the man watching her distress just caught hold of her hair and held her still. The ordeal went on and all she could do was gaze with tearful eyes at the man kneeling and watching her. Silently she begged him to make it stop. The man had her head lifted by her hair with one hand so he could see her expression. He was plainly enjoying watching her torment. He was her only hope and with her sorrowful eyes she pleaded with him to make it stop.

'Just a little longer Lara and he'll be finished with you.'

Lara gazed pitifully at the man and tried to shake her head in dismay. Sensing her attempt again to shake her head he tightened his grasp on her hair.

'Does it feel too good?'

Fresh tears pricked her eyes and she groaned through the gag as the cock drove relentlessly in and out of her acutely distended anus, the heavy balls slapping rhythmically against her pert buttocks. To her shame, mingled with the pain was a shameful enjoyment of what she was being subjected to.

'You're liking it, aren't you Lara?'

The man grinned at her and Lara gazed, nodding sorrowfully

at him as he stroked her face sympathetically.

'Take her deeper, she wants it.'

The man holding her head encouraged his accomplice and immediately the anal fucking increased in ferocity. Lara looked imploringly at the man watching her.

'Just what you wanted, isn't it!'

Lara felt herself fainting again and once more, as her eyelids closed and her head went slack, she was jerked back into consciousness by the powerful smelling salts.

'Oh no, we can't have you missing out on any of this. After all you wanted it so badly to start with!'

The man laughed softly, smiling with amusement at her distress and a moment later Lara felt the cock embedded in her aching body erupt, shooting copious amounts of semen into her.

At least now it was over, she sighed, as the cock was withdrawn from her. The man grasping her hair released his grip and stood up, grinning sadistically.

'Now, you can enjoy that all over again.'

Lara gazed in utter dismay as the men exchanged positions. She had no strength to resist and lay passively as her legs were easily pulled apart again. Fingers sank into her pussy, finding her wet with arousal and Lara groaned desperately.

'The randy little thing is loving this!'

'Give it to her then.'

Powerful hands grasped her hips, lifting her body effortlessly and dragging her backwards until she was impaled her on another thick, hard shaft of engorged cock flesh.

'God, that's good!'

This cock was thicker than the previous one and Lara weakly tried to pull herself away as it stretched her achingly wide.

'Come on darlin', don't be shy. You want it really.'

The hands grasping her waist drew her backwards and more of the shaft slid into her. The sensation was so intense Lara came, her body jerking and bucking as an exquisite climax shook her.

'Is that feeling a little too good for you darlin?'

The cock sank further into her arse then withdrew and was pushed back in again with determined force. Lara writhed and shook her head, groaning through the rubber that filled that her mouth.

'Just what a horny little girl likes you wants, isn't it?'

* * *

Doctor MacKennan and his nurse exchanged conspiratorial glances. Illuminated by the pale green light the Dreamscape sleep room was eerily quiet. The only sound was coming from the young woman strapped down over the padded couch. Through a broad strip of adhesive tape that covered her pretty mouth could be heard her muffled whimpering. Although asleep she seemed to be crying out in distress.

MacKennan stood directly behind Lara Lustral, his hand furled around a small rubber pump that was connected by a tube to a butt plug which he'd inserted into the woman's rectum after he'd withdrawn his own spent cock. Having pumped the plug up to a size he knew would force her rectum wide, he had flicked the switch that made the device vibrate. The butt-plug generally brought women who enjoyed such stimulation to orgasm within minutes and kept switched on would often force them to have a second and third orgasm, although after five or ten minutes most were begging him to switch it off and take it out. But of course, Lara Lustral was immersed in her dreamscape and she was gagged. Begging was impossible: both in her imagination and for real. For Lara there could be no respite: no escape.

'How many times has she tried to surface please nurse?' MacKennan asked his assistant.

'Four, Doctor.'

'And what level of emothome is in her blood stream now?'

'Thirty five percent, Doctor.'

'We can't give her any more, it's too risky.'

MacKennan crossed to the monitor screen. The second

guard was still relentlessly using the captured Lara. MacKennan adjusted the visual cursor to swing the dreamscape viewer so that he had a better view of Lara's face. She was conscious and clearly all too aware of every thrust of the cock in and out of her slender young body.

For a moment he became absorbed by the image on the screen.

The computer imagery constructed from his client's imagination was so real and vivid that for a moment he nearly believed his own eyes. Even sitting there in his Institute before his computer and able to glance across the room and see his client asleep on the couch, he could still believe, or almost believe, that she was really in the dungeon. So perfect was her dream in its presentation, that to all intents and purposes it could be real. She could be in that dank cell suffering at the hands of those two men. And the irony was that she wanted to be there. She had created her dream world. He had merely subtly modified it. Or to be precise: he had given her enemies a secret helping hand. Well, subconsciously Lara Lustral wanted to suffer at their hands, so if MacKennan gave them an unfair advantage, he was, he reassured himself, acting in his client's best interests.

MacKennan leant back in his swivel seat and drummed his fingers thoughtfully across the desk. On the monitor screen before him Lara the adventurer looked as if she was having another orgasm. Her body tried to arch, her muscles tightening, her eyes closed and her gagged face for a moment wore an expression of intense primal satisfaction. The man continued to pump his cock in and out of her arse regardless. MacKennan zoomed in on Lara's face. She had eyes open again now and it was clear that the man's relentless shafting was giving her as much pleasure as pain.

'What's her condition now, nurse?'

'Vital signs are fine, Doctor. She tried to surface again but she can't now. Not until the emothome level is reduced.'

MacKennan nodded and picked up a pen from the desk.

He pressed its tip down on the desk, letting his fingers slip down the barrel before he flicked it over and slid his fingers back down it again. He stood up and went over to the couch. The young women's body was bathed in perspiration. He ran his fingers over her delightfully firm and smooth bottom and pressed his fingertips around where the butt plug protruded from her anus. He could feel the vibration clearly. He moved his thumb lower and drew it across her swollen vulva. She was slick with sexual arousal. He hadn't bothered to count the number of times she'd come: her hips gently bucking, her body trembling. The delicious conclusion of her wet dreams: orgasm while asleep. What if he just left the plug in her and kept her emothome level topped up as necessary? She'd stay trapped in her dreamscape, enjoying her suffering relentlessly. What would she dream? That after the second guard had come then the first would want to take her up the arse again? Then after him his accomplice would take over once more? And so on without end? MacKennan slipped his fingers into his client's sex. She was very hot and very, very wet. And she was at his mercy. To think she was paying him for this! It really was incredible.

'I think nurse, we'd better give her a rest. Increase the Pro-oxygen by ten percent and reduce the emothome by fifteen percent.'

'Will that be enough for her to wake, Doctor?'

'Oh no, certainly not. I've no intention of waking her just yet. She's enjoying herself far too much. No, let's just give her a rest from her present suffering.'

MacKennan switched off the butt-plug and deflated it. Grasping the protruding flared end, he withdrew it from the young woman's arse.

'Give her a chance to sleep off her ordeal in her cell, then we'll see what she wants to happen next.'

* * *

As the assault on her aching body continued relentlessly Lara soon lost track of time and drifted in and out of consciousness. She was vaguely aware of more semen filling her then the cock sliding out. The restraints around her arms were unfastened and removed. She sighed and tried to open her eyes and focus but her body and mind were too dazed. The rubber ball in her mouth shrank; fingers prising the gag from her, the rubber straps slipping from around her cheeks. She lay, her face in the straw, gasping for breath and grateful that it was over. Slowly she recovered her senses enough to lift her head and focus on her surroundings. The cell was empty, the door closed. They had gone! With a grateful sigh, Lara sank her head into the straw and closed her eyes.

The clattering of the key in the lock and the door grinding open on its rusty hinges woke her. She had no idea of how long she had been left alone. She hauled herself up into a sitting position, rubbing her aching jaw as one of the Doctor's female assistants stepped into the room, flanked by two guards. They were the same two who had gagged and used her for their own pleasure. Now they stood to attention, clearly at the command of the sultry young girl in her provocative uniform.

The girl stalked into the room, the pointed toes of her black boots flicking the mouldering straw aside as if she loathed even stepping on it. She looked down haughtily at Lara, her steely blue eyes cold and cruel. Lara glanced at the two guards and saw one was gazing lasciviously at the young girl's smooth, bare thighs that were well exposed thanks to the shortness of her tight skirt of black leather.

'What a sorry sight!' the girl sneered contemptuously.

Her generous cleavage was contained by a tight black leather bustier. A broad, black PVC belt was drawn around her narrow waist. Slid into a holster was a truncheon besides which, clipped to the belt, a pair of wristcuffs dangled ominously. The girl wore long black gloves that fitted her to her elbows, the PVC glistening in the pale light. In one hand she held a blindfold and in the other a broad leather collar and chain leash.

Lara stumbled to her feet. Naked and bruised she knew how pathetic she looked in comparison. No wonder these brutish guards stood in awe of this young girl. But for her they showed such contempt. She had imagined that she could take on the Doctor and win. She'd entered his secret dungeon confident and determined. But she'd been too arrogant and now she was paying the price. Stripped of her weapons and clothes, she'd been stripped of her power and self-esteem. Naked and defenceless she was no more a threat than the other eleven young Alpha Class girls that the Doctor had abducted.

So just like them, he had impregnated her and thrown her in a cell. Worse though, he was intent on torturing her. He would use her as his sex slave while he bred from her. Unless she could find a way to mentally resist him she would end up submitting herself to him. Already though, she wondered if she had any chance at all. Maybe she deserved to be treated like this?

'Blindfold and collar her!'

The young woman snapped out the command, holding at arm's length the blindfold and collar that she had ready. The guards quickly moved to carry out her instructions and Lara knew that to resist was folly. Meekly she stood still, her head bowed as they fastened the leather collar around her throat and buckled it fast. Her head was drawn back, the soft darkness of the blindfold enveloped her and she stood obediently still as the material was Velcro fastened at the back of her head.

'She's starting to learn to behave properly. If I didn't know better, I'd say she's been having a rough time of it lately.'

There was a moment's silence and blindfolded, Lara could only guess at the exchanged glances between the girl and two guards. Did she know or guess what they had done to Lara? Before she had any more of a chance to wonder about the girl's complicity in the men anally fucking her, there was a sharp tug on the leash and Lara was jerked forward by the collar around her neck.

'I'm not even going to bother tying your hands,' the girl informed her in her icy, peremptory tone.

Lara stumbled forwards, her shoulder banging against the doorframe as she was led into the corridor.

'Owww!'

'Careful you dumb bitch! The Doctor won't appreciate you bruising yourself. He likes his property kept in pristine condition.'

The cell door slammed shut. Lara stood shivering, her bare feet in a shallow puddle of water. The cold stone underfoot was freezing and she began to shake with cold and nerves.

'Something the matter Lara?'

The girl drew Lara forward by her leash. She could sense the girl was close in front of her and she had a sudden impulse to bring her knee up into her pretty body and have the satisfaction of hearing her groan in agony. She fought down the urge to retaliate though, all too aware that the consequences would mean extreme suffering for herself.

'Feeling cold or feeling afraid?'

The girl was almost whispering. Lara could feel her warm breath against her face. She could smell peppermint in her breath and for a second the dank air smelt of her perfume.

'Cold,' Lara answered.

She could sense the two men standing close behind her and wondered if the girl was trying to coax her into doing something that would justify some draconian action on her part. She could just imagine her justifying her actions to the Doctor. "She tried to escape in the corridor Doctor. I told the guards to punish her but I never meant them to be so rough."

Lara stood rock still, her hearing straining for every sound.

'Would you like it if you were taken somewhere warmer? Would you like me to look after you Lara? Or shall we keep you here?'

Obviously a trick question, Lara decided and for a second she didn't reply. That was enough of an excuse. A stinging pain across her right breast made her gasp in alarm and clutch

81

her arms defensively across her chest.

'Answer my questions bitch! It's bad manners not to reply when spoken to! Do you want to be left here or shall I move you to somewhere nicer?'

'I'll stay here,' Lara answered, certain that otherwise she'd be letting herself in for something worse.

'Well then,' the girl's voice was sickeningly smug, 'Back to your cell then Lara, if that's what you prefer.'

Lara was drawn abruptly around by a pull on the leash. She heard the door grind open again and she was led stumbling back into the cell.

'You see Lara, whilst down here, all you pretty Alpha girls are in my care. You can look on me as your protector as well as your jailer.'

The girl's voice came from someway behind where Lara had now been led. She guessed that the girl had handed the leash to one of the men and she'd remained in the doorway. A sharp downward tug on the leash brought Lara to her knees. Thankfully the collar was so broad and made of such supple leather that it didn't choke her.

'That's it baby, on your knees. If you're staying here then you can look forward to us giving your arse another working over,' laughed one of the guards.

'No, please...'

Lara was pushed forwards. She put her hands out to break her fall. One of the men dropped down directly in front of her, his thighs astride her face. Before she could move, he pressed his legs together, immobilising her head. Frantically Lara clutched at his thighs with her hands, struggling to prise them apart and extricate her trapped head.

'Spread your legs for us honey, there's a good girl.'

Lara refused, crossing her ankles together and clamping her thighs together. There was a soft swishing sound and a sharp pain across her arse made her yelp in alarm.

'Spread you legs, Lara!'

Still she refused and again she was struck across her rump.

'Oww!'

'Come on now, open wide.'

Thwack!

The muscles in her thigh throbbed agonisingly. Why resist, she told herself. She knew what was going to happen, she knew how it was going to feel... it wasn't that bad, she reminded herself, guiltily fighting down the memory of how delicious she'd really found the experience. Already her pussy ached expectantly.

'Come on, spread your legs!'

Thwack!

'Uhhh...'

Thwack!

A pair of hands roughly grabbed her ankles and she allowed them to be pulled apart. Her thighs felt like jelly and as they parted her legs she shivered with expectation. Ashamed that she was giving in so readily to her captors and to her darker nature, she shook her head, sobbing for them not to do it.

'Be quiet darlin, or we'll have to gag you.'

'No, please!' Lara begged, tugging half-heartedly at the thighs trapping her head with both her hands.

Someone else's hands caught her by the wrists and pinned her arms down across the back of her neck. Her legs were jerked wider apart and she felt the weight of one man drop into place between her spread thighs.

'Not again...please!' Lara cried.

'Silence the bitch, before the Mistress hears her!'

The thighs pinning her head quickly parted and a hand jerked Lara's head back by her hair.

'Help! Stop it!' Lara screamed. 'Let me...'

A hand clapped across her mouth muffling her protest but to her relief she heard the bootsteps in the corridor and then the door grind open.

'What do you think you boys are up to?'

The haughty and commanding tone of the girl seemed like the answer to Lara's prayers.

'Well?' demanded the girl imperiously.

'We were just going to play around with her for a bit, Mistress.'

'And mess up the Doctor's impregnation programme no doubt! You idiots. Let her go!'

'We were only going to...'

'Shut up! I've heard enough! I should have known I couldn't trust you alone with her. Don't worry, I won't punish you, doubtless the bitch egged you on. Well, bring her with me to the exercise room!'

Immediately the two guards released her and still blindfolded and panting hard, Lara was hauled back to her feet.

'Okay, bring her along but cuff her wrists first.'

Lara stood trembling and obediently passive as leather cuffs were wrapped around her wrists and buckled snugly tight. With her arms then pulled behind her back, the two cuffs were clipped together. Lara was left wondering whether the whole episode had been pre-staged. For all she knew, being blindfolded, the girl could have been watching all along. Maybe they were just tormenting her?

They led her from the dank and dark deeper tunnels upwards. The air smelt fresher and cleaner and the stone floor was dry underfoot. This was all Lara could tell because they'd kept her blindfolded. Once inside the room where the young girl wanted her, the blindfold was removed.

'The less you know your way around the dungeons the better,' the girl told her, watching as Lara blinked and grew accustomed to the brighter light.

The room they'd brought her to was dominated by a long narrow swimming pool. The water was lit by submerged lights and at one end Lara could see a shallow slope leading down into the greeny-blue water. Glancing around she saw exercise bicycles, weights and all the equipment normally associated with a gym.

'The guards like to keep fit,' the young girl explained. 'And the Doctor likes to make sure his prisoners get plenty of exercise.'

The girl unclipped the leash from her collar then walked down the length of the pool, her boots inches from the edge, the heels clicking over the tiles.

'It's heated.'

At far end she stopped and swung around on one heel. She smiled at Lara and gestured that she get in the pool.

'You want me in there?' Lara asked, suddenly nervous again and instinctively mistrustful of the sadistic girl's motives.

'It'll warm you up. Stuck down in the dungeon isn't at all healthy. You don't seriously imagine the Doctor would jeopardise his investment in you all by leaving you to suffer cold and damp endlessly, do you?'

Lara made no reply. The truth was that she had imagined that she would be forced to spend her days and nights in the foul cell.

'Just to put your mind at rest Lara,' the girl continued, 'the Doctor has all his breeding girls take regular exercise here, under my supervision. You all have a cosy, dry dormitory cell to sleep in normally. The lower dungeon cells are just used to remind you how uncomfortable life can be made if you misbehave.'

'But I've seen all the girls in those cells,' Lara replied.

'Sure, they were all put there as punishment for you trying to rescue them.'

'But that's not their fault!' Lara protested.

'No, but after forty eight hours in solitary and a whipping, they've all decided they hate you for intruding into their lives. I'm afraid that the Doctor has made sure that your fellow prisoners have a grudge against you. Your first night in the dorm might be warm but the girls probably won't be too friendly. Some of them may even want to pay you back for what you've put them through.'

'Damn you, if you think...'

'Stop whinging Lara and get in the sodding pool! My orders are to exercise you.'

Lara glanced around her. The door to the gym was a sliding steel affair with a security-coded lock. The two guards were standing watching her. She didn't really have any choice in the matter.

'Would you tell your henchmen to unfasten my wrists then so I can swim please?'

'Untie her.'

The wristcuffs were left on but the clip connecting them was released.

'Can I take this off?' Lara fingered the collar that was close around her neck.

'No.'

Lara glanced around mistrustfully then gingerly made her way down the slope into the shallow end of the pool. The water was deliciously warm and she gratefully waded in up to her waist then threw herself forwards and struck out, breast-stroking her way down the pool. The girl and the two guards watched her as she reached the far end then turned and started back.

'How long can I stay in for?' Lara asked, reaching the shallow end and standing up.

'Twenty lengths. You stay in and swim twenty lengths.'

'Okay, fine by me.'

After completing the task set her Lara was more than ready to climb out of the pool. Since being in the dungeon she'd had precious little exercise and for much of the time her arms and legs had been bound. Now, emerging from the pool, she could feel her limbs aching satisfyingly after the gentle exertion.

'Right, get on the exercise bike,' the girl ordered.

Lara, dripping wet, did as she was told. The girl glanced at the dial on the bike handlebars.

'Ten kilometres. Get on with it.'

Dutifully Lara pedalled away. The two guards settled themselves down to watch her, while the blonde dominatrix stretched herself out along an old fashioned leather sofa, resting her heeled boots over one arm and propping her back against the other. She had a remote control to the bike in one hand and after Lara had completed five kilometres she pressed a button on the remote as she pointed it at the bike. Immediately Lara felt the resistance as she pedalled increase. By the time she'd managed eight kilometres she was sweating, her thighs aching acutely but she pressed on. The girl smiled and with a simple press on her control increased the resistance even more.

By the time Lara had done ten kilometres she was ready to slump exhausted over the handle-bars.

'Right, onto the running machine, Lara.'

'Give me a minute to get my breath back,' Lara gasped.

'Guards, take her to the running machine!'

Lara knew there was no point in resisting. She was led onto the machine and her wrist cuffs clipped onto the handle bar at one end so that she couldn't step off. With a flick of a switch on the remote control, the girl set the rubber platform in motion and Lara was forced to jog or face falling over as her legs were swept back from under her. After a few minutes she realised that the speed at which the running platform was moving was increasing and soon she was gasping then struggling to keep up with the demands made on her.

'Too...fast...please...'

The platform kept swishing backwards and Lara stumbled, her wrists jerked painfully as the leather cuffs that held her to the steel bar at the front of the platform pulled her forwards.

'Can't...keep...up...please...'

The sweat was running down her body, her legs were like lead weights now and her arms were at full stretch as she struggled to keep herself upright.

'Come on Lara, keep running!'

'Oww!'

Lara glanced over her shoulder. The girl was behind her, a long, thin cane in one hand. Laughing she flicked it again so it snapped down across her arse.

'Owww!'

'Tired already are we?'

'Yes...very...'

The platform slowed then stopped and Lara gratefully sank to her knees, gasping and faint.

'Take her to the weights. Put her under the chest press!'

The two men hauled her to her feet, unclipped the wrist cuffs from the running platform and marched her across to a weights machine. Pushing her down onto her back they made her grasp two rubber-gripped handles that were fixed to a steel bar that was swung into place above her chest. On either side of her were powerful steel coiled springs and measured counter weights. As Lara lay trying to recover her breath the collar around her neck was clipped onto the base of the headrest.

'Now let's see just how strong you really are.'

As the girl spoke the men extended Lara's legs and wrapped belts around both her ankles. The belts were then fed through buckles and fastened. Another set of belts was slipped over her thighs and pulled tight then fastened so that her legs were held securely down on the bench. A final belt was drawn across her hips and tightened so there was no way she could extricate herself from the bench and the girl nodded with satisfaction.

'Excellent. Fit the impaler bar.'

Lara, pinned down on her back was forced to watch as the men screwed a second metal rod to the steel bar poised across her chest. This bar ran above her body from her chest down to about half way along her spread thighs. As the men then screwed another section onto the device, pointing diagonally downwards and aimed at her sex, Lara had a horrible realisation of what was going to happen. By the time the men had added the last piece to the machine, Lara was panting hard and writhing against the belts that held her down, all too aware of what was about to happen.

'What a pleasing sight,' the dominatrix said, standing and looking down at Lara who was sweating and struggling frantically. She could feel the head of the steel phallus just touching the lips of her vulva. Shaped like a cock, though thicker and longer, the shiny metal instrument of torture had been the last part of the machine to be fixed in place.

'You can't be serious?' Lara gasped, glancing fearfully at the girl stood over her.

'Feeling ready for some weight training, Lara?'

Without bothering to wait for a response from her helpless victim, the girl pressed a button on the remote control she held and Lara suddenly felt the weight of the bar pressing down. Urgently she grasped a tight hold on it with both hands and pushed upwards.

Using all her strength she forced the bar away from her body, lifting the steel phallus high above her and with a snarl of determination she managed to lock her arms.

'Very impressive,' cooed the young girl stood beside her. She licked her lips thoughtfully and walked slowly around the machine.

'My my, what a strong girl you are Lara.'

The young girl idly pointed the remote at the machine and smoothed her thumb over one of the dials.

'Uhhh...no...damn you...'

As the weight increased Lara was forced to exert all her energy to keep her arms locked. Gritting her teeth and panting hard she focused on keeping her arms fully extended. As long as she could do that...

'And a little more...'

'No...no...uhh...'

The downward pressure became too much, her elbows buckled and the steel bar came sliding down slowly but inexorably. In eager anticipation the blonde squatted at her waist, watching as the steel phallus got closer and closer to Lara's tethered and writhing body.

'Uh, damn it...not going...to...let...'

Lara felt the girl's soft hands either side of her sex and realised that she was holding her in place for the descending object.

'No...stop...uhh...'

The cool steel of the device slowly pushed between the lips of her vulva then guided by the girl's hands it penetrated her sex.

'Please...no...'

Lara pushed with her hands and arms against the bar but she was exhausted from the swimming and running and the weight pressing down was too much. She felt the steel phallus slipping smoothly into her, filling her and going deeper and deeper until she was certain she couldn't take anymore and she'd faint.

'Come on Lara, push. Push or it won't stop.'

'Uhh...can't...too hard...'

Sweating and groaning Lara fought to hold the thing at bay but it was hopeless. Tears poured down her cheeks and perspiration ran from her writhing body as the steel phallus embedded itself still deeper.

'Just imagine what would happen if I wasn't merciful.'

The girl flicked a switch on the remote and the machine stopped. Lara lay panting hard and too afraid to relax her grip on the bar she was grasping.

'What the hell are you two staring at?' snarled the girl, glancing up at the two guards who stood over her.

'The Doctor said she mustn't be fucked for forty eight hours or it would put the impregnation at risk,' said one of men sullenly.

'And you idiots do as he says. Well so you should! But if I want to play with our new prisoner that's my business! So what if her impregnation fails? She'll just have to go through it again! She's going to have to get used to it, he'll be breeding from her continuously until he's got enough slaves to supply all his contacts in the Barbarian countries.'

The girl stood up and smoothed her short skirt down her shapely thighs. Flicking her blonde hair clear of her face she turned her back on Lara and snapped out an order to the guards to release her.

'If it will make you both happy you can take her into the sauna. I'll come back for her in half an hour!'

Lara watched in dismay as the girl stalked across to the entrance to the gym. Pausing as she punched in the pass code to the door panel, she glanced back over her shoulder.

'Well Lara, I think you should enjoy quite a steamy session with the lads. Have fun, I'll be back for you later.'

The door hissed softly open and the girl stepped out of the room. Lara watched the door slide shut again. She was on all fours beside the machine she'd just been strapped to. The two guards were standing close by, swiftly discarding their clothing. Lara stumbled to her feet and ran with what energy she had left to the main door. It was locked. She randomly punched in some numbers on the lock control but nothing happened. There was an amused laugh behind her and she heard the men approaching her from behind.

Lara glanced around her. The idiots had left all their discarded uniforms and weapons lying in a pile on the ground. If she could only get past them and reach them, she'd teach them a lesson! After all her exertions though her legs were weak with fatigue. As the men closed in on her and with no hope of getting to the discarded weapons she retreated instead to the swimming pool and ran down the far side.

She paused at the far end of the pool to assess her chances. She was already out of breath, her legs felt like jelly. If she could just keep them at bay until the girl returned! As the men closed on her from both sides she jumped into the pool and swam out to the middle. One of the men jumped in after her and desperately she tried to swim across the pool before he caught her up.

Even as she reached the far side though a hand clutched at her ankle and she only just kicked her legs free. Frantically she lunged for the edge of the pool but the other man was waiting for her and snatching her wrist, he hauled her half way out of the water.

'Come on then Lara, reckon after all your exertions you'll

be ready for a nice relaxing sauna!'

Laughing as they dragged her by the arms, the two men hauled her across to the sauna room.

'Now, you just relax in here for ten minutes then we'll come in and join you!'

Lara was tossed into the sauna and the door was slammed shut. The ominous sound of a bolt sliding across the door made Lara stumble to her feet and peer out of the glass window. The two men were grinning at her. She snatched at the handle and pushed against the door. Nothing! They'd locked her in! Even as she rattled the door furiously, steam began to swirl around her feet and she felt the temperature leap. She stumbled around the room, pummelling her hands against the wood walls and bursting into tears. She came back to the door and banged frantically on the glass. Of course MacKennan had built this for sweating his prisoners in, so the controls were on the outside. She thumped the glass with her fist but all she achieved was to bruise her hand. Gasping, she slumped down on the wooden bench and hung her head in her hands. Her hair was soaking; the perspiration was running off her and pooling at her feet where it rose again as steam. She felt giddy and faint now and she gazed forlornly at the door. The window was steamed over now.

'Help!'

Her voice sounded pitifully weak and the dry air rasped her throat painfully. She tried to stand up but her legs buckled under her and she sank to her knees.

'Please...' she gasped, slumping forwards.

She crawled towards the door but it was too much effort and she gave up. She collapsed onto her back and put an arm against her eyes. The heat rolled in waves over her prone body and she sighed quietly, her arm sliding from shielding her eyes and dropping limply alongside her sweat-drenched body.

Chapter Five

Lara stepped under the shower and tilted her head back so the water from the overhead jet hit her full in the face. The dried facemask quickly dissolved leaving her skin feeling taut and fresh again. The middle jet of water splashed against her breasts and the lower jet against her stomach. She fingered the dial and increased the temperature fractionally, turning around so the water pummelled her back.

After washing her hair she dribbled shower gel across her body and rubbed herself all over. As she rubbed her hand between the globes of her bottom she felt her anus ache dully. Gingerly she touched herself there, remembering her dream. So vivid her body ached...

She turned around and adjusted the rake of the lower nozzle, pushing it down a little so the water splashed against her pussy. She closed her eyes and focused on the pleasurable sensation of the powerful jets of hot water hitting her breasts and between her legs. She reached out again to the lower jet head and twisted it so the shower of water became narrower and more intense. Resting her back on the tiled wall she focused on the pleasurable feeling the water made and tried for a few moments to think about nothing else. Closing her eyes though, the memory of her time at the hands of the two guards was vividly clear and fresh. And with the dull ache in her anus as a reminder, it was impossible to forget. It felt as if it had happened, even though it was just a dream!

Lara sighed and pressed a finger into her pussy. She'd always been sexually ravenous but since starting her sessions at the Dreamscape Institute sex was on her brain constantly. And oddly too, she was less interested in anything ordinary. Now, compared with dreams, her string of casual lovers seemed to offer very little that was really stimulating for her. She rubbed her fingertip against her clitoris repeatedly, disappointed at how mild the stimulation felt now. She remembered the exquisite ache she'd felt as her breasts had been clamped and weighted. Well, as she'd dreamt and imagined it. Glancing down she caressed her breasts and wondered what it would really feel like. Gingerly she fingered her nipples, then experimentally trapped one between her thumb and finger, applying pressure until it ached pleasurably. Damn it... she'd have to book in for another session with MacKennan. Thankfully, his high fees were well within her financial reach.

She'd tried to recapture her fantasy dreams asleep at home but they had eluded her. It was like having to wait for the next episode of a screen serial, she decided. Only, she was too impatient to wait. The last thing she'd dreamt was the time in the sauna. How the two brutish guards had locked her in there. She remembered the oppressive heat, then she'd lost consciousness and to her annoyance she'd then been woken up by Doctor MacKennan. She suspected he'd done that on purpose. Bringing her back to the dull real world just when she was about to reach another good bit in her dream. She tried to imagine the guards lifting her prone body from the sauna. They would surely take her again just like they had in the cell. Or maybe this time they would ram their cocks into her pussy. She sighed and switched off the warm cascading water. There was only one way she'd find out. To pay MacKennan and to have another session at the Institute.

Dripping wet from the shower, she snatched up her phone and tapped in the Dreamscape Institute number.

'Good morning, the Dreamscape Institute, can I help you?'

'It's Lara Lustral, get me Doctor MacKennan. Please.'

She added the please as an after thought. She'd never seen the relevance of saying "please" and "thank you" to mere Delta Class workers, but she knew that her superior tone often rubbed them up the wrong way and she didn't want them trying to exact some petty revenge. The last thing she needed now was to be put on hold or told the Doctor wasn't available, just because some stupid worker girl objected to her tone of voice.

'Just connecting you Miss Lustral.'

Lara didn't bother to say thank you — she'd got what she wanted and a second later she had the satisfaction of hearing MacKennan's smooth voice.

'Lara, good morning. How can I help?'

'I need... I mean, I'd like to check in for another session please Doctor.'

'Of course, delighted. When might suit?'

'Well, today, this afternoon perhaps?'

'I'm so sorry, I'm fully booked this afternoon. Tomorrow perhaps?'

'Tomorrow...' Lara couldn't disguise the acute disappointment in her voice.

'Unless this evening is of any use to you? Though I expect...'

'No. No, this evening would be fine. What time can I come round?'

'Well, shall we say seven?'

'Perfect.'

'I'll look forward to you coming. Until then Lara, enjoy your day.'

'Thanks.'

The line went dead before Lara could switch the phone off. She hated that. She hated ringing off last. She always wanted to be the one who seemed busier, never the one to linger. And God, how pathetic she'd allowed herself to sound. Practically begging him for admission to his damn Institute! She tossed the hand phone aside and went through to her kitchen to pour herself some fruit juice. Well, what the hell was the point in play-acting? He knew she was desperate to have the sort of dreams he could offer and he knew that she knew.

She drained a tall glass of fresh mango juice in one go, took a small bar of chocolate from the fridge and walked back into the lounge. Her favourite breakfast; mango juice and chocolate! She slumped down onto one of her beautiful soft, white sofas and stretched out her legs. Noticing that her toenails needed repainting, she decided that she would have to go and visit her beautician today. A pedicure, a manicure, a facial and a full body massage. Lunch at a restaurant with a girl friend, then a few hours beauty sleep back at home before her appointment this evening. For a moment, her legs curled up under her on the sofa, she nestled into her dream, trying carefully to recreate it piece by piece. She could remember dreaming that she'd lost consciousness in the sauna and in her mind she could sketch in the men and the room, but it all seemed so... so unsatisfactory now. So contrived. Sat here, her eyes closed, or lying in her own bed dreaming, all she could experience was at best a dream. Somehow though when MacKennan had her on his couch and her body was taped up to his computer, when she drifted asleep she really felt as if she was transported into her dream world. The sounds, the smells, the feel... She wiggled her body on the sofa, feeling behind herself with one hand. Her long fingers slid between the globes of her bottom and timidly at felt she fingered her anus. Closing her eyes and forcing herself to concentrate she could recall how it had felt as the guards in her cell had forced her to kneel, head down and with rump exposed. Lara sighed and exchanged her fingertip for her thumb and she gently pressed against the seemingly firm crater of flesh. Insinuating her thumb she struggled to picture the men, the dank cell, the pungent smell of their maleness, their arousal. How had it felt as the man had forced his massive cock into her? She tried but failed to recapture the sensation. With a sigh of frustration she gave up, slunk through to her bedroom and tossed herself down on her bed.

She knew what she wanted to happen next. The guards would drag her out of the sauna. She'd be exhausted from the heat; too weak to resist them... they'd toss her perspiration-soaked body down on the gym floor...

Closing her eyes she tried to picture it but she couldn't hold the picture in her mind properly. She could get bits right... but only bits. The only way she could have her dream brought to life was to submit herself to MacKennan and his damned machine! It was still humiliating to know that he could watch her private, darkest dreams on his computer monitor. But at least he assured her that it was for her own safety, in case something went wrong and that no one else would ever know. Except of course the two nurses. Sultry, smug little tarts they were! She didn't really trust them and for a moment she'd been daft enough to wonder whether there was even something going on between them and MacKennan. Of course that was ridiculous: an Alpha male like him bothering with Delta girls. Why waste his time with them when he could enjoy the stunning looks and desirability of an Alpha woman? She smiled, wondering what MacKennan had thought of her incorporating him into her fantasy dream. Probably a bit of a turn-on for him, she decided. She'd noticed him gazing at her cleavage as she'd lain on his couch. The randy bastard, given half a chance, if she let him, she could have him feeding out of her hand, desperate for a fuck, just like every man who saw her. Well, he could dream on, he wasn't her type. There was something faintly sinister about him that disconcerted her. Little wonder she'd made him into an evil Doctor in her dreams! She laughed and jumped up from the bed. Well, she had the next session of her fantasy to look forward to this evening, she reminded herself.

'What to wear?' she asked herself out loud, snatching up the discarded briefs she'd worn the day before. Holding them to her nose she inhaled her own arousal. She'd gone to bed desperate for a fuck and had masturbated herself to sleep but she'd still woken feeling horny as hell. She opened a drawer and picked up a white lacy thong. She slipped it on and sighed as the thong slid up between her buttocks and pressed against her anus. Christ, she felt so tender there! How was it possible for a dream to translate itself into a physical feeling like that? She scratched her head and gazed at herself in her full-length wardrobe mirror. I am more desirable, more fuckable than I was when I was eighteen, she told herself proudly. So what if it's cost me? What's money?

As she snuggled her generous breasts into a matching lacy bra then wriggled into a tight, low cut top, Lara wondered briefly about her finances. She'd inherited a fortune from her parents; her father having expanded a business his father had built up. Now she just received occasional letters and phone calls from her chief accountant. Max, her father had told her, would take care of everything if anything should happen to him. Well, her father had been right, Max had been wonderful. He managed the businesses and her funds and every three months told her how much richer she'd become.

Lara sighed and slipped on a pair of high-heels, decided they weren't right and discarded them in preference for another pair. Glancing at herself in her mirror as she bent to fasten the straps on her shoes she could see how desirable she was for any man. Her body was a succession of curves that called attention to her sexually rapacious nature. Her mane of golden hair, her generous cleavage and sultry expression was a clear signal that she wanted sex. And it was true; she was aching for it. How the hell was she going to last until this evening without masturbating? She gazed in her mirror at herself then closed her eyes. For a brief second she imagined she could feel the heat from the sauna. She remembered how in the dank cell the men had held her down; how good it had felt.

* * *

Lara lifted her head weakly; her body drained by the heat; her throat dry, her limbs weak. As the steam swirled away through the open door of the sauna, she could see the two men stood regarding her. Stripped of their guards clothing, their powerfully muscled torsos were clearly apparent. Aside from their height what set them apart from any ordinary men were the size of the genitals. It was not just in brutish strength that these men resembled bulls.

They caught hold of Lara's arms and dragged her out of the sauna. Without pausing, they dragged her across the gym floor to an exercise bench, pushing her belly down against it. Lara grunted as the wind was knocked from her. One of them took hold of her wrists and drew her arms taut, pulling her body hard against the bench.

'Please... leave me alone...'

She was too weak after her exertions to offer any resistance as the other guard encouraged her legs apart with two sharp tugs.

'Come on darlin', get those legs spread!'

'No...don't...'

Lara tried to keep her thighs pressed together but she had no strength left and the man easily parted her legs then jammed his body between them to keep them spread.

'Now, let's have a feel of what's on offer.'

Lara squirmed as the man grasped her buttocks with both hands and drew them apart, exposing her sex. She felt his thumbs spread open her labia then before she had a chance to react, his cock was rammed into her. Lara cried out, trying ineffectually to wrench her arms free from the other man's vice like grip.

'Nice and tight, does that feel good?'

'Uhhh...too big...please...' Lara panted, shaking her perspiration-drenched head in desperation.

The cock was withdrawn a little then promptly driven back deeper into her.

'For a girl with such big tits and a generous arse, you've got a tight little pussy haven't you?'

'Please...please...too much...' Lara struggled against the body that pinned her against the bench, gasping as the thick cock sank even deeper into her aching sex. The sensation was so intense she suddenly felt the heat of orgasm rushing through her and moaning wildly, her body bucking, she came.

'That's it darlin', good girl...'

The man withdrew his cock and while Lara was still trembling as her orgasm subsided he rammed his massive shaft back into her, driving it into her up the hilt, his balls slapping against her arse and Lara howled frantically.

'Make as much noise as yer want,' the man laughed, drawing his cock out and shoving it back into her.

'Uhhh...stop it... can't bear it... please...'

The shaft slid back and forth now with the relentless force and rhythm of a piston, Lara writhing and thrashing with each thrust, frantic to escape but pinned and held against the bench.

'That's it, have a good cry, no one'll hear yer so it doesn't matter.'

The man grasping her wrists increased the pressure on her stretched arms and grinned maliciously at her.

'Stop...no more...please...'

'Hush now...nearly there...' the man tightened his grasp on her wriggling waist. The urgency of the cock pounding in and out of her increased and then with one last thrust he came.

'Good girl... nice little tart's doing the business. Now keep still while my mate has his turn.'

'No...can't take anymore...'

Lara tried to pull away but a hand shoved her back against the bench as the men exchanged places.

The second man quickly plunged his cock into her aching pussy and the relentless assault was resumed. By the time he'd finished with her Lara was exhausted, her whole body awash with the sensation of being fucked repeatedly by massive cocks. When the hands released her wrists, she slumped onto the gym floor.

'What a sorry state she looks in!'

'Delicious little body, just about the best of the twelve I reckon.'

'Yeah and so obliging with the way she struggles and protests. Nothing like a girl who pretends she doesn't want it, to give you a decent hard-on.'

'Look at her! What a sight; she unconscious or what?'

One of the men caught hold of Lara's hair and hauled her head up off the tiled floor. Dazedly she looked up, tears blurring her vision, her mouth open slackly as she panted to recover her breath.

'Nah, she's just tired.'

'Well, I reckon she can't be too tired to give us a suck.'

One of the men crouched down beside Lara and slapped her cheeks lightly with the back of his hand.

'Come on, stay awake, bit more work for you. Get those lovely lips around this.'

Lara groaned as her head was forced into the man's lap. His cock was semi-flaccid, spunk still dipping from the giant head, the shaft softening but still longer than any normal fully erect male.

'Lick us clean Lara, then get us nice and hard. Do it nicely and you'll not get a beating from us.'

Lara sighed and did as she was ordered. Gingerly at first she began to lick the semen that had dribbled down the shaft but soon her natural eagerness reasserted itself and she immersed herself in the task. After being whipped, buggered and fucked doing this was no hardship, she told herself, enthusiastically sucking the now clean and shiny cock.

'Good girl... very good. Yeah, that's it...'

The shaft was thickening as she bathed it in long slow strokes of her tongue. She would break off licking to spend a moment sucking the tumescent head and then she would return to the shaft, licking, kissing, gently biting so the man groaned and sighed. She tried to suck one of his balls into her mouth but it was too big although she was able to cup his scrotum with one hand and rolled his testicles together, gently squeezing them until the man was groaning loudly.

'Horny bitch... so good...' the man muttered under his breath as Lara furled her lips over the tip of his shaft and sucked hard with her mouth while playing with his balls in her hand.

'Enough...enough! Get on your hands and knees girl!'

Lara did as she was told: eager now for the cock to be inside her. Playing with the massive organ she'd aroused herself. Now she was aching with the need to come. Bent doggy fashion, she gave a sigh of encouragement as the man grasped her hips and pulled her arse back against his heavily engorged cock. The shaft slid between the globes of her arse and slipped between the slick folds of her vulva. A second later and the cock was buried in her madly aroused pussy and Lara was panting and sighing feverishly as the man started to fuck her all over again.

By the time he'd finished with her Lara had come twice and her sexual hunger was satiated. The other man though, having watched the spectacle, was wanting his second turn. Lara pleaded to be allowed a few moments' rest, complaining that she was exhausted.

'Perhaps you'd like a dip in the pool then to refresh yourself?'

Her pussy throbbing from the repeated hammering it had just taken and her limbs aching from all her forced exertions, Lara shook her head negatively.

'Too tired... just let me rest, please.'

The men though had different ideas and grasping her by the wrists they dragged her across to the edge of the pool.

'What are you doing? What's happening...'

Lara lifted her head weakly as the men rolled her onto her stomach and drew her arms behind her back. Her wrists were pulled together and the leather cuffs clipped together.

'Please...no, don't!'

Lara craned her head back trying to make eye contact with the two men.

'Come on guys... I'll do whatever you want... there's no need to tie me, please...'

Lifted by her arms she was dragged along the poolside until they were at the deep end.

'No... you can't...don't...'

The men stood up and with their bare feet nudged her naked body closer to the edge.

'Come on guys, I'll do anything, just don't...'

Ignoring her pleading, they pushed her over the edge of the pool. With a resounding splash Lara plummeted under the water. With her arms bound behind her she could only use her legs to kick herself back to the surface. Summoning what strength she had left, she swam to the shallow end and stumbling, collapsed over the edge of the pool.

'So Lara, ready for another shafting or would you like to swim for a little longer?'

'Can't swim... too tired...please, don't make me!'

She was all too aware that with her arms tied behind her back and her legs feeling weak from so much enforced exercise she'd be struggling before long to keep her head above water if they pushed her back into the pool.

'So you're game for another fuck then?'

Lara nodded affirmatively and the men caught hold of her arms and hauled her from the pool.

'Obliging little tart, isn't she?'

'Such a willingly submissive slave girl!'

One of the men crouched down beside her and stroked her face reassuringly. She was panting breathlessly and lay on her back, her arms secured behind her making her feel as helpless and vulnerable as an upturned turtle.

'What a lovely sight...'

One of the men stroked his hand down over her breasts. Lara sighed and looked up apprehensively at the two men. Surely soon the girl had to come back? The man moved his hand lower down her body, stroking her panting stomach. Her poor little pussy ached so much from her last shafting, she was sure she'd faint if one of them rammed his enormous cock back into her tender sex again now.

'Please guys...' she sighed breathlessly, 'give me a rest and I'll be so grateful I'll be really good to you. I promise... it's just that my little pussy is so tender now.'

'Okay then Lara, we'll give it a rest. There's another way for us to get satisfaction from you... and it's just as good!'

'No! Please, don't!'

Lara gave a cry of dismay as the men lifted her easily and turned her face down.

'Onto the bench with the bitch I reckon.'

'Reckon she must like being taken up her behind!'

Lara was hauled effortlessly from the floor and carried across to one of the room's benches. The memory of the guards anally fucking her in the cell came back to her all too vividly and she began pleading desperately with them as they pushed her down over the bench. Just as Lara was certain that she was about to be subjected to another punishing session, the gym door opened and the girl strutted in.

'So what have you lot been up to? Had a nice time?'

The blonde dominatrix walked across to where Lara lay panting nervously.

'Been enjoying yourself with the lads, Lara?'

Lara nodded and glanced at the three faces staring down at her. Perhaps, she thought, she would just have to submit herself to these people's sadistic whims? After all, as long as she toed the line, how much worse could her time as the Doctor's prisoner become?

'Right guys, get her up on her feet. Time for Lara's next impregnation session!'

* * *

MacKennan gave the monitor screens and the computer data banks one last glance; then, satisfied with everything, he made to leave the room. Under the pale green light, stretched out on her back, Lara Lustral lay dreaming. Her gentle breathing and relaxed appearance was in marked contrast to her dream persona. MacKennan was amused by how eagerly Lara had incorporated into her dream sequences the butt-plug that he'd used on her. Of course, blissfully unaware of what he was doing to her, Lara had merely dreamt that the brutish guards had forced her to submit to anal sex with them. And it was so satisfying to see that she was even beginning to allow her dream persona to admit that she got off on being treated as a submissive. Here she was, on only her third session and Lara the adventurer was practically encouraging her gaolers to use her body for their own pleasure.

'Zara, stay and keep an eye on her. Suzi, come with me.'

MacKennan left the room and followed by the nurse made his way through the corridors of the Dreamscape Institute. In the ten years since he had started the business he had seen it enjoy a meteoric financial success. But the Dreamscape Institute that the public saw, accounted now for only a fraction of the business turnover. The serious money was made behind not just closed doors, but behind security controlled closed doors that few clients ever saw. And those who did never got to tell anyone about what went on behind them.

Taking the lift with his nurse close on his heels, MacKennan pressed the button marked "Basement Two". In a few seconds the lift door glided open to reveal a plain, white-tiled corridor ending in a smoked glass door. Behind the glass, a man in a dark suit could be seen seated on a chair reading a magazine.

'Good evening Doctor, working late?'

The man stood up and spoke through an intercom.

'Another randy client who can't wait until tomorrow,' MacKennan explained with a smile.

'So when might we be meeting her then?' the man asked, suppressing a lecherous grin.

'Soon. Pretty soon.'

MacKennan punched in a security code and a yellow light flashed on the door's electronic lock. The guard keyed in a number on the lock on his side and a second yellow light started flashing alongside the first. He then keyed in a second number and the lift door behind them slid shut and a red light lit up above it.

'Lift secure. Two in the corridor, Doctor MacKennan and nurse Suzi.'

Whilst the man spoke into a microphone attached to the lapel of his suit jacket, MacKennan exchanged glances with his nurse. Both knew the security precautions were excessive but MacKennan was taking no chances. Of course the highly valuable computer mainframe which he'd developed was housed behind this layer of protection, so the security was easily explained to the curious. However, the real moneymaking side of his business was here too. Well out of sight and closely guarded because it was totally criminal.

The smoked glass door slid silently open. MacKennan and Suzi stepped through and the door glided shut behind them. Only by glancing at its edge, as it was momentarily open was its strength revealed: four centimetres thick bulletproof glass.

'All quiet I presume?'

'Yes, Doctor.'

'Where are they?'

'The new recruit is in "Discipline" and the other girl is "Conditioning" just now. She's coming on very nicely from what I hear, Doctor.'

'I'll take a look. Suzi, go to the office and check to see if we have any more purchase requests.'

MacKennan left his nurse outside the first door they'd come to marked simply "Office — Security Cleared Persons Only". He watched as Suzi keyed her pass number in and the slate grey door slid open for her. He made his way down the corridor past two doors marked "A" and "B" until he reached a door marked with a simple "C". He keyed a number into the door lock and the door slid open. Inside, a metre beyond him, was another door. Once the first was closed the second slid open automatically.

Seated at a plain, chrome legged, glass topped table was a young girl. Hearing him enter, she glanced over her shoulder. In the act of leafing through a folder of pictures, she paused and looked expectantly at him.

'Doctor, it's you! Did they tell you I asked to see you? Please, tell them I'm ready. I've done everything they wanted, I know you were right now.'

The young woman looked beseechingly at him and he smiled reassuringly at her.

MacKennan moved to behind her chair and glanced down at the folder spread before her. Each page displayed a large colour photograph of this very girl and in each she was naked.

In the right-hand photo she was hanging upside down, suspended by her ankles. Her legs and arms were bound together repeatedly with shiny black ropes and her long dark hair trailed down, just brushing the floor. The picture on the left showed her kneeling, her arms bound behind her back, her calves were pulled up and roped to her thighs so it would have been impossible for her to stand. A man, naked except for a black mask that covered half his face, stood before her. The photographer had caught her in the act of licking her tongue against the underside of the man's erect cock.

'So which of these did you enjoy the most Pippa?' MacKennan rested his hands on the girl's shoulders and looked down at her. Wearing nothing more than a loose and low cut white vest and white briefs, he could see her young breasts rising and falling as she breathed. The skin of her supple shoulders was smooth under his hands and he stroked down her bare arms appreciating their softness.

'The one on the right, Doctor.'

'Why?'

The girl looked up at him and smiled coyly.

'I felt all dizzy when I was hung upside down and they kept me like it for so long my legs really ached. But the other time... that was okay.'

'Just okay?'

'Nice. They've told me I'm good at it and the man says I'm one of his best pupils.'

'That's what I've heard Pippa.'

MacKennan patted the girl's head affectionately and moved closer to the table so he could leaf through the folder.

He glanced down at the girl, noting the cuffs that bound her ankles to the legs of the chair. The cuffs were padlocked shut so she couldn't remove them or leave the chair. When they'd started on the conditioning sessions with her, they'd had her arms and legs tightly bound with tape to the chair; two men with her, one turning the pages, the other gently punishing her when she refused to answer their questions. Now simple anklecuffs were enough of a token reminder for her that she was their slave.

It was curious, he thought, how humans once in a uniform quickly adapted to what the clothing proclaimed them to be: schoolgirl, businessman, soldier. Each individual quickly losing a little of their own individualism as they conformed to the role their clothing placed them in. It was the same with the young women that he abducted. Take a wealthy girl, used to being pampered and given every material luxury she wanted: strip her of all that; dress her and treat her like a sex-slave and soon, surprisingly soon, she began to behave like one. Especially when surrounded by other girls in a like situation.

Business with the Barbarian nations was flourishing and he had just shipped out half a dozen girls who he'd been training over the last few months. Now, Basement Two was quieter than it had been for a while with just two girls left: Pippa and Annabella. Pippa, at just eighteen years old was shaping up nicely as a submissive sex-slave after just a month.

MacKennan turned the folder back a page. Again, two photos of Pippa, one on each page, but in the plain space below these the girl had already written her feelings about them, as instructed. On the right-hand page she was kneeling in similar fashion to the following page, her calves and thighs bound together, her arms tied behind her back. This time though two men stood over her, one holding her head back by her hair while the other dribbled what appeared to be milk from a fine funnelled jug into her open mouth. It looked as if Pippa was gulping it willingly enough, although some liquid had spilt down her neck and over her firm young breasts. On the left-hand page she was in similar situation but this time she seemed to be struggling. She was blindfolded and gagged with an O-ring gag that held her jaws open enabling the men to pour something into her mouth against her will. The man grasping her hair seemed to be dragging her head back hard and the man administering the liquid was tightly holding her chin still with one hand. MacKennan glanced at what Pippa had written.

"The first time they made me drink it I didn't want to. I was blindfolded and nervous. The milk had semen mixed in it so I'd start to get used to the taste. The next time I wasn't blindfolded and because I was obedient they weren't so rough with me. I didn't mind them being rough with me — it makes my pussy warm and wet being treated like that."

'So what do you want to write about the next picture, Pippa?' MacKennan asked.

The girl glanced up and smiled coyly. She then turned the page back over and wrote under the picture of her licking the hooded man's cock.

"It was easy to learn to like sucking cock. When it spurts its salty milk into my mouth I know I've done a good job."

MacKennan smiled with satisfaction.

'And what about the other picture, Pippa?'

Again the young girl put pen to paper as he stood over her.

"When I'm hung upside down I know I'm really helpless. This time because I kept crying out and begging to be released they kept me like it for ages. My legs ached so much I started crying."

'Turn over to the next page, Pippa.'

The girl turned over to reveal two more photos. In the left one she was dangling and bound just as on the previous page but now she had been gagged with black tape. In the right hand photo she was on a large bed on her hands and knees, her arse thrust back for a man who was just about to take her doggy-style. She had ankle and wrist cuffs but none of them were fastened to anything and the camera had caught her in the act of glancing back over her shoulder, an expression of eager anticipation on her face.

'What about these two, Pippa?'

'Well, they gagged me because I was crying, which I deserved. The picture on the right was taken a few days later. The men said they wanted to fuck me and ordered me to get on the bed and bend over. They said they were going to fuck my arse and after that they'd whip me.'

'And you didn't mind the prospect of that?'

'No...I don't mind... I like it really.'

MacKennan could clearly recall how Pippa had protested the first time in the Basement that they'd told her she was going to be treated like that. Two men had to exert some considerable force to get her strapped down on the bed before they'd set to work on her. He was very pleased with how quickly Pippa had accepted her new life as a submissive.

MacKennan left the young and obedient Pippa, ankles tied to her chair and dutifully writing her feelings about each picture. He went to the door marked "D" and after passing through a similar set of security-controlled doors he came to a room where he found his most recent acquisition in a state of considerable distress.

Annabella had arrived in Basement Two just three days ago. Twenty nine, the daughter of a multi-millionaire, she was just like Lara Lustral — bored with her sex life. It had not been difficult to get her addicted to dreamscape sessions and it had been even easier to lay a trail of false clues to make her family think she'd eloped abroad with a man, when MacKennan decided that she would be his next little money earner.

One Tuesday morning, she had come into the Dreamscape Institute ready to enjoy another dream episode. Annabella, tall, fit and with a voracious sexual appetite dreamt that she needed a sex-therapist who'd decided that the best treatment for her was to give her more sex than she could take. Of course for Annabella the treatment was just what she craved: a chocoholic in a chocolate shop with no intention at all of making herself sick but with every intention of savouring every tempting bar of chocolate in sight.

In her dream her therapist was MacKennan — inevitable because of the computer programming. So on Tuesday she'd dreamt that this time her therapist had strapped her into a gynaecologist's chair to examine her sex. With her muscular thighs strapped wide she could do nothing to prevent him from calmly pegging and taping back the lips of her vulva. MacKennan, watching the monitor screen could hardly contain himself, so arousing was the girl's dream. He gazed at the screen as his alter-ego, in white surgical coat and facemask, began to torment the girl's exposed sex with a succession of shiny steel surgical instruments. The beautiful girl was soon shaking her head, her long dark hair cascading around her face, tears welling up from her dark brown eyes, her soft luscious lips trembling as she was brought sighing to orgasm after orgasm. Under broad black canvas straps her arms and legs twisted ineffectually, her skin glowing with perspiration and warmth from her exertions to free herself.

'No more Doctor, please...don't make me come again...' she panted breathlessly. The man tormenting her ignored her pleading and taking a device that resembled a dentist's polishing tool, switched it on and stroked the soft spinning head against the exposed delicate pinkness of the girl's sex. She cried out, her hips bucking against the straps that restrained her as she was made to orgasm again.

MacKennan glanced up from the monitor. Under the tranquil green light of the dream couch, the delicious Annabella lay dreaming. The white towelling robe contrasted pleasingly with her tanned skin. Her slender wrists and ankles were cuffed and she slithered a little, sighing as she dreamed. MacKennan could wait no longer.

'Prepare a stretcher bed and increase the emothome by ten percent. We're moving her now to the Basement.'

It had been a skilfully timed transfer, he reflected. When the sultry Annabella woke it was not to find herself reclining on a couch under pale green lights, but under a cool blue light and strapped to a padded table. She was in the "Discipline Room" of Basement Two.

'Where am I?' she sighed, licking her lips nervously.

'We've moved you to another room Annabella. A quieter

111

place; where we can continue the therapy undisturbed.'

MacKennan had added a surgeon's mask to his normal coat to help convince the girl that she was still in her dreamscape. He had spread-eagled her and strapped her down with strong canvas straps. Her arms held outstretched above her head were strapped at her wrists and below her elbows. Her legs spread-eagled were strapped at her ankles and just above her knees. The canvas straps were fed through some of the numerous narrow slits in the padded tabletop. With four sets, Annabella was utterly helpless but she could still writhe and move her deliciously curvaceous body to quite a degree.

'Now then Annabella, keep still while I examine you.'

The moment she saw the clip she bucked and twisted, swearing and cursing. MacKennan was delighted. It was so much more enjoyable when they put up a fight, he mused, ordering the nurse to fetch some more straps.

Now, three days later, Annabella was back on the padded tabletop. The sultry young woman with her shiny dark hair and smooth perfect skin, was looking the worse for three days of hard discipline. Her hair was tangled around her shoulders and face. Her eyes were wild with fear and her lips were bruised where she'd bitten down on them repeatedly in anguish. Just as she had been three days ago, when he'd last seen her, she was strapped down on her back across the padded table. Her shapely thighs were streaked with faint red marks where she'd been whipped. Her full, firm young breasts were bound repeatedly with cord and her lovely, pert nipples showed dark purple and swollen under shiny little steel clamps.

With her legs strapped down and widely spread, MacKennan could see the outer labia of the girl's vulva had been pegged and drawn fully open. The pegs had been taped against the inside of her thighs and her inner labia were clearly exposed. Two men in smart, dark suits and dark glasses were stood over her. Both had surgical masks and clear, tight fitting rubber gloves drawn over their hands. One was holding some surgical-like instrument and the other a tube of ointment.

'How is she shaping up?' MacKennan asked, walking across to the bench.

The beautiful young woman lifted her head at the sound of his voice. It was obvious from her expression that she was trying to communicate with him. A ball-gag though silenced her and the best she could manage was to plead with her large, dark eyes that now looked so sorrowful. MacKennan looked down at her and thought that he'd seldom seen so many straps used to hold a girl down.

'She's a bit of wild thing,' one of them explained, seeing his glance and reading his thoughts.

'Annabella,' MacKennan said. 'This treatment of yours will have to continue until you stop wanting to have orgasms. Until then, my dear...' he shrugged apologetically and nodded to the men. He watched as the men applied some of the ointment to her sex. The effect was almost immediate — Annabella was going to be made to have another orgasm. Tears rolling down her cheeks, her hips trying to buck, she groaned through the gag. The cool metal of tweezers was pressed around her clitoris and Annabella, her head thrashing, eyes rolling upwards, came: an intense shuddering orgasm that left her bathed in perspiration and groaning weakly.

MacKennan knew that the ointment, a chemical compound called Gelphax, was utterly effective. The girl would quickly experience an acute tingling once the cream was smeared against her inner labia. Warmth would ripple through her pussy and her clitoris would harden and ache. In less than a minute she'd be desperately aroused. The lightest of touches then against her sex would trigger her orgasm. Gelphax could be found in strengths of five or ten percent in sex shops. MacKennan though bought it in its full strength from an unscrupulous laboratory and used it neat. He looked down with satisfaction at the panting girl tethered to the bench.

'How many times has she come this time?' he asked.

'That's her seventh. She's been strapped down for just over an hour.'

113

'Let's ungag her, see what she has to say for herself.'

The ballgag was removed and the tearful Annabella was soon pleading with him.

'Please Doctor... don't let them do it anymore...I've had enough...'

'But Annabella my dear, you are a wanton little bitch on heat who won't stop having orgasms. What are we going to do with you?'

'I don't know! I'm so sorry Doctor...'

'I think Annabella there's only one thing we can do with you...'

The girl looked up expectantly at him.

'You will have to be sold into sexual slavery and shipped out to one of the Barbarians nations.'

'No! You can't do that to me!' the girl protested.

'Well Annabella, I think we'll have to,' MacKennan smiled down apologetically at the bound girl as she writhed and struggled against the straps that held her.

'My dear girl, you can hardly deny you'd enjoy being a sex slave — think of how much pleasure you'd have...' MacKennan gave the merest nod to one of the men and a little more ointment was smeared against her labia.

'I know you wish you didn't, but the truth is you just love being treated like this, don't you?'

'Yes, Doctor...' the girl sighed, tossing her head from side to side and whimpering as the ointment swiftly aroused her once again.

'Good girl, at least we've got you to admit your wantonness. If we can't bring your sexually ravenous nature under control we can at least send you somewhere where it can be put to good use. Yes?'

'Yes, Doctor. Whatever you think best.'

The tethered girl moaned feverishly, closing her eyes, biting down on her lip and trying to arch her body. MacKennan watched as her hips started bucking urgently, her limbs straining against the restraining straps. Orgasm number eight,

MacKennan mused, smiling as he watched the girl.

'Gag her and continue the treatment,' he ordered, turning his back on the young woman writhing against the straps that held her down on the bench.

They all submit themselves, sooner or later, MacKennan mused, leaving the room. Annabella was proving an interesting challenge but he knew she'd soon surrender to her submissive nature. Next, it would be the luscious Lara Lustral.

CHAPTER SIX

Lara woke to the familiar pale green light of the Dreamscape Institute sleep room. She was looking at up the pale green lights, diffused behind the tinted glass of the couch canopy. She closed her eyes again for a moment, hoping to catch the last vestiges of her dream. Snatches came to her: agonisingly arousing but too insubstantial for her to fully immerse herself in. She desperately wanted to fall asleep again — she could happily stay in her dreamscape for longer... much longer.

Her pussy had that delicious sensation of having been screwed hard and in her dream the guard's cocks were so thick that she was made to feel exquisitely filled. The pleasurable dull ache in her loins and the sweet throbbing of her swollen clitoris, still tingling after sex, made her sigh with frustration, as she knew that her dream session had ended.

'How do you feel Lara?'

MacKennan was looking down at her from one side of the couch. On the other, one of his blonde nurses stood smiling. Lara noticed that the girl's nipples pressed erectly against the fabric of her blouse and her pupils were heavily dilated. Almost as if she's aroused, Lara thought sleepily.

'Did you enjoy your dream this time, Lara?'

'Mmm yes, Doctor. It was really good.'

'Wishing you were still asleep... that you were still there?'

'Mmm, definitely,' Lara yawned and stretched.

'You have a vivid imagination, Lara. Pity such an experience can only be found in a dream, isn't it?'

'Yes...yes, it is.'

Lara looked curiously at the Doctor who gave her an enigmatic smile. Suddenly feeling self-conscious, she drew the loose towelling robe a little closer around her.

'Would you like another session now?'

'Sorry... you mean...' Lara stammered, unsure of whether the Doctor meant right away or whether she wanted another session after what she'd experienced in her last dream.

'We could put you back to sleep. Nurse Suzi is happy to work a little late this evening, she could keep an eye on you and I have some office work to catch up on. It's completely up to you.'

For a few seconds Lara hesitated, afraid to seem so desperate. Then she convinced herself that it didn't matter what they thought of her. Damn it, they already knew what she dreamt! She was about to say yes when she caught a gleam in MacKennan's eye that stirred a primitive emotion in her that was almost unfamiliar — fear.

'I think,' she answered falteringly, 'That I've had enough for this session.'

For a second MacKennan's expression was one of bitter frustration but then he smiled approvingly and understandingly, nodding sympathetically.

'Of course. Well, I trust you had a pleasurable dream?' MacKennan smiled disarmingly.

'Oh yes, Doctor. It was...'

Lara flushed with embarrassment as she recalled snatches of what she'd dreamt. Of course MacKennan would have it all recorded. He would probably sit and watch it again in private, the dirty man!

'What you'd hoped for?' MacKennan suggested.

'Sorry?'

'Your dream, I asked if you had a pleasurable dream?'

'Oh, yes...' Lara smiled apologetically, 'It was very pleasurable.'

* * *

Her chauffeur was too well trained to raise even so much as a questioning eyebrow when she summoned him just before midnight. Lara was ready for him at the main door of the luxury apartment block where she lived most of the time. She did have another two homes, apart from the apartment she kept for casual sex, one in the country and one abroad, but she seldom used either. The young driver, smartly attired in

117

an expensive suit, held the saloon door open for her. Her full-length coat of finest cashmere hung open, its length contrasting dramatically with the shortness of her skirt. As she climbed into the car, she afforded the young chauffeur a generous glimpse of bare thighs, before whisking her coat back around her long legs. The door closed for her, she settled back into the leather seat and watched her servant walk around to the driver's door and get into the car.

'Where to Miss Lustral?'

'This is the address.'

Lara brusquely thrust a piece of paper to the man and deliberately turned her attention from him. To settle her nerves she jabbed the button that released the lid on the drinks cabinet that was built into the car and she poured herself a neat, chilled vodka. The car drew away from the kerb and she was swept swiftly down the almost deserted streets of the quarter of the city she lived in. It didn't take long to reach the address she'd given. The fact that it was so close, Lara found disconcerting. The house was in one of the wealthiest neighbourhoods and no distance from the home of one of her friends. What if she was seen, she suddenly wondered in alarm. Before she had time though to change her mind her chauffeur had turned up a private drive and they drew to a halt outside an imposing mansion.

Returning home from her last session at the Dreamscape Institute, Lara had been left longing for more excitement but embarrassed or afraid perhaps, to rush back to Doctor MacKennan for another session. She had therefore turned to that primitive yet moderately effective medium of communication, the internet, to try to find some other way of indulging her now voracious appetite for sexual adventure. She had been surprised yet thrilled to find so close to her home a possible answer.

'Shall I wait for you Miss Lustral?'

'Of course,' she answered her chauffeur in a tone even more peremptory than usual. Butterflies churning in her stomach, without a backward glance to her servant, she walked as briskly as her high heels allowed up to the front door and rang the old fashioned bell. Several minutes seemed to drag past before the door was opened.

'Might I help, Madam?'

The man was nearly elderly but straight backed, his voice strong and clear and although he was dressed as a servant, a butler no less, his tone was disconcerting: deferent but with more than an imperious edge to it.

'Am I at the right address for the "Silk Club"?' Lara asked, acutely self-conscious and already wondering if she wasn't making a big mistake.

'This way.'

Without waiting to see if she was following, the man turned and walked away. Lara followed him, giving her car and chauffeur one last backward glance. Maybe she should have told him to come in and get her if she didn't come back out after a few hours. Behind her the door swung shut of its own accord and she heard a succession of soft clicks as its security locks were obviously reset.

The butler led the way down a chandelier-lit corridor, its walls papered in dark red silk, embroidered with oriental scenes. Opening another door, the man gestured to her to go ahead of him. Lara entered the room and smiling as if he knew her well, another man stood waiting to greet her.

'Lara Lustral, I presume? Honoured.'

The young man was expensively but casually dressed and holding a glass of champagne. After shaking her hand and waiting for his butler to take Lara's coat, he offered her the glass and Lara took several large sips to calm herself as she glanced around. Opulent, decadent, expensive: she had anticipated surroundings that might have been stark, seedy or tasteless and she was pleasantly surprised with what confronted her.

'Welcome to the Silk Club. Perhaps you'd like to come this way?'

Lara followed the young man, wondering momentarily whether perhaps he had misunderstood what she was looking for, or of course, perhaps she had misunderstood what he seemed to be offering her.

'This is the Club Games Room. These two gentlemen are of course members and also my personal friends. Usually Saturdays are the busy nights, everyone wants some stimulating company, naturally. Midweek, well, things are always quieter.'

The two men were seated in deep leather armchairs, one reading a magazine while the other was smoking a cigar whilst cradling a large balloon glass of cognac in his other hand.

'Why don't you take her to see Samantha?'

The suggestion came from the man reading but without even waiting for a response he turned his attention back to the magazine. Glancing at the cover, Lara's eye caught the title and her pulse quickened. Titled "The Art of Restraint", the cover pictured a girl, naked except for her skimpy underwear, her arms tightly and intricately bound with gleaming white ropes behind her back. The girl was lying face down, her legs twisted back, her ankles bound to her wrists. Her expression showed her discomfort at having her arms and legs pulled backwards and Lara quickly took a large gulp of champagne to help her swallow the lump that had risen in her throat.

'Samantha will be surprised to find that she has some company. Perhaps you'd like to come and see her?'

Lara followed the first man through another door and into a smaller room. Whilst the first had resembled a lavishly furnished drawing room this one was quite bare. The floor was polished wood, the walls plain except for two large mirrors at either end of the room. Dangling from two cords clipped to broad cuffs around her wrists, a young woman hung, her arms outstretched above her. The cords were clipped to a wooden bar that was suspended from ropes that ran through pulleys fastened to the ceiling. The woman's arms seemed at almost full stretch and her bare feet hardly touched the floor. A latex hood enveloped her head and the only opening was a small hole for her nose. As she twisted around, writhing against the obvious discomfort she was suffering, Lara was afforded a view of her from behind. The latex hood was drawn tightly around her head at the back with laces, through the criss-crossing of which strands of golden hair escaped. The woman's back from her shoulder blades down to her pert bottom was streaked with pale red lines and realising that these had been inflicted with a whip, Lara caught her breath and took a step backwards in momentary shock.

'Is this the sort of thing you're looking for Miss Lustral?'

Lara glanced nervously at the man then looked back at the woman. How must it really feel to be treated like that, she wondered? Presumably the woman had come her of her own volition, just as she had.

'Perhaps, something less extreme,' Lara admitted, smiling coyly at the young man. She tried to imagine the pain the woman must have felt as she'd been whipped. Never having really tasted any severe pain, Lara found it hard to imagine herself in the girl's place.

'Samantha loves the taste of the whip, it is her deliverance. If you doubt me, feel her sex.'

'I'm sure... I don't ...doubt ...you,' she stammered.

'Feel her anyway. Be my guest.'

Timidly Lara advanced to where the other woman hung suspended. She could smell the girl's sweat and see her perspiration trickling down her outstretched arms and shining as tiny beads of moisture on the fine hairs around her sex. Gingerly Lara touched the tethered woman's pussy. The latex covered head shook and the legs twitched in immediate response. Lara moved her fingertips more confidently, realising there was nothing the girl could do and besides, she couldn't even see her!

Just as the man had assured her, the woman's pussy was hot and slick with her arousal.

'She loves it. You should try it. Could we tempt you?'

Lara looked at the man and glanced back at the woman uncertainly. Damn it, this was the sort of thing she'd come here looking for, why was she scared now? Silently reproving herself she drew back her shoulders and smiled as confidently as she could manage.

'Okay,' she answered. 'Let's get on with it.'

'Bravo, now tell me Miss Lustral, just what sort of thing had you in mind? Your fantasy is similar to Samantha's I assume?' the man asked matter-of-factly.

'Well...' Lara swallowed the lump that had risen in her throat. 'I'd imagined being taken forcefully... sexually... by several men...' She felt the colour in her cheeks and tried to look calmly at the man to whom she was speaking but she was too embarrassed now. Her gaze wandered the room but there was nothing to focus on except for the young woman hanging helplessly from the cords. She hadn't made any response to their voices so Lara had concluded that the hood must have deprived her of her hearing as well as preventing her from speaking or seeing. The poor girl was suspended in darkness without any way of knowing what was going on around her or what might be about to befall her next. The thought made Lara's pussy ache piquantly as if in sympathy for her plight.

'Is that all? Have you not dreamt about the delights of the whip or other punishments...'

Lara remembered her dream in the Institute but glancing at the girl and the red whip lines down her back, she hesitated.

'I'm not sure...'

'Then we must help guide you. You see, all your desires can be easily accommodated,' the man smiled disarmingly.

'Really?' Lara glanced expectantly at him, her pulse quickening.

'Why don't you wait here a moment whilst I make some preparations.'

The man didn't wait to give Lara the chance to answer and a second later she was alone with the tethered girl and the room was quiet except for the faint creaking of the cords from which she hung suspended.

A few moments passed before the young man returned and with the other two men following. The man showed her a pair of broad leather cuffs identical to those that held the other girl's arms outstretched.

'Hold your hands up.'

'What are you going to do?' Lara demanded.

'Put these wristcuffs on you. If you don't want this you might as well leave now. It's your choice?'

'I'll stay.'

Lara offered her hands and stood motionless, her heart hammering as the young man calmly folded the leather around one wrist then buckled it tight. Lara watched as he dealt with her other wrist the same way, glancing as he finished at the other two men, who smiled pleasantly at her.

'Now, this isn't so bad is it?' the young man suggested, conversationally as he encouraged her to place her arms behind her back. There was the sound of a metal clip fastening and when Lara tried experimentally to move her arms, she found that he'd clipped the wristcuffs together and her arms were now held behind her back.

'Take Samantha down, it's time for Miss Lustral to be initiated.'

'But I'm not sure I want to be whipped... I only wanted...'

'Be quiet or we'll gag you.'

'No! I've changed my mind!'

Lara took a step towards the door but the man caught her arm and pulled her backwards.

'Damn you let me go!'

'I'm afraid it's too late now to change your mind.'

'You said you would fuck me, if you think I'm going to let you treat me like you've treated her, you're mistaken!' Lara hissed. 'You bastard! I didn't come here to be treated like this, I was looking for...'

'Excitement? Pleasure? Sexual satisfaction!'

The man tightened his grip on Lara's arm, drawing her back against his chest. The other two men had removed the woman from the cords and they were marching her away, one grasping each arm.

'You came here,' the man lowered his voice threateningly, 'to get off on being treated roughly. Very roughly! You asked to be taken forcefully by several men. Well, before we do that we're going to soften you up. There's nothing like the taste of the whip to put a submissive female in the mood for a nice, hard shafting!'

'You bastard! Let me go!'

Lara tried to kick back but she missed the man who just laughed at her. The other men having led the girl from the room had returned and stood smiling with undisguised pleasure as they watched Lara struggling in the grasp of the young man.

'Right, get the posh girl's pretty little clothes off her.'

There was practically nothing Lara could do to stop them apart from writhe and twist and curse and kick as best she could. They seemed to enjoy her protests and had obviously done this plenty of times before. Between the three of them they made light work of divesting her of all her clothes. Red cheeked with shame, Lara was in no time left wearing only her high heels and her delicate silk underwear.

'Okay chaps, let's get her hung up.'

The three men dragged her kicking and swearing across to the dangling pole and unclipping her wrists. Dragging her arms up one at a time they fastened the wristcuffs onto the pole. The pole was then raised until Lara was left hanging by her wrists, her high heels just brushing the floor.

'Let me down, please!' she cried, her outstretched arms quickly aching, the tension worst in her shoulders where it felt like needles were stabbing into her muscles and was quite unbearable as far as Lara was concerned.

'Now then Miss Lustral, have you ever had the pleasure of tasting one of these against your lovely soft back before?'

Lara looked wide-eyed with alarm at the whip the man had produced. It was just like something she'd seen in old pictures from when people had ridden horses. She watched, horrified yet strangely excited as the man flexed the whip. When he touched her bare skin with the tip she instinctively shied away. The man gave a satisfied smile.

'I'm afraid it will mark your skin, though after a few days the marks will fade. You don't mind do you?'

'Yes! You can't do this to me, I forbid it!'

'Really?' The man laughed and with the point of the whip stroked under Lara's trembling chin, lifting her head so that she had to look at him.

'And how will you stop me?'

Lara glanced around her anxiously.

'Please, I've made a mistake... I don't really want to be treated like this! Honestly! You've got to let me go!'

'You have a beautiful body, Miss Lustral. I must compliment you.'

As the man spoke he circled her and Lara shivered nervously as his hand stroked down her back. Moving to face her he then let his hand slowly cross her bare skin until it was touching the silk of her bra. Lara was panting hard and she glanced down at her heaving bosom as the man licked his thumb then brushed it against the silk where it concealed her nipple. Lara sighed, her back arching. For a second she had to close her eyes; so delicious was the sensation. There was something about being tied and touched that made it so much more exquisite... she gazed down, watching mesmerised as having licked his thumb again he drew it across the silk over her nipple. As the fabric dampened, it clung to her nipple; erect now, it pressed, clearly visible against the gossamer silk.

'Such generous breasts on such a slim young lady deserve a lot of attention.'

Handing the whip to one of his friends, the young man used both hands to coax her breasts from the silk cups. With the fabric of the bra now tight under her breasts, they hung down like ripe fruit, the nipple of one glistening wetly.

'Would you like us to gag you?'

The man smiled as he asked the question, so matter-of-factly that he could have been asking her if she'd like a coffee. Lara stumbled to find an answer but she was lost. The man nodded sympathetically, as if understanding and appreciating her dilemma.

'Feel free to scream, the room is sound proofed.'

Without further ado the young man stepped back and gestured to his friend now holding the whip to proceed.

'Please, don't...'

Thwack!

The riding crop cut down mercilessly hard against her back, just below her shoulder blades. The pain shot to her brain like a searing flame that left her dizzy and gasping. Too breathless for a second to even keep herself standing upright, her legs buckled and her wrists were jammed against the leather cuffs as her arms were dragged painfully between the weight of her body and the resistance of the cords.

Thwack!

Like a jolt of electricity the whip stung her bottom making Lara yelp with alarm then struggling to recover her footing she looked around her in anguish and alarm.

'A little less vigorously I think Charles. After all this is Miss Lustral's first session.'

With a faint hiss the whip snapped against her rump again.

'Oww!'

Lara jerked against the cords that held her arms. The pain was far more intense than what she'd imagined but to her shame she already felt sexually aroused by her situation. Whether it was the knowledge that the three men planned to fuck her later or whether it was being tied and naked except for her underwear, she felt the heat of sexual longing and need burning in her loins.

Thwack!

The pain ran like a tongue of flame from her bottom, fanning out in a second to reach her pussy and her brain. She felt washed with feelings she'd never felt before. She was helpless before these strangers. Her body stretched and dangling naked before them: her breasts, aching mildly from the cutting pressure of her bra under their generous weight. She groaned and twisted, gazing up at her outstretched arms. Seeing the leather cuffs tight around her wrists stirred more emotions in her, deep down and the warm ache in her pussy she knew was quickly building into the heat of desire that she so loved.

The succession of blows from the riding crop that followed were skilfully delivered and enough to bring Lara to a fevered climax. She was unable to stop herself crying out in ecstasy as she came. After that she was beyond caring what the men did to her. She knew with gleeful certainty that whatever they subjected her to she'd enjoy herself and that was all that mattered. The next hour or so passed in a delicious daze. Aching from her beating, she was lowered and a glass thrust against her lips.

'Drink! It will wash away the pain.'

Lara didn't care about the pain, she'd enjoyed it but she did as she was ordered, too weak or uncaring to argue or question.

'Good girl.'

Hands grasped her aching arms and dragged her into another room. The bed was large and sumptuous, draped like the room itself in rich fabrics and opulently decorated. Thrown down onto the bed, they held her face down and took in turns to use her. By the end her pussy felt deliciously satisfied and throbbed pleasantly. She felt herself quickly drifting towards sleep and dreamily let her head slump against the soft pillows. Her sexual longing more than slaked she was already half asleep when she heard the men talking in hushed tones as they left the room.

'Give it a few more minutes to take full effect then we'll take her to join Samantha. Once she's had her little rest, Miss Lustral can get a taste of what The Silk Club is really about.'

The door clicked softly shut. Weakly Lara lifted her head

and shook herself, struggling to dispel the drowsiness that had crept over her. She was too shaken by what she'd heard to stop and think about dressing herself. Abandoning all her clothes except her shoes she tiptoed from the room. To her relief the house suddenly seemed deserted and it was only as she was passing another door that led off the main drawing room that she heard voices. Leaning lightly against the door she pressed her ear against the wood. She could just make out the men's voices and a female voice, pleading with them. Deciding that she'd definitely had enough excitement for one evening Lara hurried for the front door. To her relief her wool trench coat was hanging in the porch and snatching it up she fumbled with the door lock then dragging the door open she ran out into the cool night air.

To her relief her chauffeur was waiting and he had the rear door open before she reached the car. In her rush to retreat to the sanctuary of her car, her coat slipped open as she climbed in, revealing more than a glimpse of bare thigh this time to her young driver. She was driven home without so much as a word spoken between them. All the way Lara struggled to keep her eyes open as whatever the men had encouraged her to drink tried to lull her to sleep. Perhaps all they'd intended were some harmless games but she was glad to be safely back in her car with her trusty chauffeur.

As she was whisked to her thirty-second floor apartment by the express elevator, she was already feeling more confident and relaxed. She thought about how good the evening had been and chided herself for running out half way through. Back in her apartment her thoughts were full of her sexual adventure and as she pushed the door shut she already knew that she craved more attention. Damn it, she cursed silently, why had she let her nerves get the better of her? Impatiently she phoned her chauffeur.

'Yes, Miss Lustral?'

'Get your arse up here, now!'

In the time it took her chauffeur to arrive she'd dabbed on

some perfume and had slipped on a black silk camisole and panties. When the buzzer sounded, she was in the kitchen and she stabbed the front door release button then resumed what she was doing. Her chauffeur found her with two tumblers of ice and vodka in hand. She smiled sweetly at the young man and offered him one glass.

'Darling you're a wonderful chauffeur and now it's time for me to thank you properly for your loyal work.'

'Is this a trick?' the man warily accepted the glass.

'No, I'm just desperate for a fuck. Will you oblige?'

* * *

The next morning Lara woke to find her servant naked and sleeping soundly in her bed alongside her. She grinned childishly remembering the previous night then her expression hardened: of course, now she'd have to sack him. She slipped out from under the silk sheets and walked through to the living room. The sex had been good but she had to have more. She knew there was only one way she'd be assured of the satisfaction she was craving, without taking any more risks, so without any hesitation she dialled the Dreamscape number. Having made herself an appointment for the evening, she went back to her bedroom. Glancing in her mirror, she saw the pale red lines across her bottom and back. She smiled as she remembered how good it had felt.

CHAPTER SEVEN

MacKennan leant back in his chair, smiling with satisfaction as he watched the monitor screen. Lara the adventurer hissing and spitting like a wild cat dangled by her arms while the evil Doctor calmly circled her. Twisting, writhing, her naked body slick with perspiration, she stared in fear and loathing at the whip he held.

She was in a stone hall that was lit by large, flickering candles; primitive furnishings gave it the feel of some medieval torture chamber. Upon a smoke blackened iron grate, logs crackled and blazed and beside them lay several long branding irons. There were manacles and ropes littering the floor: against one wall was a cross of wood with belts and leather bracelets fastened to it. A large heavy wooden table was strewn with implements of torture.

MacKennan was impressed by her fertile imagination: Miss Lustral was evidently going to give her heroine persona a hard time this session, he mused.

He glanced across to where his client lay sleeping. They had not restrained her wrists this time: all of what he viewed sprang uninfluenced from the young woman's desires. MacKennan took a sip from his coffee and turned fractionally in his chair, settling into a more comfortable position. His cock was hard, aching for satisfaction. For the moment though he was quite content just to watch the screen.

The young heroine, naked and tethered by her wrists dangled defencelessly as the evil Doctor brought the riding crop down against her slender back. Lara gave a choked gasp, stumbling forwards under the force of the blow. The whip came down again and she groaned, twisting her arms and jerking her wrists against the tight leather cuffs. Again the whip struck her, this time against the back of her thighs.

MacKennan rubbed his jaw thoughtfully and moving aside his coffee drew his keyboard a little closer towards him. He quickly keyed in a series of commands — suggestions, he preferred to refer to them as in his notes — and leant back again in his chair his hand hovering over the keyboard, one finger poised directly above the enter button.

* * *

Lara, blinking back her tears, watched in alarm as the evil Doctor discarded the whip and taking a branding iron shoved its end into the fire making sparks leap and the logs crackle more fiercely.

'Time to brand you as my property! Now, you're not going to be silly and struggle are you?'

Lara swallowed the lump of fear in her throat, her heart hammering as the man moved towards her, the smouldering iron held before him.

'Would you prefer it if we tied you down so you don't wriggle and spoil the brand? Or can you be as tough as you like to pretend you are and keep still for a brief moment?'

'You bastard...'

Lara glanced around her frantically. One of the female servants was in the room, lounging on a chair, her slender legs raised, her feet balanced on the table of torture instruments. She was plainly loving every minute of what she was watching and Lara bitterly vowed that she would wipe the smug grin from the pretty face before she was through with the evil Doctor. Other than the girl though the rest of the henchmen were absent. The smell of the smoking brand made Lara glance back at her arch-enemy. Stood close before her, smiling sadistically, he looked hard into her eyes, revelling in her fear. Lara stared back, anger and defiance burning in her fiercer than the glowing poker of orange iron that was now inches from her bare skin.

'Feeling brave my dear?'

The evil Doctor raised the glowing end of the brand towards Lara's exposed arm. At the last second Lara tightened her hands around the ropes that stretched from the wristcuffs and pulled herself up with all her strength.

131

Her first karate kick took the man under the chin and her second struck his arm that held the smoking brand. In his anguish he dropped the poker, which clattered onto the cobbles, hissing loudly. Suspended like a trapeze artist, Lara swung forward and before the man could respond she had one leg hooked around his neck. Dragging him forward she wrapped her second leg around his throat and now at last her body weight was supported, thanks to the man trapped under her, still reeling from the karate kick she'd delivered.

Lara glanced sideways to see what the girl was doing. For the first few seconds she'd been too stunned to react but now she'd jumped from the chair and was rushing across the room, whip in hand. Lara, ignoring her for the moment, tightened her leg lock on the man's head and letting her weight sink onto his buckling back, she suddenly had a few inches of slack rope above her arms. She snatched at the buckles that held the wristcuffs but only managed to free one before the man dragged himself free from her. Dangling by one wrist she wrenched at the buckle that kept her suspended. Pain like a jolt of electricity ran through her body as the girl brought the whip down against her.

Crack!

The whip lashed across her again. The pain in her suspended arm was worse though and with a determined effort she tore the buckle free. Landing hard, her aching legs almost buckling under her, she felt the whip snake down across her shoulder. She snatched for the end before the girl could pull it back and as her adversary jerked and tussled for control of the weapon she sprang at her.

Tumbling together across the stone floor, Lara was first back to her knees and she still had a hold of the end of the whip. She glanced behind her to see the Doctor lurching towards the table and she knew he was after a weapon. She hurled herself onto the girl, knocking her backwards and wrenching the whip from her hand. With a rush of euphoric triumph she leapt to her feet and turned to deal with her arch-enemy.

* * *

MacKennan glanced at the dreaming Lara then looked across to where Suzi stood watching both patient and monitor. On the screen, Lara the adventurer, whip in hand stood facing her enemy. The evil Doctor looked more than a little afraid; his lower lip was bleeding, his face already showing the beginnings of a bruise. He was panting hard and had backed up against the table, a slender truncheon clutched in one hand and a cat-o-nine tails in the other.

MacKennan pressed the "Enter" button on his computer keyboard and relaxed back in his chair.

The girl who had been sprawled on the floor behind Lara silently gathered herself like a cat preparing to pounce on its prey. Lara never heard her until it was too late. The heel of the girl's leather boot struck against the back of her leg, directly behind her knee. With a cry of anguish, her leg buckling under her, Lara collapsed. The pointed toe of the boot thumped into Lara's stomach.

She was still doubled up in agony when the girl grasped her hair and jerked her head back. The palm of her hand smacked against her cheek with a resounding slap. A second later her head was flicked in the opposite way by a backhand slap delivered to her other cheek. The girl grinned down at her, tightening her grasp on Lara's tousled mane of golden hair.

'Something wrong Lara? Feeling a little dazed are we?'
Slap!

Lara groaned, weakly trying to lift one hand to defend herself. Laughing, the girl stood over her, flicked it aside and brought her palm down again against her cheek.

Slap!

'Well, if you will be naughty you have to be punished!'

The girl gave a scornful laugh and brought the back of her hand down against Lara's other cheek.

133

Slap!

'Poor thing, you're looking a little sorry for yourself. Feeling a bit tender are we?'

Slap!

'Good work nurse, I don't think the bitch will give us much trouble now.'

Lara saw the man looking down at her.

'Shall I tie her up?' the girl asked.

Lara tried to pull her hair free of the girl's grasp and was rewarded with another slap across her face. The man grinned and gestured for the girl to continue.

Slap! Slap!

The man grasped Lara's chin with one hand, lifting her face so he could see her anguish. She was too dazed to do anything now and the man nodded with satisfaction.

'On the cross, use all the straps. It's time to teach her a lesson!'

* * *

MacKennan stood up and walked across to the leather couch. Below the pale green lights Lara Lustral lay, eyes closed, her breathing fast and shallow. Carefully he slipped his hand under her towelling robe and felt between her legs. His fingers found the soft lips of her sex. Pushing them a little way into her he found her warm and slick. He glanced at his nurse.

'Like a bitch on heat.'

'Is it time to take her to the basement Doctor?' the girl asked.

MacKennan nodded affirmatively.

'Nearly... I think though we'll conclude this session with some hard punishment. If she responds well towards it in her dreams, then the next time Miss Lustral comes to the Dreamscape Institute, can be her last.'

'I can't wait to see her suffering for real,' the nurse admitted, licking her sensual lips in eager anticipation.

'Don't worry. Lara Lustral is addicted to playing the submissive. You won't have long to wait.'

* * *

'Would you like some water or a drink before we get under way?'

'No thanks, I feel fine,' Lara answered.

After the excitement and stimulation she'd enjoyed during her last session at the Institute, Lara had booked herself in again before she'd even left the building. To her delight, MacKennan had suggested another evening session, since his daytime appointments were full for weeks. Lara had readily agreed.

'Okay then, rest your head back and relax. Suzi, prepare the triple hypodermic for Miss Lustral.'

'My dreams Doctor... are they...unusual? I mean, they must seem...'

'My dear Lara, like I think I said before, you are not the first Alpha woman I've worked with who has displayed such dreams,' MacKennan smiled reassuringly.

'That makes me feel better,' Lara admitted.

She felt a tiny prick against her arm and glanced sideways to see the nurse had applied the head of a fibre optic lead to her arm. When she experimentally flexed her arm muscle the little head of the lead remained attached to her skin.

'What's that for?'

'So we can administer three drugs into you in controlled and varying amounts simultaneously.'

'You've not used three before Doctor, what are they?'

'They're to help you sleep and dream and admit how you feel'

'What do you mean, admit how I feel?'

MacKennan gave an ambiguous shrug then nodded to the nurse.

'Ten percent emothome and ten percent votrimal please Suzi.'

Lara relaxed her head against the padded couch and took a few relaxing deep breaths. She tried to remember where her dream had got to: she could vaguely recollect the incident in

135

the gym with the two guards but she couldn't remember any detail. It was impossible for her to visualise the men's faces, for example. It was strange how her memory was so arbitrarily selective. Closing her eyes though she could suddenly clearly see the dominatrix in every detail as she'd walked back across the gym to where Lara lay panting breathlessly. The girl seemed very tall because Lara was gazing up at her and her high-heeled black boots gave her extra height. She could remember the feel of the warm PVC elbow length gloves the girl wore as she'd caught hold of Lara's collar and hauled her up into a sitting position. She'd then fleetingly stroked her gloved hand down her neck and over the swell of Lara's breasts. She could remember the expression on the girl's face and see her face clearly. Of course, she was the real Doctor MacKennan's nurse. That must be why she could so easily recall every detail about her.

Impatiently she wished herself asleep. She could remember the incident in the torture chamber, fighting the evil Doctor, nearly winning but then his damned young female servant had surprised her from behind and between them they had subdued her and strapped her to the cross. She had been spread-eagled on it facing the wall and the Doctor had taken a whip to her entire back, from neck to knees. Lara felt herself moisten as she recalled the repeated smacks of the whip lashing her and how her screams had echoed round the chamber. And she could also recall how the vivid slashes of pain had excited her and brought her to orgasm after orgasm.

'Lara can you hear me?'

She opened her eyes to the pale green light as the Doctor's voice intruded on her thoughts.

'Yes...' she answered, feeling very sleepy now and eager to slip back into her dream world.

'Suzi is going to strap your hands above your head. You don't mind if she does this, do you?'

Although she felt very sleepy she knew she'd heard the Doctor correctly. Suzi was going to strap her hands above her head! Not the nurse in her dreams — this was Doctor MacKennan of the Dreamscape Institute, telling her that his nurse was going to do this to her! Confused and irritated that she had been disturbed just as she was falling asleep, she looked around for the Doctor, wanting to ask him what was going on.

Doctor MacKennan was standing directly beside her on her left and as she made eye contact, she felt her right arm being lifted and soft hands coaxing her shoulder from inside the towelling robe.

'What the hell is she doing?' Lara demanded, trying to sit upright but unable to.

'Just relax Lara, it's all part of your treatment. Trust me,' the Doctor soothed.

'But...no, wait a minute, why...'

Only by exerting considerable effort was Lara able to pull her arm away from the nurse's hold. Already though the girl had extricated her arms from the towelling robe and Lara modestly drew her arm across her chest to cover her breasts. MacKennan glanced across to his assistant who was looking expectantly at him. He gave her a conspiratorial nod and Lara glanced to her right just in time to see the nurse adjust two dials on a drip machine that fed the fibre optic tube that was connected to her.

'What's going on... Doctor?'

Lara slumped her head back against the couch, sighing, as the strength in her muscles seemed to suddenly dissolve.

'Lara, you have to trust me. I know what you want from your dreams and I can give that to you. There's no point in trying to deny how you feel and what you need.'

As she listened to the Doctor's calming voice she knew with appalling certainty that the drug he was administering to her was making her so lethargic, so weak, so sleepy that she couldn't galvanise herself into even trying to resist him. He had her in his control; there was nothing she could do! But what was *he* going to do? Her pulse raced, her mind filled with a jumble of images from her dreams and she found herself excitedly anticipating a dozen things that might lie in store for her. Surely though this couldn't be happening...

The nurse caught hold of her right arm and drew it up above her head. Lara looked in disbelief at what was happening to her, tried to pull away but her arm muscles felt as soft as jelly. She sighed with frustration and then stared in fascination as she saw a rubber strap being drawn around her wrist.

'You can't do this to me!'

She looked at the Doctor and tried to tighten her grip with her left hand on the side of the couch so that she could climb off it. The Doctor shook his head reprovingly, watched her as she managed to lift herself a little way up, then with a cry of frustration sink back down onto the soft black padding. She had no strength at all in her muscles! She shook her head with dismay as she felt the rubber strap tighten around her right wrist and glancing up saw the nurse pull the strap below the edge of the bench. It tightened and Lara realised that the girl must have fastened it to some concealed clasp.

'Just relax Lara, let yourself dream if that's what you want. Or if you prefer, enjoy the experience of what is really happening to that lovely body of yours.'

'I... don't... understand...' Lara whispered, shaking her head as the nurse now lifted her other arm above her head. She felt the rubber of another strap around her wrist and then her arm was drawn a little higher and closer to the edge of the couch. When she tried to pull it back down she felt the rubber around her wrist resist the pressure she struggled to exert. Realising that both her arms were now tied down she sighed despondently and looked for reassurance to the Doctor.

MacKennan smiled benevolently then allowed his gaze to be drawn to her exposed breasts.

'Now then Lara, you've been given a muscle relaxant so there's no point in struggling or objecting, you won't get anywhere.'

'You can't...'

'Be quiet Lara,' the Doctor spoke sternly, impatience evident in his voice for the first time.

Lara looked apprehensively as the nurse flicked away the towelling robe from her legs, exposing her from head to toe.

'Let me go!'

'Listen Lara, as well as muscle relaxant, I've given you something to make you sleepy and something else to make you admit what you feel.'

'What do you mean?'

'You've been administered a truth drug, so whether you want to or not, you're going to answer all my questions honestly.'

'No, this isn't fair! You've no right!'

Even as Lara blurted her objection the nurse was wrapping and tightening rubber straps around her ankles. She saw the Doctor gazing down appreciatively at her naked body and she felt her cheeks blush. Her legs were spread apart and when she tried to modestly draw them together she realised that they'd been secured in similar fashion to her arms. MacKennan bent over the couch and spoke softly, his voice hypnotically soothing.

'Relax Lara, nothing is going to happen that you don't want. Just close your eyes and think about your dreams.'

'Please, Doctor, I want to go home...'

'No Lara. No, I don't think so. You've enjoyed your dream sessions here haven't you?'

'Yes, but...'

'And you would like to have another good dream, wouldn't you?'

'Yes...'

'You see, the truth isn't so hard to tell, is it? Now, tell me what bits of your dreams you liked the most.'

'It's hard to remember,' Lara murmured, glancing anxiously from side to side.

'We both know you can remember, now tell me.'

'I liked it when the evil Doctor took me prisoner...I was

139

tied up and helpless; I couldn't stop them from doing whatever they wanted with me.'

'And what did they do to you, Lara?'

Lara felt herself blushing as she recalled the scenes from her dream.

'I was bound with ropes...they made my breasts ache...they tied cords around them and... and they made my nipples hurt.'

'Did you like that?'

'Yes. They made them ache so much I thought I was going to faint... but it felt so good...'

'What else did they do?'

'I don't want to say, Doctor, please don't make me.'

'Tell me Lara. Tell me everything. You have to.'

Lara sighed and closed her eyes. She could feel the rubber straps tight around her wrists and ankles, the tension in her limbs was arousing. She knew the Doctor could see her naked body, her breasts, her pussy... it made her wet, knowing that he could see her, that if he wanted to he could touch her and she couldn't stop him.

'What else did they do to you?' the Doctor's voice prompted.

'The evil Doctor had guards, genetically modified men, they used me.'

'Tell me how they did it.'

'They came to my cell. One of them held me down and the other took me.'

'And you let them?'

'I couldn't stop them... my arms were tied and they had me gagged...they were too strong...'

'And you were so weak and helpless...'

'Yes, they had me tied...gagged...they put something in my nostrils... made me breathe it so I was sleepy.'

'So you couldn't stop them?'

'Yes...'

'But it felt good, didn't it? You were glad that you were helpless because then you could just let them use you however they wanted.'

'Yes...'

'And how did it feel when they used your body?'

'It felt good... they were so big...such a good dream, if only...'

'And your last session Lara, when the Doctor was going to brand you; did that excite you?'

'Yes...very much...'

'You remember breaking free? You remember that? Tell me what you liked best.'

'The feeling of helplessness as the girl slapped me...knowing that they were going to punish me...'

'And you liked that?'

'Yes... feeling my arms and legs spread... tight straps against my skin... no escape...being helpless...'

'You're such a sexually frustrated young woman aren't you Lara? Ordinary sex just isn't good enough for you, is it? You need something stronger... much stronger.'

'Yes...yes...' Lara sighed.

'Well you can let me take care of you now. I hardly think there's much need for you to have to dream to find what you're looking for.'

'What do you mean, Doctor?'

'Lara, you admitted what you wanted, so now I'm going to look after you.'

'I don't understand what you're saying...'

'What you dream is what you want. Well, that's what you're going to get! Now you've admitted how much you love it, I've no hesitation in providing you with what you need.'

'But you made me tell you. You gave me a truth drug... you've forced me to admit it, otherwise I'd never have said anything!'

'But it's still the truth. The facts are that you want what you dream. What difference will it make if I give you the chance to experience it for real?'

'This isn't fair, you have to let me go!'

Lara tried to pull her arms and legs free from the restraining straps but the rubber was too tight around her ankles and wrists and after writhing ineffectually for a few moments, she sank back down with a sigh of despair.

'What are you going to do to me?' Lara asked nervously after she'd exhausted herself with a few moments of futile struggling.

'Well Lara, that depends on you. What would you like to happen? Would you like to experience your delicate little pussy being stretched wide and filled up again with an unimaginably large cock?'

'You're going to make me dream that? Can you do that?' Lara look anxiously at the man stood over her.

'Dream it? That bit of your fantasy was hardly a dream...'

'Oh my God... you mean...' Lara shook her head in disbelief.

MacKennan smiled smugly. 'Last time, since it was such a tight fit for your slender little pussy, I was very gentle.'

'You swine! You've fucked me whilst I was asleep!'

'And you loved it, you randy little bitch, so stop pretending. Well, now I know how much you loved it, I don't need to be so gentle do I?'

'No...'

MacKennan grinned as he heard her answer.

'So nice to hear the truth, I'm glad you're looking forward to the experience as much as I am.'

As MacKennan began unbuttoning his white surgical coat Lara dragged her hands against the rubber that jammed up against her wrists. There was no chance though that she might extricate her hands.

'Struggle all you want Lara, if it will ease your conscience. The fact is you're desperate for it and I'm going to give it to you.'

'If you so much as lay a hand on me, I'll scream so loudly...'

'Scream all you want. This room is sound proof and there is no-one else left in the Institute now. It's the evening and everyone's gone home. It's just you, me and Suzi. And I think you can guess from your dreams what Suzi is going to get up to with you once I've finished with your delicious body!'

For a moment Lara writhed and twisted again but the rubber straps held her and soon, panting hard, she gave up struggling. MacKennan smiled and placed his hand on her stomach.

'Relax, Lara. If you allow yourself to, you'll enjoy this as much as I will.'

His hand moved lower and she felt his fingers stroke the insides of her thighs. As he spoke his fingers slid smoothly over her skin and brushed tantalisingly close to her sex. Lara gasped and fought down the urge to arch her back and beg him to sink his fingers into her pussy. She bit her lip to stop herself from betraying her disappointment as the man took his hand from her body. God, she was desperate for it. He knew her too well! He was right, she was aching for it! Filled with shame she shouted:

'What are you waiting for you bastard? Why don't you just get on with it?'

'Why don't you admit that it's what you want then, Lara: you want to suffer just like the adventurer Lara does in your dreams.'

Her mind answered yes but she managed to remain silent. Whether it was the drug he'd given her or not, she knew she couldn't deny that she longed to experience what her dream persona had gone through. He had already watched her fantasy dreams on his computer monitor, he knew what turned her on, she told herself, so what was the point in trying to deny it any longer? Shame, that was why! But then what was the difference between her paying him to give her what she wanted through her dreams and letting him give her the real experience? He was giving her the chance to enact her darkest dreams: perhaps it would be stupid not to grab the chance. Lara lay impatiently waiting, certain that the Doctor was about to fuck her. She wondered whether he was really as well endowed as the men in her fantasy dream. Suddenly impatient for what lay in store she looked up and met MacKennan's gaze. As if sensing what was going through her mind, MacKennan smiled victoriously.

'Tell me Lara, do you want me to treat you like your were treated in your dreams?'

'Yes...'

She had said it before she could stop herself! But then maybe it was the truth drug he'd administered still working. Whichever, she'd never know and she didn't care!

'Excellent. Right then, it's time for Miss Lustral to enjoy what she's always dreamt of experiencing. More emothome, please nurse.'

Lara rested her head back against the couch. There was no turning back now. She glanced back at her outstretched arms and stared at the rubber restraints tight around her wrists. Her eyelids closed heavily and she felt herself being pulled down into a deep sleep.

* * *

The icy cold water jolted Lara abruptly awake. For a moment she imagined that she was dreaming. They'd done this to her before. She was in her dreamscape. As her breath ran out she struggled against the hand that held her down. Thankfully just as she was certain she couldn't hold her breath any longer her head was pulled up out of the water. Coughing and spluttering, Lara struggled to get her breath back. She saw the Doctor watching her and suddenly with dismay she realised that he wasn't the evil Doctor of her dreams but that it was MacKennan from the Institute and the memory of what had happened before she'd lost consciousness came flooding back. As alarm bells rang in her head someone tightened their hold again on her soaking hair and her head was pushed back down. For a moment she was submerged and struggling frantically and then she was abruptly and gratefully gulping air again. Before she could catch her breath properly though MacKennan gave the order for her to be submerged once more.

'Again.'

Lara felt rough hands pushed her head back down once more and her face was forced under the water. A few seconds later, grasped by her hair, her head was hauled back up. MacKennan was staring down at her. She lay stomach down on a bench, her upper body dangling over the edge. Glancing down she saw a large plastic container of water just below her.

'Feeling refreshed Lara?' the Doctor asked sarcastically, 'Is that the same as your dream Lara or better?'

Lara was coughing and gasping, her head left dangling now above the water.

'So tell me Lara, does this feel more convincing?' MacKennan questioned. Lara looked at the man with unconcealed fury. The Doctor gave an amused smile then gestured to the man. Her head was pushed back down again. She tried to stop them but her arms were pinned behind her back, her wrists cuffed together and her ankles too were tied. Someone had a hand pressing down between her shoulder blades and another hand pinned her lower back. The water enveloped her face and she was submerged, holding her breath, thrashing her head in protest. After a few seconds she was hauled back up by a sharp tug on her soaking hair. Coughing and spluttering and too exhausted and dazed to resist, hands grasped her ankles and her arms and dragged her from the bench.

As she lay on the floor recovering her breath, cord ropes were clipped to rubber cuffs that were already secured around her wrists. A clasp holding the two wristcuffs together against the small of her back was unfastened and Lara was hauled to her feet. The cords that were fastened to her wristcuffs were fed through hooks fixed to the low ceiling and as the cords were now pulled down, Lara's arms were drawn above her head.

'No... let me go!'

Lara frantically pulled against the cords as she realised what was happening. She was fighting against two men though and relentlessly her arms were drawn higher above her head. As her feet started to lose contact with the floor and her toes were left dragging frantically on the ground, the cords were clipped back onto the rubber wristcuffs.

'Uhh... my arms... please...'

Lara groaned in discomfort but to her relief the cords stretched just enough for her to get her feet back on the floor and take a little of the weight from her acutely stretched arms.

'Spread her legs,' MacKennan ordered.

There were already rubber cuffs strapped tightly around her ankles. The two men in dark suits carried out the Doctor's order with a ruthless swiftness. One fastened a steel bulldog clip onto the ring fixed to one of the anklecuffs. The other man had a firm hold of her leg and with sharp tug, dragged Lara's leg sideways. The bulldog clip was swiftly fastened to another steel ring that was fixed to the floor. Dealing with her other ankle in a similar fashion the men quickly had Lara's long, slender legs held widely spread. Lara gazed up and down at her acutely spread-eagled body. She could feel every muscle in her arms and legs straining.

'How do you feel now Lara?'

Lara gazed at the men surrounding her but made no reply. It was all too much to take in. This was no dream, no fantasy. This was for real. Her stomach churned in nervous anticipation.

She gazed up at her outstretched arms and saw the rubber cuffs tight around her slim wrists. Looking down her naked body she stared at her widely spread and tethered legs, similar rubber cuffs tightly bound around her ankles and clipped by powerful metal fasteners to purposefully placed rings fastened onto the floor. She looked around the room and felt a sense of fascination and horror as she realised that it was designed for just such a purpose as it was being put to now: the tormenting of a helpless girl. They'd started her on the bench and she could see the straps dangling from its sides, their purpose all too obvious. Now, hung by her arms, naked and helpless, she wondered what lay in store for her next. MacKennan's cold, hard voice gave her the answer.

'Cane her!'

'What... no...wait!'

Lara turned her head in time to see one of the dark suited men pick up a slender cane and flex it experimentally. The other henchman stepped back, folding his arms across his chest as he watched. Although his eyes were concealed with dark glasses, she saw his mouth was twisted into a cruel smile.

'Start with her arse.'

There was a faint hiss of the cane slicing the air then a sharp pain across Lara's buttocks.

Whack!

'Oww!'

'Does that feel real enough for you Lara?' the Doctor asked.

Whack!

Again the cane struck her in the same place.

'Oww!'

'Is real pain as refreshing and as stimulating as imaginary pain?'

Lara jerked her arms and legs angrily against the straps that held her spreadeagled.

'Damn you MacKennan, this is for real! This isn't a dream! Sod you, let me go!'

'But you wanted this, Lara.'

The cane swished down again and cut sharply across where the swell of her rump met the back of her thighs. Lara let out a howl of protest.

'You can't really treat me like this!' Lara protested.

MacKennan gave a scornful laugh.

'My darling Lara, I can treat you however I like!'

Whack!

The cane cracked down again, this time across the backs of her thighs.

'Oww! Hurts! Stop it!'

'Stop? My dear Lara, this is just the beginning!'

The cane whipped down across her back and the pain made Lara jerk violently against the straps that were bound around her wrists and held her helplessly dangling. Another blow across her back tore a scream from her. MacKennan signalled for the man with the cane to pause. Shivering violently with fear Lara swallowed the lump that rose in her throat as she watched MacKennan dip a hand into the water.

'You're trembling my dear.'

As he spoke the Doctor stroked his wet fingers over her forehead then meshed them into her hair so that he could control her head.

'Is the excitement too much for you? Shall we slow the pace down a little? Give you time to come to terms with what is going to happen to you?'

'You bastard... if you think you can get away with this...'

MacKennan laughed and tightening the grip of his fingers in her hair drew her head a little sideways as he leant closer to her and whispered menacingly.

'Lara, unless you think you can escape... then I will be able to get away with whatever I choose to subject your delicious body to!'

Lara looked around her disconsolately. Tears pricked her eyes and the fist that seemed to have clenched hold of her stomach tightened its grip. Her gaze travelled from the rubber straps tight around her outstretched limbs to the two men watching her: ominously threatening and merciless looking in their dark suits and dark glasses. She looked around the windowless room, the sterile white walls and the slate grey steel door gave her no comfort or hope.

'What are you going to do to me?' she asked plaintively.

'You're going to experience all the delicious things you've dreamt of tasting.'

'But they were just in my dreams... I only...' Lara blurted, tears threatening to overcome her now as a dozen images from her fertile imagination flashed through her mind.

'Hush now Lara...'

'No, please...no, don't... let me go! You can't do this!'

MacKennan pressed a single finger to her lips, cautioning

148

her to stop protesting.

'Now, you have to learn to take your pain like a good girl, or we'll gag you. Would you like that?'

Lara blinked nervously, hardly able to believe that this was really happening to her. She swallowed and shook her head as best as she could.

'Time for another taste of the cane, Lara.'

'No... it hurts...' she whined pitifully, biting back tears.

'Which is just how you like it.'

MacKennan stepped back and with the merest nod, signalled for the caning to be resumed. Lara glanced apprehensively over her shoulder just in time to glimpse the cane before it snapped down across her back.

Thwack!

'Uhh...'

She tugged frantically against the cuffs and shook her head in frustration as the man with the cane circled her.

'I can't bear it!' she sobbed, gazing up pitifully at her outstretched arms.

'Well Lara, perhaps the reality of being this submissive just takes a little getting used to. Just imagine all the things you have to look forward to though?'

'Uhh...' Lara groaned deeply as her sex was unexpectedly touched, fingers slipping between the soft folds of her vulva and stroking her. She opened her eyes and gazed at the Doctor who stood close before her, smiling with satisfaction at her condition.

'Pleasure will come with the pain Lara. Such sweet pleasure...'

The fingers slid deeper into her sex making her gasp and then the stinging harshness of the cane striking her arse made her yelp with surprise.

'Please... too much...'

She shook her head weakly, her tethered body making one last attempt to break free. Another jolt of pain shook her as the cane hit her thighs. Lara groaned and writhed, crying and shaking her head as three more blows rained down across her arse.

'Well done Lara, you've taken your first dozen strokes of the cane and I didn't hear you once ask for us to stop. That tells me quite a lot about you.'

Lara shook her head in dismay and was about to protest when the Doctor stroked his hands over the swell of her breasts.

'You have such a magnificent body, Lara. Last time I clamped your gorgeous nipples I was very gentle and you were lying on your back, asleep and dreaming of what I really wanted to do with you. Well, now...'

Lara gazed down helplessly as MacKennan lifted one of her breasts, holding its weight with one hand underneath while with his other he stroked the smooth, soft flesh. Lara couldn't prevent a sigh of pleasure escaping her lips as the man stroked her nipple, teasing and coaxing it until it hardened.

'Feels good, doesn't it? So sensitive, just imagine how exquisite the sensation of having your luscious little erection trapped by a clamp and then weighted.'

'No, please...'

'Hush now Lara, I know you've dreamt of this being done to you. Now you're going to be allowed to experience it for real.'

As the Doctor spoke, he stroked her other breast and toyed with her nipple until it too was as erect as the first. Lara stared down, hypnotised as he then flicked one fingertip against first one nipple and then the other until both were swollen to their full state of hardness.

'Now, there's no point in struggling Lara, keep still, there's a good girl.'

The man reached in his pocket and she looked in panic at the pair of shiny little steel clamps he held. Lara shook her head, pulling back as the Doctor stepped closer.

'Hold her still.'

The two men pinned her squirming body and for a moment she was forced to watch as MacKennan teased her, slowly stroking the cool metal of the clamp over her trembling stomach and then in slow circles around her breast.

'I think you can imagine just how intense the feeling is going to be, can't you?'

'Don't do it. Please, don't do this to me.'

She struggled as the cool metal stroked over her skin, around her breast and then brushed against her nipple.

'No...please...'

The two men tightened their grip on her naked body, holding her still as the cool metal closed against her right nipple. MacKennan smiled at her as she shook her head and looked imploringly at him. She gazed down at her breast as the little metal plates trapped then squeezed her nipple.

'Uhh...no...stop...no more...no!'

She sighed and gasped then whimpered plaintively as the clamp tightened against her nipple.

'Uhh...please... stop...'

She pulled down with her arms, trying to back away as the clamp tightened mercilessly around her nipple. The men behind her though held her still and a second later the task was finished. To her dismay she felt the Doctor now trap her other nipple between his thumb and finger.

'There's no point in struggling Lara, you can't escape from this or anything I choose to do to you.'

As he spoke MacKennan was toying with her nipple, coaxing it back to full hardness. Lara shook her head in despair as she felt the cold hard steel of the second clamp close around her little erection.

'No...let me go! Please...let me go...uhh...'

The clamp tightened against her nipple. The men stepped back. Lara arched her back and dragged down with her arms against the ropes that restrained her as tears ran down her cheeks.

'Hush now Lara... the best is yet to come.'

Gazing up she saw MacKennan now held two shiny little weights in the palm of his hand.

'No...please...' she sobbed.

MacKennan closed upon her at the same time as one of the men stepped close behind her. Hands reached around her and cupping a breast in each palm, her magnificent orbs of flesh were held while she was forced to watch the weights being clipped onto the clamps.

She gazed down at her trapped nipples, whose flesh showed dark purple between the shiny little discs of steel. She could see how the edges of the metal plates were grooved and designed to mesh snugly against the opposite plate. There were even four little softly serrated teeth around the outer edge of each steel circle and she could see the metal teeth sunk firmly into her delicate flesh.

Lara was plaintively whimpering as the Doctor stepped back to regard her. The man behind her released his grasp upon her breasts and retreated and the weights were left to dangle freely. Lara groaned and writhed, gazing with dismay at her breasts, now cruelly distended by the weights that hung from her clamped nipples, which throbbed and ached unbearably.

She was certain that she was going to faint. For a few moments she struggled wildly then gave up, her exhausted body slick with perspiration. She hung by her outstretched arms, her head lolling forward and gazed hypnotised by the sight of her clamped and weighted breasts.

'Please take them off... too much...hurts...'

'Relax Lara, you'll soon learn to enjoy the feeling. It's time now for your next twelve strokes of the cane. You'll find the combination of the cane and nipple clamps rather delicious. I have to say, I really rather enjoy watching a tethered girl dangling helplessly, her nipples clamped and weighted as she writhes under the sweet, sharp pain of the cane.'

Before Lara could even get a word of protest out the cane struck her rump making her jerk against the cuffs and swear with frustration at her helplessness.

Thwack!

'You've no right to do this to me!' she howled.

Thwack!

Her only answer was another stinging blow from the cane across her now achingly tender rump. Lara bit her lip and swore under her breath.

Thwack!

The cane smacked down again, this time against the inside of one of her thighs.

'Oww!'

As her body jolted in response, the aching in her breasts was intensified.

Thwack!

Another blow from the cane against her thighs made her frantically jerk her tethered legs. The weights dangling from her swollen nipples swung wildly and the pain in her breasts was unbearably heightened. Crying out as more well aimed strokes from the cane tormented her, tears poured down her cheeks.

By the time the second set of a dozen strokes was finally over, Lara hung, physically exhausted after having struggled wildly throughout the caning. Her tethered body was bathed in perspiration and her thighs and arse throbbed with pain. Her nipples felt acutely swollen and ached madly. To her shame though, her body was deeply aroused and during the caning she found herself imagining what it would be like when the Doctor or one of his men elected to take her body for their pleasure. Before the punishment session was over she was longing for a cock to be slid into her aching pussy to satisfy her. With the punishment seemingly over, Lara lifted her head weakly and gazed at the Doctor.

'What's going to happen to me now?' she asked plaintively, secretly hoping that they would untie her and her aching pussy would at least have the satisfaction of a cock filling it.

'Do I detect a note of eagerness for some more treatment in a similar vein?'

'No, Doctor...no...'

A hand furrowed into her tousled hair and tightening its

153

grip held her head back. MacKennan smiled victoriously.

'You see Lara, I knew you wanted this.'

'No...'

'Perhaps it's time for you to feel the piquant bite of a clamp somewhere even more sensitive?'

'No!' Lara shook her head; writhing and twisting as the men in the dark glasses held her still once more from behind while MacKennan drew from his jacket pocket another shiny steel clamp.

'Don't do this to me Doctor, please!' Lara begged, fresh tears welling up in her eyes.

'Hush now Lara, or I'll have to gag you.'

Fingers brushed her swollen clit. Lara tensed her body, panting fast and shallowly. She was agonisingly close to coming and was unable to stop herself from pushing her hips forwards as the Doctor touched her sex. The Doctor gave her a reproving shake of his head as she felt his fingers slip into the moist folds of her vulva.

'You're desperate for it, aren't you? This little session has made you deliciously wet. Wet and so very hot...'

'Uhhh...' Lara sighed as the fingers in her sex slid deeper.

'You dirty little girl, you're aching for more attention aren't you?'

'Yes...' Lara sighed, nodding shamefully, tears running down her cheeks as she realised what she'd confessed to.

CHAPTER EIGHT

'Well Lara, you seem to like the feel of clamps so much, I think you deserve a taste of some more.'

'No... I can't take anymore, please Doctor MacKennan,' Lara begged.

'So what would you rather experience?'

Lara said nothing, swallowing nervously as MacKennan surveyed her like some prize trophy, stroking his hand affectionately down her bare body.

'Come on Lara, tell me what you'd like, or shall we watch the tapes of your dreams to help refresh our memories?'

'You bastard...'

'Well then, it's your choice. Tell me what you'd most like.'

'Do you think I'm going to answer that? Do whatever you want to me: you're going to anyway, whether I sanction it or not!' Lara spat.

MacKennan laughed. 'How right you are!'

Lara shivered as the man's hand stroked over the bare skin of her chest until his fingers circled her aching breast. She looked sorrowfully at her breast, pulled down by the cruel weight that hung from the clamp that bit against her swollen nipple. Idly MacKennan flicked one finger against the dangling weight.

'Uhhh...no...'

Lara hung her head back and bit down on her lower lip as the weight was made to pendulum and the pain increased. MacKennan flicked the other weight into motion and Lara groaned and writhed, fresh tears pricking her eyes.

'Of course, I can do whatever I want with you. Your dreams have given me a clear insight into what you desire. So you may as well just relax and enjoy what lies in store.'

The dangling weights were given another flick and as they swung back and forth with renewed energy, Lara gazed up at her arms and pulled down frantically with all her strength in an effort to tear free from the restraints they'd subjected her to. MacKennan watched her with undisguised amusement as she writhed and struggled, tugging her legs and jerking her arms in a futile bid for freedom. Once she had exhausted herself and hung subdued and panting he caught hold of her chin with one hand and forced her to meet his gaze.

'Agonising isn't it my darling Lara?'

With the back of his other hand he carefully wiped the tears from her cheeks then stroked her tousled hair clear of her eyes. Her body was with slick with sweat from her struggling and she felt too weak now to even try to pull away from his sinister caress.

'Time to have some more clamps fitted Lara. So keep still there's a good girl.'

Lara hung helplessly from her aching arms while a strap was drawn around her left thigh and buckled snugly. A second was then fastened around her right thigh. Each of the straps was broad and on the inside of her thigh there were two small protruding funnels of plastic. MacKennan's two henchmen now slipped a metal pole between Lara's thighs. Whilst one man held her leg still, the other slid the pole end into the plastic funnel. The other end of the pole was then fixed in a similar fashion against her other thigh. The pole, which was telescopic, was then lengthened by a simple twist and pull and locked by another twist at its extended length. Lara was now left with her thighs widely spread and she knew with dismay where she was going to feel the next cruel clamp.

'Feeling rather helpless? Poor thing, you look so sorry for yourself. And I've hardly even begun...'

'Uhh...'

Lara gasped as MacKennan stroked her sex, his fingertips slipping between the soft, wet folds of her vulva.

'Rather wet... feeling rather aroused are we?'

Lara said nothing, screwing up her eyes and trying to prepare herself for what was about to happen. When she felt the man's fingers lightly stroke her sex she was taken by surprise and unable to prevent a sigh of appreciation escaping her lips.

The man laughed softly and slowly slid two fingers deeply into her pussy. Lara bit down on her lip, struggling to contain a gasp of pleasure. When the man's thumb brushed against her swollen clitoris the sensation was too intense for her control and she gave a long, low shuddering sigh of pleasure.

'That's it Lara, let your feelings out, there's nothing to feel shamed about. You see I know how much you've wanted to be treated like this. I can make you feel so good... so very good...'

With his other hand the man lightly tapped one of the weights dangling from Lara's breasts and as she whimpered the fingers embedded in her pussy were slowly twisted and withdrawn, bringing Lara to another shuddering gasp of ecstatic pleasure.

'A delicious combination isn't it my dear? We are getting very wet aren't we? Let's feel a little more...'

Again the man slipped his fingers into her sex and at the same time the weight which had just been flicked was tapped again. The biting and tugging pain produced by the clamp and weight seemed to be heightened acutely as the dangling weight was made to swing under the orb of her breast. The sensation was too intense to bear but she couldn't escape it, couldn't evade it. She felt dizzy, her whole body washed with pain and pleasure. With complete dismay she realised that she was starting to gyrate her hips, pushing against the hand between her legs.

'Give her another taste of the cane on her rump.'

Lara shook her head, begging them not to but unable to form words, or maybe afraid that if she spoke now it would be to urge them on.

Thwack!

The cane sliced across her bottom, the pain shooting through her body and exploding in her brain. Lara cried plaintively as the aftershock of the cane rippled then washed through her tethered, aching body. It was all too much... too much...

'Uhhh....uhhh...'

'Good girl... come for me, that's it...' MacKennan coaxed.

His thumb brushed hard against her aching clitoris. Lara moaned feverishly. Hands caressed under her breasts, lifting the orbs of ripe flesh, the clamps tugging deeply, sweetly against her swollen nipples.

Thwack!

The cane, like a tongue of fire, licked across the backs of her thighs where they reached the curves of her rump.

Thwack!

'Uhhh... mmm...'

Thwack!

Lara dragged her arms down against the restraints, the cuffs digging into her wrists, the pain washing through her shoulders. She ground her hips forwards, pushing her aching pelvis against the man's hand as she came, her orgasm washing over her deliciously and coming again and again like waves against a shore. The hardness of the cane was pressed against the tender softness of her buttocks, hands squeezed her breasts, her orgasm went on and on until she imagined she would faint. Then, just as she imagined she would be allowed to rest, she heard MacKennan's voice and his words made her moan despondently, shaking her head pleadingly.

'Such luscious sex lips... now, just keep still...'

'No... please...'

Lara shook her head as she felt a clasp slide over one of her outer labia. As the metal tightened against her soft fold of flesh she gasped then cried out.

'Please, no, aches so much... can't bear it...'

'Be quiet my dear... I want you to experience the feel of these while your lovely sex lips are at their most aroused and so delightfully distended.'

'Please, Doctor... this isn't fair...' Lara sobbed, shaking her head and writhing against the numerous hands that now held her still.

'Keep still Lara... you can't stop me. You are completely at my mercy, you may as well resign yourself to the fact that I'll do with you whatever I please!'

'Uhhh...no....stop...'

Ignoring her pleading, the man slid a second clamp around her other outer labia and as she felt the soft lip of her sex being squeezed she struggled urgently but to no avail.

'Please, no...more...'

She shook her head vigorously as she felt with alarm the Doctor's fingers teasing and coaxing the delicate little folds of flesh of her inner labia.

'So soft and tender...poor Lara, you're going to suffer so much...now let's hear you really begging for me to stop.'

'No! Please!'

Lara moaned as she felt the cold hardness of steel tighten against first one and then both of her inner labia. She stared down at her tethered legs, acutely spread by the steel pole and she could see four slender chains dangling from the lips of her vulva. 'How does that feel, Lara?'

The man stepped back, the hold on her body from behind was released and she was left dangling from her outstretched arms. Lara drank in the sensation of the clamps teasing her pussy lips, the tickling feeling of the little chains hanging between her legs, the cool metal lightly brushing her skin sending delicious ripples up her thigh muscles. The ache from the pressure of the clamps around her labia was, she was ashamed to admit, more pleasurable than painful. She glanced down at her distended breasts, the clamps on her nipples dragged down by the weights. They ached... how they ached, if her pussy lips were subjected to something similar... Lara sighed at the thought and then as if in answer to her fears she saw MacKennan displaying four shiny little steel weights, balanced in his palm and held before her.

'Oh no...you can't, please...' Lara shook her head, pulling fearfully with her arms again against the leather that bound her wrists.

'Hold her still!'

The four weights were clipped to the little chains but for

the moment the Doctor restrained their weight against his palm. Panting hard Lara swallowed and looked pitifully at her tormentor.

'Please Doctor MacKennan...I really can't take any more!'

'And if I show spare you this... how would you like to show me your gratitude?'

'I'll do anything...my poor breasts just ache so much and I can't bear any more. Please, I beg you!'

MacKennan smiled ruefully and slowly lowered the hand that held the weights. As the lips of her vulva were slowly stretched she looked in alarm at the man before her. MacKennan gave an apologetic smile and released the weights completely from his hand. Lara gave a choked gasp then groaned feverishly. The weights were not as heavy as she'd dreaded. The pain was bearable but the sensation was agonisingly arousing. Her pussy throbbed with the urgent need to come again and just suspended there, helplessly, the pain in her breasts and loins was, she knew, going to be enough to bring her slowly but relentlessly to another climax.

'No...uhh...no, please...'

She closed her eyes and writhed helplessly, her body agonisingly stretched, her throbbing sex stretched, her magnificent breasts stretched. She shook her head, panting hard as her sex burnt with the need to be made to come. If only MacKennan would touch her there, rub her clit, stroke her... anything... please...

She looked up and focused on the man stood watching her. Blinking away the tears that blurred her vision she gazed imploringly at the man.

'Please fuck me! Please fuck me!' she begged desperately.

MacKennan smiled triumphantly and nodded to his two accomplices.

* * *

Lara lay face down in the same as position they'd tossed her down into on the bed until she succumbed to sleep. It didn't

160

take long; she was physically and emotionally exhausted. When she came to, the room was dark and there was not a sound. She lay listening to her own breathing. Gingerly she felt between her legs. The throbbing ache in her pussy had subsided. At first when they'd clamped her sex she was certain that she was going to find it unbearably painful. The truth though was that the lightly weighted clamps had pulled her sex lips just hard enough to create the most agonisingly delicious sensation: an exquisite blend of pain and pleasure. Combined with more well aimed strokes from the cane, it had quickly brought her to a heady climax.

After they'd finished, they had rubbed some cool ointment along the lines the cane had left and the throbbing pain soon subsided. The clamps were removed from her exhausted body and with her wrists bound together behind her back she'd then been blindfold and taken to another room.

The room was tiny and the only furniture was a simple single bed. There was no window and the door was disconcertingly solid. Without doubt she was a prisoner and this was her cell. It seemed incredible that MacKennan had abducted her, but it was clear that he had and that he wasn't acting alone. What, Lara wondered, was his motive: to sexually torment her? Was that the only reason? Perhaps her dreams had provoked him, she thought. But then he'd said that other women had demonstrated similar dreams. Had he abducted them then as well? Lara laughed at the idea. He could never get away with it. He'd never get away with holding her here against her will for any length of time. Someone would realise that she was missing and trace her last movements. Feeling faintly reassured that she'd be rescued before too long, Lara drifted back into a fitful sleep. She was wide awake before long, after dreaming that she was Lara the adventurer and the evil Doctor was torturing her. Her erotic dreams of earlier now seemed disconcertingly close to reality. She rolled onto her back and with her hands folded behind her head, she gazed up into the darkness. She could feel a cool current of fresh air circulating from some unseen air conditioning unit and now she was lying still and breathing quietly she thought she could hear sounds from the wall to her left. Cautiously she sat upright in bed and twisted her body sideways so her legs dangled over the side of the bed.

The floor was warm under her bare feet. Gingerly she tiptoed across the room and put her ear against the wall. There was someone on the other side of the wall, or more accurately several people, she could just hear them now: a female voice from the sounds of it and a man. Straining to listen, the best she could work out was that the man seemed to be barking out orders and the girl was crying or protesting. She didn't sound happy at any rate and given what Lara had just been through, it dawned on her that perhaps she really was not the only young woman that MacKennan had abducted. Lara crept back to her bed and lay down. What were they doing to the girl? She rubbed her wrists, remembering the feel of the cuffs they'd bound her with. She felt between her legs and touched her labia again. They still felt a little delicate after being clamped. How it had made her writhe, how it had hurt and yet... tentatively she trapped the sensitive flesh between her thumb and forefinger and gently applied pressure until the memory of the sensation from the clamping came flooding back. Now though, she could control the amount of pressure and without that sense of helplessness, the experience was dulled. Sighing, she fingered herself, closing her eyes and focusing on the feelings that stirred in her body. When the door was abruptly opened and light flooded into her cell, she was taken completely by surprise.

The two men both wore the same dark suits and dark glasses as before. They moved into the tiny cell fast and purposefully, giving Lara no time to react. Caught by one wrist she was jerked off the bed. Dragged sideways she was sprawled across the floor, struggling to find her feet as one man pushed her to the ground and fell astride her. With lightning speed, her arms were quickly pulled behind her back and steel handcuffs snapped shut around her wrists. Lara knew in that instant that resistance was futile but something drove her to struggle. She remembered the muffled sounds of the girl next door and wondered if now it was her turn. The thought excited her and as she tussled with the two men for a moment before they completely overpowered her, she knew that a part of her was already embracing whatever punishment lay in store for her. But not all of her, not yet.

Once they had her wrists cuffed together behind her back, the men relaxed, confident that their victim was helpless. Lara seized her chance as the man sitting astride her stood up. Bending her legs together up to her body, she rolled onto her back, aimed her feet at the man's groin and kicked out as he bent over her. The force of her blow sent him reeling backwards and for a second the other man hesitated, caught by surprise and frozen by indecision. Lara saw her chance, rolling backwards then springing to her feet. For a fleeting moment she felt as strong, defiant and self-assured as her heroine adventurer. As the man lunged at her, she twisted sideways and delivered him a stinging single footed kick to his stomach. The man crumpled to his knees. Lara saw the open door and light-filled corridor and without a second's hesitation, she fled. A hand grabbed hold of her leg as she burst through the open doorway but she tore free and flung herself out of the room.

Left or right the corridor gave her no clues as to the best way to run. As she glanced over her shoulder to see the men stumbling to their feet she saw the electronic keyboard on the wall beside the cell door. Her was back already facing it and it was low enough for her to reach despite being handcuffed. The panel had luminescent touch pads numbered one to nine and a green and a red button. With no time to think about the choice, she strained her fingers to reach the pad and jabbed one finger against the red button. She saw the man's mouth almost snarling as he lunged to reach the door but the steel panel slid shut too quickly. Lara let out a sigh of relief as she listened to the men banging on the inside of the door. For a second a wave of despondency swept over her. What hope did she have of escaping? But then she remembered Lara the adventurer: she'd never have given up without a fight!

The corridor yawned emptily in both directions. Sterile, white and eerily deserted. Lara quickly dropped to the floor and wriggled her cuffed arms from behind her under her bottom and into the crook of her legs. Rolling on her side and pulling her legs tight into her chest she was just able to get her cuffed hands out from under her feet one at a time. Flushed with success, she sprang back to her feet, her hands still cuffed together but at least not trapped behind her back. She set off down the corridor at a quick jog.

The first two doors she came to were on opposite sides of the corridor. One was labelled "C" and the other "D". The door to the room marked "C" stood wide open and Lara peered in. There was a second door at the end of a short lobby, which was also open. The room beyond was about four metres square and all that was inside was a chrome legged, glass topped desk and a matching chrome chair. There was a folder on the table. Just as she was agonising what to do next, she heard footsteps approaching from the direction she had been going in. Not more than half a dozen metres ahead of her the corridor turned a corner and she realised that she had perhaps only seconds before whoever was approaching turned the corner and saw her. She ducked into the roomed marked "C" and pressed herself back against the wall to one side of the open door.

The footsteps came quickly past the room just a moment later. Peering out, she saw the rear view of one of Doctor MacKennan's nurses walking briskly on down the corridor. High heels, short white PVC skirt clinging around her thighs and ending well above her knees. White blouse, blonde hair tied in a ponytail, tiny white nurse's hat perched jauntily at an angle on her head. The girl swept on down the corridor, oblivious to Lara staring at her back.

She had to find a way out before the nurse found the two men locked in her cell. She was about to dash from the room when she remembered the folder lying on the desk. It would only take a second to glance at and perhaps it would offer her some clues as to where she was or how to get out of the place. She darted across to the desk and flicked the folder open, catching her breath in shock as she saw the photos that it contained.

The pictures all showed the same person: a young girl, perhaps eighteen or twenty years old. She was very slim and had shoulder length dark hair and a pretty face, with high cheekbones and large, dark eyes. The photos at the front of the folder showed her bound, gagged and variously tormented. Below each photo, there was handwriting in a large, carefully formed, immature script. As Lara read one caption she realised that the writing was the girl's own. Lara flicked through the pages, shaking her head with disbelief. By the time she reached the last of the photos, the girl's narrative confessed more than her acceptance of what was being done to her. She declared the enjoyment she derived from her suffering! Lara stared, hypnotised by a picture of the girl kneeling, her thighs bound to her calves and her arms bound with shiny black rope behind her back. The two men in the dark suits and dark glasses were making her drink from a funnel. It reminded Lara of her dream of how the evil Doctor of her dreamscape had impregnated her. It was all so familiar she began to suspect that her dreamscape was perhaps not entirely of her own design. Perhaps MacKennan had interfered with her dreams, using his computer to make her dream in the way he wanted. If he had though, Lara realised, he'd given her dreams that had been what she'd wanted. Maybe he knew her better than she knew herself!

She hurried down the corridor, passing two doors marked "A" and "B" and then a third marked, "Office — Security Cleared Persons Only". Just beyond this the corridor ended in a plate glass door beyond which she saw another similar barrier. These doors were code number locked and she realised that she'd come to a dead end. Looking through the glass doors, beyond them she could see what looked like a lift door and she gazed in frustration at the door lock panel, suddenly guessing that the lift was most probably her way out. She must be in a basement below the Dreamscape Institute, she thought, with dismay.

'Surely you're not thinking of leaving us so soon?'

Lara swung around at the first sound of the sneering female voice behind her. Flanked by the two men, the nurse gave her a malicious smile.

* * *

'And you really think you can get away with this?' Lara demanded, glaring at MacKennan as he watched his men finish securing the straps that held Lara forcibly to the chair.

'My dear Lara, you are just yet one more of many girls who have allowed themselves to fall into my hands.'

'You smug bastard...just wait...'

It was too late though to attempt to resist. Canvas straps were tight around her calves and thighs holding her legs snugly against the frame of the heavy chair that was bolted to the floor. Her arms were drawn and held by another set of canvas straps to the chair and even as she verbally expressed her contempt for MacKennan, one of his minions was fastening another strap around her chest, just below the swell of her breasts. Pulling the strap taut and buckling it behind the chair, he ensured that Lara was now held immobile, forced to sit and await her fate.

'Now then Lara, you must remember what brought you to the Dreamscape Institute; your insatiable carnal needs. Well, you are going to be truly satisfied, once I have finished with you. What we just have to do is put you in touch with yourself. It's time for you to remember and learn who you really are. Or should I say, who you want to be.'

As MacKennan spoke he was toying with a remote control

and at the press of a button a screen which dominated one wall of the room they had brought her to, flickered to life.

'Nurse, kindly prepare Miss Lustral.'

The sultry blonde in her provocative white uniform moved across to where Lara sat bound and helpless.

'Relax, you'll enjoy this...'

Instinctively Lara struggled as the girl bent over her, but she could barely move her arms or legs, let alone extricate them from the tight straps. The blonde showed her a small jar of creamy ointment, into which she delicately dipped her middle finger.

'Please... what are you going to do to me?' Lara shook her head, glancing apprehensively at the girl then at MacKennan and then back at the girl.

'There's no point in struggling darling... there's no escape from this.'

Lara squirmed ineffectually as the ointment coated finger reached between her tethered legs. The ointment was cool against the soft flesh of her sex and she sighed as the girl slowly insinuated her finger into the folds of her vulva.

'Sitting comfortably Lara? Excellent. Time for a some enjoyable viewing then.'

MacKennan pressed another button on the remote control he held and on the screen that Lara was facing a film started which she immediately knew to be the computer simulation of the first dream she'd experienced at the Institute. When she tried to look away the blonde nurse caught hold of her tousled hair with both hands and turned her face, forcing her to watch the screen.

'This isn't fair... leave me alone...' Lara cried, struggling ineffectually against the girl then whimpering as an arousing warmth and ache spread in her pussy. Whatever the ointment was that the girl had anointed her sex with, it was making her swiftly feel intensely randy.

'No...oh, God...no...' Lara moaned and writhed, biting her lower lip and squirming in the seat of the chair. Glancing down at her tethered body seemed to increase her state of arousal but looking at the screen was even worse. The more the heat in her sex built the harder it was not to watch the film. The image soon had her spellbound and she gave up struggling and sat, desperately wishing she or the girl would finger fuck her or rub her clit and make her come. On the screen, Lara the adventurer had woken to find herself in a desperate plight.

* * *

Lara looked forlornly up at her outstretched arms. The ropes were bound so tightly around her wrists they burnt and they were drawn so taut that her arms were held at full stretch, her feet barely able to touch the stone floor. The ropes were threaded through iron rings set in the ceiling and her arms were held outstretched.

The two blonde girls, who looked to be no more than teenagers, laughed as Lara groaned in discomfort, struggling to gain a purchase on the floor with her bare toes.

'Something wrong baby... feeling a little uncomfortable, are we?'

They each wore high black leather boots and short black leather skirts. Their generous cleavages were contained by tight black leather bustiers. One wore elbow length black gloves whilst the other wore delicate white lace mittens that left her long fingers exposed. Her nails, shaped like talons and painted blood red, trailed down Lara's arm. Her glinting blue eyes sparkled cold and cruel and her generous bow shaped lips were twisted into a sadistic smile as she stroked the end of a riding whip over Lara's bare skin.

'Poor little Lara has got herself in deep trouble, hasn't she?' the girl taunted.

Lara grunted with despair as the girl trailed the plaited leather of the whip over her bare back. She shook her head, hissing at the girl as the leather stroked from her collarbone down over her breasts.

They had stripped her completely naked and she could see

her discarded clothes along with her guns laying in the far corner of the room.

'Keep your whip to yourself bitch or you'll be sorry when I get free from here!' Lara snarled defiantly.

The thought of the whip against her soft bare skin was too excruciating to seriously contemplate but Lara reassured herself she'd turn the table on her enemies soon enough!

'You'll wish you hadn't said that!' the girl warned, jabbing Lara in the ribs with the handle of the whip. Lara pulled and twisted frantically against the ropes but only succeeded in burning her wrists. The whip's tip trickled across her ribs and stroked up her back. Lara shook her head in frustration and gazed up desperately at her outstretched arms.

'Does this excite you? If I touch you like this...'

Lara shivered as the hard handle of the whip traced the line between the globes of her arse.

'Would you like to take it up your little pussy?'

Lara felt the handle rubbing her sex from behind, the warm leather teasing her vulva. She shook her head, clenching her teeth and shaking her head with despair, furious that she couldn't as yet free herself.

'Come on... relax... you'll learn to enjoy it, if you just let yourself go.'

* * *

'Come on... relax... you'll learn to enjoy it, if you just let yourself go.'

'No...no...uhhh...' Lara sighed feverishly as the nurse lightly stroked her neck, coiling strands of her golden hair around one finger and pulling it progressively tighter.

'Time to come for me, honey, I know you want to.'

'No...' Lara shook her head weakly, gazing helplessly at the screen where her alter-ego was shuddering as she climaxed, she felt the nurse slowly trace her fingertip across her cheek and then over her trembling lower lip. Moaning feverishly, Lara parted her lips allowing the girl to slide her fingertip just

169

inside her mouth. The ache in her pussy was too exquisite, and hypnotised by the scene on the screen before her, Lara cried plaintively, her whole body shuddering and twisting against the straps as a violent orgasm whipped through her tethered body.

'Good girl... you enjoyed that, didn't you?' the young girl standing over her laughed softly, caressing her trembling shoulder then stroking her hand slowly over her breast. Lara was still panting breathlessly as the girl caught her nipple between her finger and thumb and gently at first, then more firmly squeezed. Lara whimpered and writhed.

'Look at the screen, Lara,' the girl told her.

Lara obeyed and saw herself tied, legs spread astride a bench. Her wrists were bound by a rope around her waist and as she struggled against her captors another rope was drawn around her biceps and pulled taut forcing her arms back and tight into the small of her back.

Unable to tear her gaze from the screen, which held her spellbound, she felt the pressure on her nipple ease as the girl released her from the hold of her finger and thumb. The girl then flicked her fingernail against her now tender nipple and the piquant sensation brought Lara to another shuddering orgasm.

'Good girl...'

Lara gazed forlornly down. The straps were tight around her arms and legs and held her snugly against the chair. Under her heaving breasts, as she struggled to recover her breath, she could glimpse the strap that held her back against the chair. There was no escape and there was going to be no let up from the exquisite torture she was being submitted to, she realised with dismay as she watched the nurse dip her finger again into the little jar of creamy ointment.

'Feels so good doesn't it? Lucky Lara's going to get to have another delicious orgasm. Now keep still, honey.'

A second later and the fingertip had brushed against her sex, this time leaving her clitoris glistening with the potent cream. The effect was almost immediate.

'Oh God, going to come again... no...no...' Lara panted, tossing her head from side to side as her exhausted body was swiftly propelled towards another climax.

'Look at the screen Lara.'

She lifted her head at MacKennan's command and saw herself being made to swallow the impregnation mixture the evil Doctor had elected to force-feed her. The sight, combined with the ointment smeared against her clit, was enough to make her come again and even more intensely than the last two times. Before her climax had subsided, Lara felt herself fainting and her body, held against the chair by the straps went slack, her head lolling forward, her tangled golden hair trailing down over her breasts.

CHAPTER NINE

'On your knees Lara.'

Lara obeyed without hesitation, all too aware of how keen the nurses would be to punish her given half a chance. She knew what was expected and held her arms out before her, offering her wrists submissively. She had not been surprised to find that MacKennan's nurses were armed with weapons no less effective than those of the evil Doctor from her dreams. As the nurse named Suzi, fastened the familiar rubber cuffs around her wrists, the nurse named Zara stood close by, booted feet planted firmly apart, a short rubber-handled truncheon grasped in one black-leather gloved hand while from her other dangled a collar and leash.

'Good girl. Turning into a very obedient slave, aren't you?' Suzi sneered, buckling the first cuff snugly around Lara's left wrist.

It had been three days since they'd first taken her to the Conditioning Room and made her watch the film. Three, or perhaps four... Lara couldn't be certain. Confined underground, her sleep patterns purposely disrupted, she had already lost an accurate track of time. What was certain was that they'd taken her back to the room a total of three times and she guessed this was to be her fourth. Naked, she had been strapped into the chair and ordered to watch the film. To her shame, she'd found playing voyeur to her own erotic adventures deeply arousing. During each session Suzi had smeared a little of the ointment onto her sex. It was potently effective at bringing her to a climax. Each time though, Suzi had waited longer and longer before applying the cream and Lara was desperate for the deliverance it offered after being titillated by viewing her own sexual dream adventure.

'Now put your hands behind your back.'

Lara did as she was told; kneeling patiently as she felt Suzi clip the two wristcuffs together.

The first time the nurses had come for her, she had resisted.

With a pre-cursory flick of a switch, Zara had done nothing more than take a half-hearted swipe at Lara with her truncheon. The electric shock it had delivered though mild was enough to bring Lara momentarily to her knees. The nurses had then quickly both caught hold of a wrist each and jerked her arms behind her back. By the time Lara had recovered her senses, her arms were bound behind her back, rubber cuffs clipped together at her wrists and above her elbows. Her ankles too were cuffed and clipped to either end of a slim rod that held her legs well apart. The girls then forced a ring-gag into her mouth and secured its strap tightly behind her head.

Groaning in protest, Lara was rolled onto her belly. Hands grasped her buttocks, the slender fingers sliding between her globes. She cried out through the gag, shaking her head as, with one girl holding the cheeks of her arse drawn apart, the other girl smeared a slippery gel over her rectum muscle.

'You're a bad girl Lara, so you've got to be punished.'

'Lie still now.'

The girls dropped their weight astride her wriggling body and the fingers applying the gel to her rectum now slid inside her anus, first one at a time, then as her muscle was made to soften, several at once. Lara felt something being insinuated into her bottom. Her legs slithered across the ground as she struggled frantically, the object sliding deeper into her squirming body. She cried out for them to stop but her pleading, made incoherent by the ring-gag, went ignored. The butt plug that had been driven into her expanded and with her buttocks now acutely distended, Lara was forced to suffer a dozen punishment strokes across her rump, delivered by Suzi's truncheon with determined force.

So with the memory of what the nurses had subjected her to the first time they'd come to collect her from her cell, Lara made no protest at all as they first cuffed her wrists behind her back and then fastened a leather collar around her neck.

Naked, hands bound behind her back, Lara allowed herself to be led by the collar and lead down the corridor to the

Conditioning Room. MacKennan was absent, as he had been last time, and Lara wondered whether he had turned his attention to another client who was destined to become his next victim. Had he decided that the conditioning of Lara Lustral into a dutiful submissive was already so well advanced that his attention was no longer required? A part of Lara felt piqued that the Doctor had already seemingly lost interest in her.

There had been something deeply exciting about being forced to submit to whatever he chose for her and to have him stand watching her as she was subjected to whatever practice took his fancy. Lara had always assumed it was natural, as an Alpha One class female to take a dominant role with any other person. She had been brought up and tutored to think of herself as superior: socially, financially, physically, sexually. But her physical relationships had always left her feeling mildly dissatisfied. She craved something else, but had only begun to learn what, when she had put herself in MacKennan's hands at the Dreamscape Institute.

After her first dreamscape experience, even before she had walked out of the doors of the Institute, she knew she would have to go back for more. It had become swiftly addictive. At home in bed, she'd tossed and turned, fitfully dreaming poor substitutes for what MacKennan had delivered at his Institute. Her ordinary life: shopping for new clothes and new jewellery, meeting friends for meals in restaurant, going to nightclubs and parties: had quickly paled into a boring interlude between the heady sessions she'd come to crave on MacKennan's couch under the soothing green light of the dreamscape machine.

The nurses led her into the Conditioning Room and without having to be coerced, Lara sat on the leather seat facing the screen. The younger of the two nurses confidently drew the straps around Lara's arms and fastened them so her arms were held snugly over the arms of the chair. Her legs were then secured and Lara was ready. They had dispensed with the restraining chest belt and Lara made no attempt to struggle or object now when Suzi smeared Gelphax cream over her sex. On the contrary, she was desperate for it.

The screen flickered into life. Lara the adventurer, her naked body slick with sweat, lay dazed and helpless on the floor of the gym. Lara glanced down at her own body and deliberately tried wriggling her arms and legs so she would feel the tightness of the straps against her skin. There was now something disconcertingly reassuring about the feeling of being bound. It almost seemed to absolve her from anything she now experienced. Or at least that was what she tried to convince herself. She turned her attention back to the screen.

* * *

Lara lifted her head weakly; her body drained by the heat; her throat dry, her limbs weak. As the steam swirled away through the open door of the sauna, she could see the two men stood regarding her. Stripped of their guards clothing, their powerfully muscled torsos were clearly apparent. Aside from their height what set them apart from any ordinary men were the size of the genitals. It was not just in brutish strength that these men resembled bulls.

They caught hold of Lara's arms and dragged her out of the sauna. Without pausing, they dragged her across the gym floor to an exercise bench, pushing her belly down against it. Lara grunted as the wind was knocked from her. One of them took hold of her wrists and drew her arms taut, pulling her body hard against the bench.

* * *

Lara glanced across to Suzi. Alongside her companion she was focused on the screen, neither girl paying any attention to their captive. Lara could feel the dull ache of arousal beginning in her pussy. She leant her head back against the chair and moaned softly, wriggling her bum against the leather. On the screen the two brutish guards were taking it in turns to fuck her. God, how she wished they were here now. How she wished she could feel a thick cock driving hard into her pussy. She needed to be screwed, just having to sit and watch wasn't fair... she felt so frustrated and never before in her life had anything been withheld from her! Why didn't Suzi come and rub some Gelphax into her poor, aching pussy?

'Please... make me come!'

She'd said it before she could stop herself. She ground her teeth in frustration and looked down in humiliation, averting her gaze from the two young girls who were now watching her and grinning at her plight. God, how desperate and pathetic she must sound! But she couldn't help it, she was so desperate for sexual attention now, she didn't care what they did to her — just as long as it satisfied her craving for sexual gratification! She looked at the two girls in their ultra short skirts and tight blouses. She remembered how the first time they had come to her cell she'd fought them. How ruthlessly they'd dealt with her. The helpless feeling of lying shackled, legs spread and one girl's soft, long fingers forcefully insinuating their way into her squirming body. How excruciating it had felt as the butt plug had been forced into her. Then, how deeply, shamefully arousing it had been as they'd held her down and punished her.

'Is pussy ready for some nice cream?' Suzi taunted.

Lara nodded shamefully.

Licking her lips with satisfaction, Suzi walked across the room and picked up the jar of Gelphax cream that had been displayed all along to torment her. Lara watched the girl then walk back to where she was strapped helplessly to the chair in the centre of the room. On the screen before them, the adventurer Lara was pleading and begging with her two assailants. The camera had zoomed in on her face to show her anguished look as, one man having finished with her, the second took his place and plunged his mammoth cock into her pussy. Lara the adventurer howled and cried, struggling pathetically as the man then proceeded to fuck her: his giant cock driving in and out of her slender body with complete disregard for his victim.

'How badly do you need this?' Suzi asked, tauntingly.

'Very... please...' Lara sighed, gazing hopefully at the other girl's fingertips which were already glistening and sticky from where she'd dipped them into the jar she held.

'Okay then honey, keep still...'

The coolness of the cream against the folds of her vulva contrasted deliciously with the warmth of the girl's touch as she slowly stroked with her fingertips the length of Lara's aching sex.

'Uhh, yes...yes...'

Immediately the tingling sensation, she'd come to so love, started and then the warmth quickly seeped into her sex and seemed to fan out through her loins. Her clitoris hardened, aching madly and her vulva became acutely sensitive. When Suzi touched her again, Lara sighed gratefully and leaning back in the chair, closed her eyes, her breathing now coming in short, ragged gasps.

'Please stroke me... please...'

'No.'

The nurse laughed softly and Lara ground her teeth in frustration. She gazed down at her pussy and looked at her arms bound to the chair. She couldn't bear it any longer...

'Not fair...please make me come!' she begged, tears pricking her ears

'I'm not going to stroke your pussy but I could do other things to you... if you'd like that?'

As she spoke, the young girl stood behind the chair and with both hands stroked her fingertips lightly over Lara's chest, all around but carefully avoiding her breasts.

Lara begin to cry softly as her body was overtaken with excruciating, sexual frustration.

'Anything...' she sobbed, 'just do anything to me that will make me come!'

The girl stood behind her gave a short triumphant laugh

and abruptly stopped caressing Lara, who tilted her head backwards and gazed imploringly at her not to stop. The girl though, had paused only to pick up a shiny steel nipple clamp that she had awaiting use concealed behind the chair.

'Would you like it if I put a pair of these on you?' she asked, dangling the device before Lara.

'Yes...'

Lara swallowed the lump that had risen in her throat as she nodded affirmatively.

Breathing fast with nervous expectation, she watched, mesmerised as the clamps were fitted to her already erect nipples. The figure of eight shaped pieces of steel dangled down brushing her ribs and as Suzi pulled experimentally on them, Lara could feel the clamps tightening against her aching nipples.

'The more weight that is applied the tighter the clamps become. Ingenious device, don't you think?'

Lara could only managed a groan in response. The sensation of having her nipples tormented had brought her agonisingly close to coming. It was with a shameful feeling of longing and gratification that she watched Suzi fasten two weighted chains to the clamps. The increase in pain brought Lara's long awaited climax and she jerked and twisted against the straps that held her in the chair as her body was bathed in the most delicious orgasm.

Panting hard, she opened her eyes and gazing down saw the weighted clamps still fastened to her trembling body. She stared, breathless and disbelieving as Suzi dipped a finger back in the jar of Gelphax cream and delicately dabbed a little over the end of each of her swollen nipples where they were exposed beyond the tight jaws of the steel clamps. In almost immediate response her nipples throbbed, attempting to swell even more and turning from deep crimson to a dark purply blue.

'No... can't bear it... please... take the clamps off!' Lara moaned, tossing her head from side to side and frantically tugging and twisting her arms and legs against the straps that held her down.

The two girls now stood back and watched as, bathed in perspiration, Lara was left to writhe helplessly. Held by the straps, she could do nothing but endure the exquisite torture until with a plaintive cry, she was brought to another orgasm.

'Okay Lara, time for some more viewing.'

Suzi picked up the remote control and pressed a switch. The image of Lara the adventurer being taken by the two guards in the gym was abruptly replaced. Lara caught her breath and gazed in disbelief at what she now saw on the screen before her.

They had filmed her whilst she was asleep in the Dreamscape Institute! She looked at the screen in angry amazement then fascination. She was asleep on the leather couch under the green lights. Doctor MacKennan and his two nurses were standing over her. The white towelling robe lay open and discarded, her whole naked body exposed. Her arms were held above her head, rubber rings around her wrists fastened to fine cords that stretched away tautly across the top corners of the couch. Likewise her legs were held spread in an identical fashion. MacKennan was fingering her nipples, coaxing them to a state of erection. Her sleeping self, stirred and moaned faintly but did not wake.

'The bastard...' Lara muttered under her breath. She glanced down at her clamped nipples, shaking her head in despair. It was impossible not to look back at the screen. She watched, spellbound as MacKennan asked Suzi to "peg her" and the nurse swiftly fastened two small steel pegs to her nipples. MacKennan then stroked her sleeping body, working his way from her face down to her breasts. Her pegged nipples had turned purple though not as dark a shade as they were now. MacKennan moved his hands lower, ending up at her sex, which he calmly opened and admired while the sleeping Lara lay oblivious to what was happening to her. MacKennan then announced that he "needed milking" and in no time he was reclined on a chair, his trousers and pants pulled down by the obliging Suzi, who began stroking and licking his cock. His tool was massive and Lara now knew where in her dreams the idea of the guards' genetically modified cocks had originated. MacKennan himself had just such a monster organ!

As, on the screen Suzi jerked off the Doctor, alternating skilful handwork with eager licking and sucking, Lara, strapped to the chair found she was now frantic to come again and her clamped nipples throbbed unbearably.

'Please Suzi...make me come...please!'

The nurse smiled with malicious satisfaction while on the screen the smiling and devoted Suzi furled her lips around MacKennan's cockhead and made him come. The image on the screen was so taunting, Lara couldn't bear to watch it and she screwed her eyes shut. The unfulfilled ache in her sex though remained and when she opened her eyes again she saw the nurse, having evidently made MacKennan ejaculate was now eagerly licking and sucking the massive cock until it was brought back to a condition of ramrod hardness. As Lara watched, unable to tear her gaze away, MacKennan had Suzi fasten some tape across the sleeping Lara's mouth.

'No...' Lara stared in disbelief, squirming in the seat, aching to come, acutely aroused but unable, without some more physical stimulation, to actually climax.

'Keep watching Lara, the best is yet to come.'

Suzi was stood behind the chair where Lara was bound. She had one hand resting on her bare shoulder and the other was stroking her neck.

On the screen, the rear section of the bench was then lowered, leaving Lara's rump just balanced over the edge.

'Oh my God...no...'

Lara shook her head as she watched MacKennan calmly slide his cock into her sleeping body. The sight of witnessing herself being screwed while asleep was too much for Lara in her aroused condition. All it needed now was for her to writhe and twist and the excitement of struggling against the straps that held her triggered her orgasm. Watching her, Suzi and Zara exchanged knowing glances.

'You're doing very well Lara; the Doctor will be pleased with your progress.'

* * *

'There's three new purchase requests come through Doctor MacKennan?'

'Talk me through them then.'

MacKennan was sitting in the basement office with Karl, the man to whom he entrusted the day to running of his secret business. He noticed that the young man was wearing another new suit, black as always, but this one cut in the newest fashion style which somehow reminded MacKennan of a popular style from his own more youthful days.

'Well, I think the first we can reject out of hand,' Karl announced, with the confidence of someone who loved his job and knew he had his boss's admiration for his business acumen.

'Briefly...' MacKennan prompted, curious to at least know what it had been.

'A Warlord from one of the old Chinese empire provinces wants to buy a dozen harem girls. His only stipulation is that they are all Alpha 1 girls, not older than twenty.'

'How vulgar,' MacKennan shook his head and gestured for Karl to go on to the other requests.

'Item two: Governor of a pacific island wants a Girl Friday: ideally not over twenty and completely submissive. Willing to entertain house guests, do light work in the house and service him and his wife as required.'

'Sounds perfect for young Pippa, don't you think?' MacKennan suggested.

'My thoughts exactly,' Karl agreed, 'but there is the third request...'

'Which is?'

'From His Highness the Emerald Tiger, he wants three more

girls for his Palace,' Karl announced, leaning back on his chair and smiling with the knowledge that the person in question was easily one of the Doctor's wealthiest and most valued clients.

'Excellent,' MacKennan nodded with satisfaction. 'Pity though, I've just sold off all my stock.'

'Annabella and Pippa...' Karl suggested.

'Yes, obviously... but we need a third,' MacKennan commented.

'Perhaps he'd be content with just two?' Karl suggested but without much conviction.

'If we fail to fulfil the order this time he may look elsewhere next time. I can't afford to lose such a customer. We'll have to give him Lara as well.'

'She's hardly completed Conditioning, let alone...'

'It doesn't matter. There's no option. Tell His Highness that he will have three delightful specimens of Alpha One Female Slaves dispatched within forty eight hours.'

'Two days! But what if Lara doesn't accept her new role?'

'She won't have any choice in the matter. Besides, she'll love her new role; just trust me.'

'You're the boss and besides, you know their minds, if you think she's ready, she's ready.'

'Karl, I think I still detect a note of doubt. Come with me, I think you need convincing.'

'I believe you boss, honestly.'

'Well, follow me anyway. You deserve a reward for the extra work you've put in lately.'

* * *

Lara glanced up at the sound of the door opening. MacKennan and another man she'd not seen before looked down at her where she lay on her little bed. MacKennan smiled and stepped aside.

'Bring her to Discipline.'

Lara swallowed nervously as Suzi and Zara moved

purposefully into the room.

'Stand up Lara!'

Knowing there was nothing to be gained by refusing, Lara quickly stood up. Suzi moved swiftly behind her, took hold of her wrists and drew her arms behind her. Instead of the familiar feel of rubber or leather tightening around her wrists she felt the coolness of steel sliding around the base of first one thumb and then the other. Experimentally she tried moving her arms and found her thumbs were pinned together.

'Open you mouth.'

Lara obeyed. Zara showed her a ring gag and without prompting, Lara opened her mouth enough for the girl to insinuate the rubber. Lara patiently stood still, tasting the familiar taste and experiencing the familiar feel of the broad rubber ring as it jammed behind her teeth and pushed her jaws wide. Behind her, flicking her long hair out of the way first, Suzi fastened the gag's strap snugly at the back of her head. Lara swallowed nervously. In a way she hated this gag more than any that they'd used on her. Whilst there was always the alarm of feeling the pump up ball gag expanding in her mouth or there was the smothering feeling of the other gags they used, this one was the most unsettling. The rubber ring was hollow, so although Lara could still make herself heard to an extent, she felt acutely vulnerable. With her jaws held open, anything could be inserted through the ring into her mouth. The thought seemed to trigger a nervous ache in the pit of her stomach. Or perhaps in truth lower than her stomach... yes, if she admitted it, being gagged like this made her sex ache with eager expectation. The gag presaged torture and her body now was so keyed up with feverish anticipation at how she might be made to come by being tortured, that she loved the feeling of being gagged.

The young man was watching her and for a second Lara imagined that he could read her thoughts. She felt herself blush but then she told herself she didn't care; it didn't matter. Whoever he was, he was plainly with MacKennan and would, like the Doctor, clearly take delight at seeing her distress. Perhaps that was why they were taking her now to the Discipline room — to be tortured for his amusement.

The two teenage girls led Lara down the corridor and she could hear the men talking as they followed. Once in the Discipline room Lara was pushed down to her knees.

'Help yourself Karl... she's awaiting your command.'

Lara glanced at MacKennan then at the young man. The two girls stood watching. For a second the young man hesitated and then he moved quickly to stand in front of where she knelt and he hurriedly unfastened his trousers and pulled out his cock. It was already fully erect and now as he stood close before her, Lara could see how aroused the man was. His eyes gleaming, his cock swaying almost with a life of its own, he caught hold of Lara's hair with one hand and with his other hand he took his cock and thrust it through the rubber ring of the gag into her mouth.

'Do your best to look after him Lara, there's a good girl,' MacKennan ordered, trying not to let the amusement in his voice be too transparent.

Lara, although her jaws were held immobile still had the freedom to move her tongue and she dutifully set to work licking the cock that filled her mouth. The young man sighed appreciatively then after a minute or so he withdrew his shaft and looked down at her, a gleeful smile across his flushed face.

'Bend over!'

Lara did as she was ordered and with her cheek pressed against the floor and her rump thrust high, she eagerly awaited what she knew would come next. Grasping her hips with both hands he pulled her back onto his shaft and Lara felt it slide easily into her sex. To her disappointment, he was so aroused that he came too quickly for her. Whilst he was now quite satisfied, Lara was left frustrated as the man tidied his clothes.

'She looks like she wants more,' the young man commented dryly.

'Lara can never get enough. Now do you believe me? She'll be just what the Emerald Tiger is after.'

'You're right of course, Doctor MacKennan.'

'I know my girls!' MacKennan laughed then gestured to Suzi. 'Lara looks like she is in desperate need of another shafting: I haven't time, perhaps you and Zara could find a way of satisfying her?'

'It would be a pleasure, Doctor.'

Lara pulled her body weight backwards so her face was lifted clear of the floor again and she could lean her weight more comfortably on her legs as she remained kneeling and awaiting what was wanted from her next.

'How will the girls deal with her?' the young man enquired.

'Stay and watch, if you'd like Karl. You'll have to excuse me though, I have other matters to attend to.'

Lara watched the Doctor leave the room. Once he was gone and she was left staring at a closed door she turned her attention back to the others. The young man was staring wide-eyed across the room and Lara swung her gaze to see what had riveted his attention. It was Suzi. She had removed her skimpy skirt, but retained her high heels and stockings. From the locker where all the restraining equipment and whips were stored, she had produced a massive strap-on dildo. When she caught Lara gazing at her and read the alarm on her face, the girl threw back her head and laughed.

'Right then Zara, give me a hand to strap her down on the bench. Time for the bitch to get a proper shafting!'

With her arms held behind her Lara knew resistance was useless and she allowed herself to be led docilely across to the bench. The girls pushed her chest up against the padding and a collar was strapped around her neck. The collar was then clipped to a ring on the bench preventing her lifting her head more than a few inches.

'Uhhh...'

'Hush now baby, it'll all be over soon enough,' cooed Zara as she slipped a leather strap around one of Lara's thighs and tightened it then clipped it onto the leg of the bench.

'Don't worry Lara, we girls know just how to give each other a good time, don't we?'

Suzi fastened a matching strap around Lara's other thigh and drawing her leg sideways clipped it to the other table leg. Lara shivered nervously as the girl's hands stroked down the exposed inside of her spread thighs. She was breathing hard now and sensing her fear, Suzi stroked her face reassuringly.

'Don't worry darling, I promise not to stop until you tell me to! Now, have a good look at what I'm going to treat you to.'

Dangling the strap-on dildo before her face, Lara now saw clearly just how big it was. She jerked her body urgently, trying to pull away from the bench but with her thighs strapped to the table legs and her neck collared and held down it was already too late.

'Nuuhh!'

'Let's take those silly little thumb cuffs off her before she bruises herself with them. Fetch some wristcuffs Zara.'

Lara's arms were soon stretched and secured above her head and for good measure, Suzi put a leather strap across the small of her back as well. Now completely helpless and watched by the young man, Lara waited while the girl strapped the dildo on, standing in front of her so that she could see what was happening. To Lara's shame, the realisation of what she was about to be subjected to aroused her intensely and to her relief, when Suzi speared the rigid latex shaft into her pussy she was already slick with arousal juice and the phallus entered her easily. Through the gag, Lara emitted a long, low groan. As Suzi settled into a determined rhythmic thrusting into her tethered body, Lara quickly felt her aching sex being brought to a much needed climax. Just before she came she saw the young man watching her. His cock pressed hard against the material of his trousers and she guessed that he would be ready again to use her, given half a chance. She closed her eyes, imagining him taking over when Suzi was finished with her. She would be well and truly satisfied by the time this session was over, she thought dreamily. MacKennan was right... Lara admitted to herself, gazing at her outstretched, tethered arms: he knew just how she liked to be treated.

CHAPTER TEN

The runway shimmered, glossy black in the blistering heat. The noise of the wheels hitting the tarmac was echoed by the harsh cry of an animal from some unseen place in the high savannah grass, which rippled in the warm breeze blowing in off the emerald sea. On a high plateau of rock, stacked like a precariously balanced deck of playing cards, three dark skinned natives stood motionless, resting their lean, sinewy bodies against the tall shafts of their spears. A mile below them the small jet plane seemed to skim the surface of the black line the tarmac drew. The plane came to a halt at the very end of the landing strip, where half a dozen buildings of gleaming glass and chrome and steel clustered in a defensive crescent against the desolate landscape that encircled them.

Men in military uniforms emerged from one of the buildings and in open top jeeps sped across to where the plane had come to rest. The three natives watched, unblinking against the ferocious midday heat as the plane's passengers disembarked. A handful of people in crisp white clothes first from the front of the plane and then from a rear door, one man, leading three girls. Apart from high black leather boots and black blindfolds the girls were quite naked. They walked close together, each collared and tethered to the next, their hands roped behind their slender backs.

* * *

'Your Highness, the plane has arrived safely, your new toys should be here by this time tomorrow.'

As the man spoke, he prostrated himself on the marble floor, hardly daring to glance up towards the person he addressed.

'And they are good examples, as we were assured?'

'I spoke with the commander of the airfield, he tells me they are magnificent. He is sending them under armed guard as instructed at first light tomorrow. They should reach the Palace by late afternoon.'

'You reminded him to double his watch tonight and keep a patrol out until dusk?'

'Yes, your Highness. He says there is no sign of any bandits.'

'He's being naive if he imagines that the arrival of my new toys will pass unnoticed. Very well, leave me... I have affairs of state to attend to '

The messenger stepped back and rose, bowed twice and walked backwards towards the double doors by which he had entered the hall. A moment later and he was gone and His Highness the Emerald Tiger was alone again.

Slipping behind a large wall hanging of brightly woven silk, he left the hall by a small door concealed behind his throne and walked slowly down a narrow, faintly lit corridor. Occasionally he would pause at a small spy hole to peer in upon one of the many rooms that he could watch from his secret corridor. Sometimes if the activity in a particular room took his interest he would flick on a small switch adjacent to the spy hole and the conversation of the room's occupants would be revealed to him. After satisfying himself that his ministers, secretaries and servants were all loyally performing their expected duties he moved swiftly down to the end of the corridor. The carbon fibre door slid open the moment he rested his palm against it and stepping into the room beyond, it slid smoothly shut behind him.

Two men, powerfully built and shaven headed, quickly stood to attention then relaxed again once their ruler gestured for them to do so. Both the men who were dressed in nothing more than emerald green, silk pantaloons turned their attention back to the task they were performing.

The naked girl made little objection as one man grasped her hair and pulled her head back from where it rested on the small leather covered bench. The Emerald Tiger watched as the second man drew a black silk blindfold across the girl's eyes. The wide, blue eyes that registered her excitement and apprehension so clearly were promptly covered and the silk knotted firmly at the back of her head.

The girl was crouched face down on the couch with her legs drawn up under her so that her knees were close to her breasts. A white silk rope bound repeatedly around the bench and over her back, just below her shoulder blades, held her down and a second rope lashed tightly over her slender calves, pinned her legs. Her firm young rump was thrust high, her skin, smooth and pale. The girl's arms hung down over the sides of the bench, her hands just reaching a crossbar of wood below the bench, to which they were bound by a silk sash wound around her wrists. It was only when the men coaxed her jaws open and began to feed a fine silk scarf into her mouth that the girl started to struggle against the restraints that held her. Her efforts to object though were futile and with one fine silk scarf filling her mouth a second was drawn across her face to complete the gag.

The Emerald Tiger wandered around the bench, stroking the girl's body affectionately. So delicate, so tender... and so helpless... he smiled to himself as she wriggled under his touch. Her arms jerked a little as he traced his hand along her ribs, she was delightfully slim and yet her breasts were more than full enough to please him. She gurgled something incoherently through the gag as he caressed one of her breasts and lightly squeezed her nipple between his thumb and finger. Saliva already soaked the silk gag and drops were shining on the black leather of the bench. He gestured for the men to continue.

One of the men slid his palms, extended fingers first between the globes of the young girl's arse and then drew apart her buttocks. The second man took an elephant tusk, shiny with some grease or oil and pushed the pointed end, which had been pierced to make a small opening, into the girl's anus. As the tusk was driven progressively deeper, its increasing girth forced the girl's rectum steadily wider and soon she was shaking her head and groaning urgently through the gag. One of the men then brought a small bowl across to where the girl lay writhing.

The Emerald Tiger glanced at the earthenware bowl, noting

the bright red berries, their skins burst and weeping juice. The bowl was then upended above the tusk and the berries tumbled down the ivory tube into the prostrate girl's anus. The tusk was then withdrawn. Soon the girl was groaning through her gag, writhing madly, pulling frantically against the silk cords that bound her. Beads of perspiration ran down her face and her tethered limbs were soon glossy with sweat as she struggled futilely against her restraints.

There were two other girls in the room. The ruler of Pashkent had got to know all three very well during the year that they'd served as his toys. But now he was growing bored with them. They knew all his ways of teasing and torturing them. They'd grown used to his punishments just as he had become too familiar with each of their responses. All three had arrived at the same time, American students who had strayed too close to the Pashkent border once on an adventure trekking holiday. He had happily disposed of the girls he'd had in his Palace previously and had since devoted many pleasurable hours to amusing himself with these new Alpha girls. They had come to Africa for adventure and he had given them a year that none of them would ever forget.

So the time had come to exchange these for some new girls and having now enjoyed the delights of forcing wealthy, privileged, arrogant Alpha females to his cruel ways, he wanted three more such girls. He had bought similar females on previous occasions from MacKennan, mostly to give as presents to loyal servants or to some of his male relatives. Those that he'd kept for himself he'd enjoyed, but as always, he'd grown bored with them eventually and had given them away.

So now he had ordered three new females from the British Doctor. There was a plentiful supply of slave girls around the world but there was a certain satisfaction in buying an Alpha One female. Whilst they were well enough trained, if provoked sufficiently he could usually make them break. The veneer of devoted slave would crack: a defiant, spoilt young girl would

191

emerge, spitting fury at being treated like a caged, wild animal. And that was when the games really became fun.

These three American girls had at first been defiant but soon learnt to toe the line. The blonde in fact demonstrated a penchant for submissiveness and she'd become the focus for his attention. The other two had become so meek and obliging as to be boring. Doubtless they imagined he would tire of them and perhaps they fondly, naively imagined he'd release them. He turned his attention from the blonde girl bound to the bench and looked across the room at the two other girls.

Both were bound side by side in similar fashion. Knelt on the floor, their arms were held stretched above their heads by silk cords bound around their wrists and fastened to ropes suspended from the ceiling. The girls were naked and sat with their legs folded under them. Leather belts were bound around their thighs pinning them against their calves. They watched silently as the third of their number was subjected to the latest of their master's whims. These two thought that they were being clever, being so subservient. Well, he would give them to a couple of his army officers as rewards for good service. Then they would learn how kind and gentle he had been with them.

He turned his attention back to the blonde who was still writhing madly. He stroked his hands over her raised bottom, finding the skin warm and wet under his touch. Feeling between her legs he found her sex moist and hot and his fingers slipped easily into her soft, wet folds. The girl groaned the gag and thrust her rump backwards against his hands.

'How are we feeling, my little blonde tiger?'

The girl gurgled something incoherently, trying to lift her head as best she could given the silk drawn tightly across her shoulders which held her down against the bench.

'Are you feeling in need now of some attention?'

The girl nodded affirmatively and the Emerald Tiger gestured to one of his servants. Quickly the man moved behind the girl a short whip in one hand. Stepping aside, the Emerald

Tiger signalled for the man to go ahead.

The pain of the whip would for a brief time distract the girl from the terrible ache in her body that the juice from the berries was inflicting. After she'd been whipped and the sensation had subsided, she'd still be left with that maddening ache in her body, like an itch that could only temporarily be assuaged by fierce scratching. Her rump streaked with red whip marks, he would then ask her if she wanted to feel one of his men ram his cock up her delicate, young arse. He knew she'd agree enthusiastically, naively believing that such attention would quench the excruciating throbbing ache that the berry juice had brought upon her. But the juice from the berries would also, once it had soaked into his servant's cock, prevent him from ejaculating. Her pert little rump would be subjected to a very long session of anal sex before the man using her might eventually manage to shoot his load.

'Was that good? Would you like us to do something else to you now?'

As he posed the question he stroked his hands over the girl's quivering rump. Some of the berry juice was trickling from her anus and he smeared it with his fingertip across the softness of her sex lips. The girl groaned feverishly through the gag and jerked hard with her arms against the silk that bound her.

'Perhaps if one of my men was to sink his cock into your aching body, it would help to relieve the sensation of distress?'

The girl nodded with frantic agreement and a moment later the Emerald Tiger watched with satisfaction as one of his men stood behind the girl, grasped her hips with both hands and speared her rump with his heavily engorged cock.

'As hard as you like,' the Emerald Tiger gestured for the man to get on with the task of shafting the tethered girl.

The man needed no more encouraging and the Emerald Tiger settled back to watch as the young white girl was mercilessly sodomised. Gagged and blindfolded, bound so her arse was kept forcibly thrust high, there would be no way she could signal for the man to stop. The Emerald Tiger smiled sadistically as the assault on the defenceless girl got under way. For the moment she was enjoying the attention... soon enough though through the silk that gagged her, he would have the pleasure of hearing her gurgling, pleading for the man to stop. Her words would be incoherent though and ignored. Her ordeal would only end when it pleased him to show her some mercy. And that would not be for quite some time...

* * *

Lara gazed around the room in which they had been locked. There was only one narrow window, barred with primitive metal tubes, and the heat was oppressive even though it was now dark outside.

The other two girls had both pounced on the two narrow bunk beds that provided the tiny cell with its only furniture. This had left Lara standing but she didn't care. She didn't feel tired and at least she could lean against the wall by the open window and enjoy a little fresh air.

MacKennan had told her he was selling her to a client named the Emerald Tiger, who ruled one of the many small kingdoms of eastern Africa. She was to live at his court and serve him as he demanded. He was buying three submissive slaves from MacKennan and Lara was to be one. When MacKennan had asked her if she objected to what was to befall her, Lara had stumbled to answer. The simple truth was that while a part of her abhorred the idea of being sold into slavery, the darker side of her nature was eagerly revelling in what might lie in store for her.

Her new companions soon, despite the humid warmth, drifted asleep. By the pale moonlight that spilt through the open window Lara was able to gaze at them and she wondered what had been going through their minds since MacKennan had sentenced them to life in one of the Barbarian nations. The man called the Emerald Tiger, a self-styled King, ruled a tiny country called Pashkent that was built around a handful of diamond mines. From what MacKennan had told her, Pashkent was a far cry from the safe and wealthy Europa of which Lara was a citizen. The country she was now in had reverted to many of its tribal practices from a century or more ago. As a white Alpha 1 class girl she would be a novelty; a plaything to amuse the despot who ruled mercilessly over his arid, semi-desert country.

Lara was gazing dreamily out of the window, breathing in the unfamiliar smells of grass and earth, when a movement in the dark caught her eye. A darker shadow in the shadows; a fleeting glimpse of fast moving, stealthy figures, men surely but maybe, she wondered, some form of wild animal. As if in response a spot light suddenly came on and swung a beam of pallid yellow light across the ground, illuminating briefly thick, high grass, boulders and gnarled, stunted trees. The beam of light swung back and forth again but showed nothing more than empty arid earth as it swept close around the buildings.

A few moments later two men with guns and torches moved past the window and headed into the undergrowth. They returned after a short time and marched purposefully towards the window that Lara was watching from. When they peered in she had retreated to the far wall. The beam of a torch flashed into the room, illuminating the bunk beds it lingered over the naked bodies of the sleeping girls. It then swung across the room, exposed Lara and shone full in her face. As she shielded her eyes with her hand she heard the men talking, their language completely unintelligible to her.

Lara didn't have long to wait before, preceded by a rattling of primitive metal keys in locks, the two guards let themselves into the cell. One of the men caught her by the hair and jerked her towards the door. The noise had woken Annabella and Pippa but they remained silent as Lara was shepherded from the room. With one man holding her firmly by the arm and the other grasping her hair, she was marched quickly down a series of narrow, dimly lit corridors before being ushered into the room. Stumbling in the high-heeled boots, which was all she had been given to wear, Lara found herself in a room that obviously served as the living quarters for a handful of guards, who now circled around her, grinning with eager expectation.

As the men caught hold of her wrists and dragged her across to a broad wooden table, Lara remembered how it had felt to be the adventurer as the evil MacKennan's guards had taken her body by force. How they had come to her cell, gagged her and used her body. But that had been a dream, her fantasy... now this was for real! Instinctively she struggled but her resistance only served to taunt them and when two of them found it difficult to control her, several more eagerly joined in the game. It took them only a moment before they had her waist jammed against the edge of the table, her chest pulled down over the top, her arms held fully outstretched by two of the men grasping and pulling her wrists from the far side.

'Please... let me go!'

Lara writhed and struggled as from both sides, hands grasped her bare thighs, drawing her legs apart.

'Uh, no... please...'

She knew what was going to happen next and secretly wanted it but she was too ashamed to openly admit it and there was something conditioned in her now to struggle. MacKennan and his dream machine had taught her that her sexual satisfaction was heightened when she had no control over what she was being subjected to. Her heart hammering, her body slick with perspiration, Lara struggled frantically against the numerous hands that held her down. Someone was behind her, powerful thighs jammed between her legs, the hardness of his body pressing against hers. She shook her head, trying to twist and writhe but they were holding her firmly still now.

She felt the cock nudge against her sex then sink into her. A shiver of delicious pleasure ran through her body and she moaned feverishly as the cock partially withdrew then sank back. Afraid that she might call out begging the man to fuck her hard, she screamed for him to stop and was grateful when in response a ball of cloth was forced into her mouth silencing her. She gazed around her at the grinning faces and guessed that she wouldn't be returned to her cell until she had serviced all the men. She looked at her outstretched arms, her slender wrists grasped firmly by numerous hands. The sensation of the man ramming his cock back and forth had her close to coming already and this was just the start... Lara sighed through the gag and closed her eyes.

Her aching body was lathered with sweat, her pussy throbbing from a relentless shafting by half a dozen of the men when she realised that she'd had enough. She had lost count of how many times she'd come, but she felt washed with sexual satisfaction and now she just longed to be left alone. Her captors though had other ideas. As another man took his place behind her spread legs, Lara groaned and struggled as his cock was driven hard into her now acutely delicate pussy.

'Nhhh!'

Lara shook her head vigorously, trying through the cloth that filled her mouth to tell them that she'd had enough. For a moment she willed herself to wake up then she remembered with dismay that this was no dream. This was no fantasy scenario created for her by MacKennan. This was really happening! In alarm she began to try to expel the cloth from her mouth but a firm hand was quickly across her mouth and then a second later it was replaced by one of the dark green neck scarves the men wore. The material, tightly rolled was jammed between her jaws and drawn closely around her head then tied above her nape. Lara thrashed her head vigorously, groaning her objection at what was happening. She felt the cock in her pussy draw back then thrust into her again. The hands holding her down tightened their grasp. She gazed despondently at the grinning faces surrounding her. She guessed there must be a dozen of them: that meant she was perhaps no more than half way through her ordeal. She blinked back the tears and reminded herself that she'd chosen this. She'd wanted to be treated something like this; well, now she had only herself to blame for her sorry condition!

* * *

When she came to, she opened her eyes to see Pippa looking down at her. Seeing her wake, she smiled and flicked her long, dark hair clear of her face. Lara sighed and closed her eyes again. Her leg muscles throbbed dully and the gentle ache between her legs reminded her of her ordeal from the previous night.

'How are you feeling?' Pippa asked.

'Never felt better!' Lara managed a smile and lifted herself up onto one elbow. She was in the lower bunk bed of the cell and from above her Annabella's face and shoulders dangled over the side of the bunk whilst Pippa sat perched on the end of the tiny bed.

'They had you for hours, we were really worried... they didn't you whip you or anything?' Pippa asked, her hazel eyes wide with concern.

'No,' Lara shook her head, 'they didn't lay a finger on me. They just fucked me senseless instead!'

'God! How many?'

'I'm not sure, I lost count. Maybe a dozen.'

'You poor thing!'

'Oh, I don't know. It wasn't so terrible. I'm still in one piece.'

'When they brought you back, they took Pippa,' Annabella announced, with more than a hint of jealousy in her voice.

'Their commanding officer wanted me,' confessed Pippa, 'He made me look after him.'

'You mean he fucked you?'

'No, I offered to suck him and he agreed. I like doing it that way. I told him he could punish me if I didn't satisfy him but he said he didn't dare risk marking my skin. If it was found out he'd had me, he said he'd lose his job if not his life.'

'So if we tell...' Lara mused out loud, but her thoughts were quickly dashed by Annabella.

'Tell him what the man said Pippa.'

'The officer said that if any of us breathed a word of what's happened he'd have us murdered. I think he meant it too, these people seem pretty ruthless.'

'I think we should just shut up and forget about it,' announced Annabella.

'Okay, if that's the consensus,' Lara shrugged.

'They're moving us to the Palace today. We should have left at first light but there's been a problem with bandits, so things have been held up.'

'Bandits...'

'Apparently they're after the bounty which came in on the last plane.'

'What bounty?' Lara asked.

'Us, you idiot!' laughed Pippa.

The girls' chatter was brought to an abrupt end by the arrival of the officer who seemed in command. He was escorted by four of his men, all of whom were armed with old-fashioned bullet firing guns. Whilst Europa Federation troops had for ages carried laser guns, these soldiers were equipped with nothing more than late twentieth century machine-guns.

'It is time for you to be transferred to the Palace, follow me!'

The girls were ushered from the cell and led outside to where a rusty open-roofed truck stood flanked by two military jeeps. The sunlight was so fierce Lara had to squint and desperately wished she had some sunglasses. Back in Britain she'd worn them mostly as a fashion accessory but now she really could have done with some! The heat seemed to ripple from the metal of the vehicles and rise in a shimmering haze from the baked earth. Immediately Lara felt the perspiration begin to trickle from her armpits and down her back. When she touched the wheel arch of the truck as she prepared to clamber on board, the metal was so hot that she yelped, snatching her hand back in alarm.

'It is only mid-morning: in another three or four hours, then it will get truly hot.'

The officer grinned with satisfaction and a perverse sort of pride as he spoke and Lara glowered at him as she nursed her burnt fingertips. Before she was allowed to get into the truck she was made to hold her arms out before her and a pair of leather cuffs was fastened around her wrists. Once in the truck she and the other girls were made to sit on a crude wooden bench. Above their heads, running the length of the truck was a steel bar and they were each made to lift their hands to touch it. A chain was then coiled around the bar and clipped to each of the girl's wrist cuffs and they were left now effectively manacled to the bar and prisoners in the truck. Without any further preamble four men clambered into each jeep, a driver jumped up into the cabin of the truck and another soldier climbed into the back to sit opposite the girls. Before they had even set off he had discarded his machine-gun and turned his attention to rolling himself a cigarette. Belching diesel fumes and throwing up a cloud of dust, the three vehicles roared away from the airport buildings. The road they took was no more than a dirt track and as it climbed a steep incline to traverse a broad ridge, the truck quickly lost power and its speed was reduced to a crawl.

On the highest point of the ridge, crouched motionless amongst a jumble of rocks, three natives watched the convoy. As the vehicles rounded a bend in the track and disappeared from view, the natives stood. Spears in hand, without a word, they set off at a jog down the hillside.

CHAPTER ELEVEN

They had been driving for perhaps an hour and the first jeep had just driven across a rickety wooden bridge that crossed a dried up river course when the attack came. Lara was gazing disconsolately at the surrounding savannah when an explosion directly in front of the truck made her shriek with alarm. The bridge timbers erupted in a cloud of acrid smoke and dust and before the driver could react, with the bridge in tatters, the truck ploughed into the dried up riverbed. The ground dropped only a couple of metres thankfully and the front of the truck took the impact of the crash. The girls were thrown forward then the truck lurched sideways and slowly toppled over. Screaming in alarm the girls were left dangling by the chains that held them by the arms to the pole they'd been secured to.

As Lara came to her senses the gunfire broke out on all sides. As the smoke cleared she could see the jeep that had been behind them. Halted at the edge of the shallow ditch the soldiers had jumped out and from behind the cover of their vehicle they were now firing furiously into the undergrowth on both sides of the track they'd come down.

Her arms aching unbelievably as she dangled from the pole, Lara struggled to gain a foothold on something solid below where she hung suspended. At last, her shoulder muscles in agony, her right boot caught hold of the upended edge of the bench seat and a moment later she had got both her feet balanced on it and she could give her arms some slack and relieve the screaming pain in her muscles. Beside her the other girls were crying and flailing the air with their legs. Lara was about to tell them what to do when the sound of tearing metal above her head gave a second's warning before the rusty pole sheared off and all three girls tumbled into the well of the truck.

'Let's get under the truck and take cover before someone accidentally shoots us!'

Encouraged by Annabella, the three girls crawled on their

hands and knees out of the back of the truck then scurried underneath the overhanging debris that was all that remained of the bridge. Above their heads the gunfight already seemed to be dying down. There were two loud explosions like thunderclaps close by and after that the amount of gunfire subsided abruptly.

'Perhaps we should try to...'

Lara never caught the rest of what Annabella was saying. There was a deafening bang around her ears and something like an invisible wave seemed to wash over her. She was vaguely aware of stumbling then dropping to her knees. She remembered a ringing in her ears and dizziness, then darkness.

* * *

At the Palace of the Emerald Tiger the morning calm was about to be shattered. The first rumblings of the impending storm came as a bedraggled handful of soldiers stumbled through the Palace gates. Whispers of what had happened rippled through the Palace even before the soldiers were ushered into the Palace and led to the King's throne room.

The shouting could be heard beyond the closed doors of the throne room and any servant, soldier or minister who caught the first rumblings of their monarch's fury, quickly absented themselves from the fallout zone. The only man who remained unworried was the King's executioner, Salim the Silent. He merely checked that the blade of his great axe was sharp and then he sat back with a small cup of treacle-thick dark coffee and a bowl of sherbet and awaited his summons.

By late afternoon, the King's most favoured General had left the Palace at the head of a small convoy of crack troops bristling with the best weaponry that the diamonds of Pashkent could buy. At about the same time, from the army barracks outside the capital a squadron of helicopters jammed with more of the King's crack troops took off in pursuit of the bandits that had robbed the Emerald Tiger of his prized new toys.

In a quiet courtyard tucked in a corner of the Palace grounds, Salim the Silent shouldered his great axe and without so much as backward glance left his workplace. The old hunch-backed woman, like a raven in her tattered black robes, had already gathered the heads into her wicker basket and two of the Kings eunuchs had tossed the bodies onto the cart. A few moments later and the courtyard stood deserted.

* * *

Still dazed from the explosions of the stun grenades, Lara gazed up disconsolately at her tethered arms and legs. With her ankles bound together with rope, like her wrists, she hung by her arms and legs slung below a long wooden pole that was carried by two natives. Squinting against the overhead sun she looked around her as best she could.

Annabella and Pippa were slung in a similar fashion; the petite, young Pippa being carried behind her and ahead of her, still unconscious, Annabella was carried by two more natives. Walking a short way ahead of them were several white men in safari clothes, hunting rifles slung over their shoulders. Bringing up the rear of the party were half a dozen natives, all armed. Lara lifted her head and looked at herself. Apart from a few scratches and bruises she was fine. She gazed up at her bound wrists; the rope was wound repeatedly around them and the pole and mercifully, because of the way they'd tied her, her wrists and ankles bound over the pole, the strain of hanging from her arms and legs wasn't too bad. We look like game hunter's trophies, Lara reflected, glancing at the other girls.

The captive girls were carried for less than a mile before reaching a rough clearing in the bush, in the middle of which was a small jet helicopter. The girls were deposited in the back, the natives paid off and a moment later the white men had climbed aboard and they were air-borne. The flight lasted for less than an hour; all the time the helicopter flew very low and for the girls thrown in the back and deprived of ear protection the noise was deafening. When they eventually landed Lara felt like every bone in her body had been shaken loose. Dragged legs first from the cramped rear of the helicopter Lara discovered that the chopper had actually landed on the helipad of a ship.

'Put them in the secure hold and get cast off, I'm sure by now The Emerald Tiger will have every available soldier hunting us. There's no point in hanging around inviting trouble.'

Lara glanced at the man, wondering who he was and what was now to be their fate. As if guessing her thoughts the man raised his hand, gesturing for the two crewmen who had just hauled Lara to her feet, to wait for a moment before dragging her away.

'Wondering what's going to happen to you now?' the man strolled across to stand before her and calmly he swept his eyes over her, as if only now for the first time having the opportunity to survey his newly acquired trophy.

'What do you think!' snapped Lara angrily.

Instinctively as she made the merest move towards the man, the hands grasping her arms tightened their hold to restrain her more effectively.

The man smiled and flicked some of Lara's tangled golden hair clear of her face. She stiffened as his hand then moved over her body, his fingers stroking first her neck and then her breast.

'Where are you from?' he asked but with so little real interest that Lara was immediately and cruelly reminded that now all that mattered about her was her body. She was a living trophy: sold as a slave to one man, she'd now been stolen by another. For a moment she felt furiously indignant but then as she saw the man's appreciative gaze lingering on her, she felt pride that her physical desirability had provoked men to not just pay for her but to fight for her.

'I asked you a question girl! Where are you from?' the man repeated his question with more than a trace of impatience in his voice now.

Lara glanced down at her roped hands before her and then looked disdainfully at the two lackeys holding her arms.

'What does it matter? I'm here now. What have you got planned for me?'

'You know I really don't like your insolent tone,' the man warned.

Lara could feel the gazes of the other two girls and the surrounding men on her. Goaded by her bruised and aching body, her temper frayed by everything she'd been put through in the last forty eight hours, her patience snapped.

'Well, I don't like you: I've got no idea what you've got planned for me but I think I'd rather have ended up a slave to the Emerald Tiger!'

The man's face turned from a frown to a snarl.

'Take the other two down to the secure hold. Bring this one with me!'

The men holding Lara promptly dragged her by the arms after the man. With her ankles still roped together, her feet trailed helplessly, her heels dragging across the polished wooden decking then banging down a short flight of chrome steps. Lara was then dragged along a corridor and into what was evidently a dining room.

'Put her over the table on her back!'

The two men holding her quickly obeyed the instruction, Lara landing on her back with a hard bump that sent pain shooting through her shoulder blades as the men virtually tossed her onto the table.

'You bastard... you'd better hope that I never get free from here, or you'll be sorry!' Lara snarled.

'A defiant young lady like you needs to be taught some good manners. I'd have thought if you'd ended up in Pashkent you'd have been taught how a slave should behave properly.'

'Maybe I'm not a slave!' protested Lara, grunting and writhing as the two men tied another rope around the one that bound her wrists.

'Tie the slave down. Time for her to have a lesson in good manners!'

'Damn you... just you wait!'

Lara glanced over her shoulder to watch with dismay as her arms were stretched above her head and the rope pulling them taut was dragged over the edge of the polished tabletop and fastened to one of the table legs.

'Untie her ankles: spread her legs: as wide as she can bear!'

Lara jerked her arms ineffectually then tried thrashing her legs as ropes were drawn around each of her ankles.

'Bastards...get your hands off me! If I ever...'

The man laughed scornfully.

'You'll never have the chance girl. From now on I'll keep you roped and tethered. If you want to be bad tempered then you'll be treated accordingly!'

As the man spoke the rope binding her ankles together was removed and the two men quickly pulled on the ropes they'd applied. Lara felt her legs being jerked apart then spread painfully wide. The dining table, which would have seated a dozen people, was broad enough for them to spread Lara's legs as wide as they'd go. As they secured the ropes Lara fought down the urge to cry. For a while she'd imagined or believed herself to be the defiant tough girl adventurer of her dreams, but now her real self was resurfacing. What chance did she have against these men? Now she was going to be severely punished and she had only herself to blame! Why hadn't she just kept quiet like Pippa and Annabella?

'What a pleasing sight,' sneered the man, 'I think perhaps her arms should be spread-eagled as well. After you've done that, blindfold her and leave her. It will do her good to contemplate what might lie in store for her.'

Five minutes later and Lara was alone. Or at least she assumed that she was alone. Blindfolded she couldn't be absolutely certain. She had heard the men walk to the door, heard the door open and close and then the room was silent except for her nervously fast breathing. They'd blindfolded her with black tape. It only adhered to itself and was only a few inches wide but wound repeatedly around her head across her eyes it had proved utterly effective. Plunged into darkness her other senses had immediately become needle sharp. She could feel the warm air coming from an air conditioning unit somewhere beyond her feet. She could smell the beeswax polish from the table. She was acutely aware of the tightness of the ropes around her wrists and ankles and if she slithered her arms or legs she could hear the dull rubbing sound of the rope against the table edge. With her arms and legs spread-eagled and blindfolded she felt extremely vulnerable and could imagine what a sight she must look, naked and tethered in such a fashion.

When the door latch clicked Lara jerked her head in the direction of the sound. Her pulse quickened and she felt, in her nervousness, her tethered body begin to perspire again. The sound of footsteps, one person, circled the table. She fought down the urge to speak, to ask who was there, knowing this would betray her fear. A hand touched her ankle making her try to jump in surprise. Tied down though, her limbs stretched taut, she managed no more than a nervous jerk of her leg as the hand slowly moved upwards from her ankle. Lara swallowed as the hand moved above her knee and the fingers stroked on upwards across the soft, sensitive inside of her thigh. To her shame she was already more aroused and excited than scared. Sexual attention, she realised with a flush of shame crimsoning her cheeks, was what she really craved. As the fingers reached the sensitive tops of her inner thighs, Lara gave an expectant murmur and silently urged the person, she guessed it was the man, but wasn't sure, to stroke her sex.

The fingers though, merely whispered around her anus and then glided tantalisingly lightly over her aching pussy. Lara sighed with disappointment and a female voice softly laughed.

'She's aching for it. Any ordinary girl would be quivering with fear but this one's desperate for it. She's been well conditioned. Either that or she's a natural submissive.'

The hand, and now Lara chided herself for not appreciating the softness of touch as being obviously female, moved across her taut stomach and up her chest until it reached her nervously heaving breasts.

'Superb breasts. The highest quality modification I would say,' commented the female voice, 'Most probably genetic. A very expensive job: I'd say this girl is an Alpha One. They probably all are, though this one is easily the best example.'

The fingers stroking over Lara's breasts toyed with her nipples bringing them quickly to full hardness. Lara moaned softly, her body now aching for more attention. She knew how inviting her nipples would look and she remembered in her dreams what the evil Doctor had subjected them to. Then she recalled what MacKennan had really subjected them to. With a pang of fevered erotic longing, Lara silently hoped that the woman inspecting her would treat her in some similar way.

'If she weren't tied down so firmly she'd be writhing now. Look at her hips, her parted lips, her back wanting to arch. She's desperate for some attention. Aren't you?'

The woman's question hung unanswered for a moment; Lara too ashamed to admit how she felt. Then the woman, gently at first then progressively more firmly, squeezed both Lara's nipples between her fingers and thumbs. Lara sighed then groaned in response, trying to drag her arms down against the restraining ropes so she could arch her back. The woman laughed softly again and then the man, who had been silent all the time, spoke.

'Do you think she's too good to release into the game park?'

'She'd attract a lot of hunters. You could charge plenty for her. The other two would make amusing quarry also.'

'But you think it would be a waste of her talents?' the man suggested.

The woman released her grasp on Lara's nipples and she sank back down against the table with a sigh.

'Wouldn't you rather keep her for yourself?' the woman

suggested.

'I think the bitch will just be too much trouble.'

'She just needs training. I could work on her,' suggested the woman.

'Do you know,' the man laughed, 'she said that she'd rather be a slave to the Emerald Tiger than here?'

'She's just a silly little girl, who doesn't know when she's well off,' said the woman drawing her fingernails down from Lara's chest to her stomach and then lower. Lara bit her lip, holding her breath as she felt the woman's fingers hover very close to her sex.

'Lovely lips, very full. And that delicious smell of arousal...'

Lara tensed as she felt the woman's warm breath against her pussy.

'Well darling, I think you're in need of some attention, aren't you?'

The woman's question went unanswered again. Lara tried to steady her breathing but for a moment she'd imagined the woman was going to kiss her between her legs and her fingertips were still resting close to her pussy.

'So, what shall we do with her?' the woman asked.

Lara gave a gasp of surprise and pleasure in response as a slender finger slipped deeply into her aching sex.

'Sell her back to the madman who rules Pashkent?' the man suggested icily.

'Did the Captain tell you that some of his helicopters had been detected on the radar cruising the coast?'

'Yes, I told him if they started across the lake just to shoot them down but they've turned back. You know that country is so pathetically defended, I could be tempted to take it over just to enlarge the game park.'

'Don't be silly darling,' the woman said, her tone softly reproving. 'The eastern side of the lake is nothing but trouble. Thank heavens the lake itself is the size of a sea and we can keep them at arm's length. Now, what shall we do with this little vixen?'

The woman withdrew her finger from Lara's aching sex, making her sigh softly with disappointment at not receiving more attention. The sensation of helplessness and expectation which came with being naked and tied down had become so synonymous with sexual torment that Lara was now feverishly aroused. How she wished that they would use her body or punish her in some deliciously painful way that would bring her to a climax. She thought of all the things that she'd suffered at the hands of MacKennan: despite all the tears and torment he'd put her through, she was secretly deeply grateful. How dull her life had been until the day that she'd walked into the Dreamscape Institute!

'Well, we've got the best part of two days before we get home, so there's no rush to make a decision,' the man said.

'You're right darling,' the woman agreed. 'And meantime, just to pass the time, I'll amuse myself with her. That is if you don't mind?'

'Just don't leave any lasting marks on her skin,' the man cautioned.

'That still give us plenty of scope for fun,' the woman laughed.

'I'll see you later then, enjoy her.'

The heavy bootsteps of the man moved across to the door. Lara heard the door latch and then sound of the door clicking softly shut.

'Now, just to make sure we don't get disturbed.'

A dull metallic clunk from the door told Lara that the woman had locked the door from the inside.

'What's your name?' the woman asked, her voice now disconcertingly soft and friendly. Lara cleared her throat and turned her head in the direction of the voice. Whichever way she twisted her head though she remained plunged in darkness and when she tried to move her eyelashes she could feel the tape tight against her face.

'Lara,' she answered.

'Well Lara,' the woman's voice now came from directly

behind her head and as she spoke she gently rested the palms of both hands against Lara's cheeks. A fingernail brushed lightly across her lips making Lara shiver and have to fight down the urge to try to capture the finger with her teeth and suck it into her mouth.

'What... are...you.. going to do to me?' Lara stammered nervously.

The woman laughed softly.

'I can't tell you that. It would spoil the surprise. You don't mind anyway do you? You'd be happy for me to do anything with you, wouldn't you Lara?'

Lara made no reply, swallowing nervously.

'Now, if you're not going to answer me truthfully, if you don't want to talk to me, well...'

Lara squirmed as the woman placed her palm across Lara's mouth.

'Does that feel nice?'

Lara moaned and twisted her head sideways. The hand though remained clamped firmly over her mouth.

'There's no escape darling... so why don't you give a little nod to tell me that you're going to answer my questions?'

Lara refused to give in so easily to the woman and as reward for her stubborn behaviour the woman edged her hand a little higher so the edge of the palm began to smother Lara's nostrils.

'Nnnnhh!'

Lara shook her head vigorously but the grip merely became firmer.

'Feeling a little breathless? Would you like to talk to me now?'

Lara squirmed ineffectually as the woman's thumb and finger pressed her nostrils closed. For a second Lara couldn't breathe at all and then the hand was gone and air rushed into her lungs. Even as she recovered her senses the woman slid two fingers into her sex and Lara gave a plaintive moan as she felt herself being brought to a climax.

'That's it baby, time to come...time to come.'

The fingers sunk in her pussy twisted deliciously and at the same time the woman's thumb rubbed against her clitoris. With a breathless cry, Lara came, her whole body shuddering, her arms and legs writhing against the ropes that held her. It was so exquisite, so intense that when her sensations that had washed over her ebbed, she lay panting breathlessly and oblivious to the unseen person looking down at her.

'Well Lara, you seem to be enjoying yourself; I wonder what else you'd like me to do to you?'

The woman gave an ominous laugh. Lara listened to her footsteps moving across the polished wooden floor before returning a moment later. Relax, she told herself, whatever the woman had planned for her it couldn't be anything worse than what MacKennan had subjected her to. Or come to think of it, Lara thought, what I made myself suffer in my dreams. Anyway, the truth was that the woman was right — she had enjoyed what she'd been subjected to. Perhaps even before MacKennan had encouraged her imagination to search out her darkest fantasies, she'd known deep down what she'd craved. Well, now there was surely no turning back. She really had become a prisoner to her own desires.

The woman's footsteps returned and Lara stiffened as she felt the strands of a whip trail down across her stomach and briefly caress her sex; cruelly exposed between her wide-spread thighs.

'I think a few strokes on that lovely pussy of yours should help with your manners. And then we'd better see to those gorgeous tits. I wonder how many it'll take to make you come again.'

'No!' Lara just had time for the one word before hearing the Smack! of the whip and being overwhelmed by a fierce stinging which erupted from deep inside her loins. Her back arched and her wrists tugged frantically at their bonds.

'One' the woman's voice counted calmly. 'Are you ready for number two?'

'No! Please........Ahh!'

* * *

The six men had nothing in common except their considerable wealth and penchant for hunting. A hundred years ago the safari park where they had been brought would have been witness to similar men hunting. Then, the idle rich of the western world came and hunted wild game, but now all the big cats and wild animals were extinct. At least in their natural habitat. But there was another creature on offer.

'There! Down there!'

As the men pointed excitedly the helicopter swooped lower over the savannah. Any reservations about the massive fees they'd paid for the hunt dissolved at the first glimpse of their prey.

The girl was naked except for a leopard print bikini and short; high heeled brown leather boots. Apart from the skimpy material of her bikini briefs and top, her tanned skin was covered only where her long, dark hair cascaded over her shoulders. She had one slender arm raised, her hand shielding her eyes as she watched the helicopter speed towards her. The men could see her lean body was beaded with perspiration. For a moment she watched them approaching and then she turned and ran, jumping down from the rocky outcrop and sprinting into the nearest undergrowth, long legged, sleek and fast. At the first sight of the girl, the men's primal instincts took over. Back at home they could buy and enjoy anything they wanted but here was the chance to hunt for what they wanted. Their adrenaline pumping like mad, before the helicopter had even landed the men were congratulating themselves on choosing to come on such an adventure. Why had they ever doubted how good it would prove? As the helicopter called by radio for ground support, the hunters made themselves ready to disembark.

The quarry was intending to go to ground and the men exchanged amused glances as the helicopter rushed them closer to where their prey had last been sighted. Two of the men quickly clambered from the helicopter as it touched down.

213

With their hunting rifles in hand they hunkered down while the jet helicopter rose and swept in an arc for a quarter of a mile then lowered again, coming to rest just long enough for two more of its passengers to quickly disembark. The last two hunters were deposited about half a mile away so that the three groups now formed the points of a triangle, somewhere in the middle of which was the girl.

It was blisteringly hot and the sun was almost directly overhead. They had left the camp late in the day after a leisurely breakfast and a lazy morning exchanging stories: it was nearly midday before they'd set off. It had been stuffy enough in the helicopter but at least with the windows open they'd enjoyed a cooling breeze. Now on the ground the heat bore down on them and the backs of their safari suits were soon drenched with perspiration and clung to their skin. After the helicopter had swooped away, each team of men was left coated in a fine film of dust thrown up from the whirling blades of the helicopter. And whilst from the air, the landscape seemed easily navigable, down on the ground, surrounded by scrub and bush, the men were quickly disorientated.

'So which damn way are we meant to be heading?'

'Hang on a minute!'

A compass was impatiently pulled from one jacket pocket and consulted. The drone of flies and insects was all around them. The man without the compass swatted at those around his face irritably. The other man shoved the compass back into his pocket, looked around and pointed to the high ground to their right.

'That way. We came in from the east, she was up there.'

The men checked their rifles. The guns fired tranquilliser darts. One hit would be enough to bring the girl down; they'd been assured. Though she might keep running for ten or fifteen minutes, the park's owner had added with a wry smile.

'Her name, gentlemen, is Annabella and if you capture her, she's yours to enjoy for the rest of your safari,' he had told them. As the men shouldered their rifles they thought about what they might subject the girl to when they brought her back to the camp. Their host had thoughtfully provided plenty of accessories with which they could indulge their fancies. Already, a dozen natives would have left the camp not five miles away and would be heading in the direction of the hunt. They would have the nets and ropes to subdue the prey once she was caught. Then they would carry her back to the camp. The men of course, would call the helicopter to come back in and pick them up. They could then have a drink and shower and relax back at base and await the arrival of their prize. With this satisfying picture in mind, the first two men to have been dropped by the helicopter began to slog their way on foot through the undergrowth towards the hills ahead of them.

* * *

'And you are certain that my slave girls are in his park?'

'Beyond a shadow of doubt your Majesty. Quite how much of the trouble with bandits has been actually his work, we cannot be certain. However what is beyond any shadow of a doubt is that the man who claims to be your friendly neighbour has been stealing from your Kingdom.'

The Emerald Tiger nodded as he digested this fact. He had long courted the friendship of the ruler of the independent province that lay on the western shores of the lake. The man had many international business contacts within the civilised Alpha nations. He had been courteous and helpful in return or at least that was the impression that the Emerald Tiger had drawn. And now it turned out that the man had been orchestrating the bandit raids throughout Pashkent and had on at least one and probably several occasions, stolen slave girls that he himself had bought and imported. Well, no one crossed the Emerald Tiger and got away with it! At least not once they had been found out!

'Does your Majesty have any orders?'

The Emerald Tiger swung around and pointed an accusing finger at his Foreign Secretary.

215

'I don't know whether I should congratulate you on your spy network for finding this out or lose my temper with you for having taken so long to discover this!'

'Your Majesty has every right to execute me for not finding out sooner,' the man answered with astonishing calm, 'but I would humbly point out that I have worked unstintingly for you and my men are totally loyal to me and try their best for me.'

The Emerald Tiger nodded, trying not to smile. The man's words were clear enough: 'kill me and the intricate network of spies and agents I have built up will not serve you.' Doubtless his Foreign Secretary had structured his network of agents so that if he were killed they would melt away for fear of punishment themselves.

'I know how hard you work for me, don't worry,' the Emerald Tiger answered with the smile of a shark, 'For this valuable piece of information I would like to give you an estate in the south — see to the necessary details and come back to me. Meantime, on your way out tell General Kazunga I wish to see him: it is time for us to sell some of our diamond reserves and buy some decent weaponry. I think we've got a good use to put it to!'

'I will convey the message. Good day your Majesty.'

The man bowed and walked out. Once alone the Emerald Tiger turned and drawing aside the hanging tapestry behind his throne opened the concealed door and made his way down the secret passageway. Sadly he had given away two of the three American girls in anticipation of his new slaves being delivered. Thankfully though he had kept the blonde; the most pleasing of the three. Right now he wanted to wreak his revenge on the man who ruled the province across the great lake. But he would have to wait. He could though, vent some of his pent up energy on the girl. It had been a while since he'd spent much time with her.

The girl was sleeping on the floor on the mattress they'd given her. A locked collar and leash was secured around her throat, the leash being anchored to a large iron ring bolted to the floor. There were leather cuffs fastened and padlocked around the girls wrists and ankles but these were not clipped together so the girl was able to enjoy the freedom to move her arms and legs while she rested. His two servants who looked after his slaves were gone and the room was still and quiet. The door to the room had glided silently open and the girl remained sleeping peacefully, unaware that she was being watched. The Emerald Tiger pressed one of the switches on the wall and it took only a few moments for his two eunuchs to come running in response to his summons. The girl remained asleep; blissfully unaware of what was about to befall her. The Emerald Tiger quietly, calmly told his servants what he wanted and the men nodded to show their understanding. Silently they collected the equipment they needed and then they closed in on the sleeping girl.

The Emerald Tiger watched as the girl was abruptly woken, a ball gag being forced into her mouth before she even knew what was happening. She was still sleep- dazed as one man fastened the gag's strap at the back of her head and the other man jerked her arms behind her back. The man then deftly clipped her wrist cuffs together, pinning the girl's arms behind her slender back. The Emerald Tiger felt his cock hardening quickly as he watched the girl being forced onto her chest and her legs bent backwards. Her ankle cuffs were then clipped to her wrists and the girl was effectively hog-tied before she'd even had time to come to her senses. So unexpected and ruthless was the assault that the girl was in a wild panic and struggling frantically. The Emerald Tiger smiled with grim satisfaction as he watched his men pick her up and haul her up onto the bench that served so well as the platform for many tortures. She was shaking her head vigorously and her pretty blue eyes were wide with fear. He smiled at her with insincere sympathy.

'Now, I wonder little girl, can you guess what's going to happen to you next?'

The girl groaned through the gag and though her words were quite incomprehensible her alarmed expression clearly demonstrated that she knew all too well what sort of ordeal she was about to be put through.

* * *

'You've no idea how lucky you are Lara. With me to look after you, you've nothing to fear. But if you had fallen into the hands of the Emerald Tiger, well...'

The woman left her sentence unfinished and smiled as she regarded Lara. Lara closed her eyes for a moment, savouring the deliciously heady feeling of the whip trailing across her bare back. She shuddered, knowing what was about to happen and pulled nervously with her arms against the straps that held her arms stretched above her head. The straps twisted and being toughened rubber they gave a little against her weight. Lara glanced down at the floor as her bare toes managed, for a brief moment, to gain a better purchase on the polished wood.

The pull exerted on her stretched body gave her just enough pain to make her feel breathless and helplessly vulnerable without actually making her suffering unbearable. The pain in her acutely stretched arms was complemented by the piquant pulling on her nipples by delicate, silver weights. She gazed down at her naked body and stared mesmerised for a moment by the shiny little weights dangling from the clips that squeezed her nipples. At first the tightness had been too painful and as her nipples had swollen and darkened to a deep purple, Lara had cried out and writhed, certain that it was more than she could bear. It wasn't though: her training at MacKennan's hands had been no worse and she already knew deep down that after the initial shock of the clamps biting into her delicate flesh, the pain would quickly become as much a sexual stimulant as a form of torture.

'Okay Lara, time for your morning orgasm.'

Lara sighed as she felt the familiar latex girdle being fitted

218

around her slender body. The plastic was cool against the bare insides of her thighs and she groaned as she felt the first phallus brush its broad, smooth head against her sex. She had already lost track of how many days had started this way... the routine ritual kept her now in a continued state of expectancy and her pussy seemed perpetually aroused. Doubtless this was just the effect that the woman wanted.

'Uhhh...mmm...'

Lara squirmed more urgently as the second phallus was pressed against the crater of her anus. The latex shafts were slick with lubricating oil and as the woman pulled the girdle up at the back Lara sighed, tossing her head in ecstasy as both her passageways were speared then filled.

'Doesn't that feel good?'

'Yes...' Lara answered breathlessly, nodding her agreement. She dreamily watched the woman as she fastened the girdle just below her waist. Obligingly she tightened the girth strap as far as it would go, leaving Lara a little breathless and the shiny latex snug between her legs and firm against her sex, just the way she loved it. She could feel the lubricating gel trickling out of her pussy and seeping between the folds of her vulva, that were pressed against each other by the rubber girdle. The woman stepped back and picked up the little black remote control box that worked the electric motor chips in the girdle. Lara gazed expectantly at the woman, wondering what she might subject her to first.

The woman was perhaps ten years older than Lara and from the Europa State Fifteen, that had once been called Sweden. She was tall, with long platinum blonde hair and bright blue eyes. Her pale skin was accentuated by her penchant for black clothes: today high leather boots, a short lycra shirt and an acetate T-shirt that clung to her body exaggerating her breasts and emphasising her narrow waist. Kristina was the mistress of the man who owned the safari park and like him she enjoyed nothing better than sexually tormenting the young girls he captured and stocked his park with.

219

'Now then darling... which way would you like to feel the pressure today?'

The woman lightly brushed her thumb over one dial on the device she held and Lara gasped, twisting against the cords that held her dangling helplessly as the phallus in her anus expanded.

'Please... enough... too big...' Lara sighed, tossing her head from side to side.

The woman smiled and flicked a little switch then brushed the same dial again with her thumb. This time the phallus in her anus lengthened and the head thickened even more. Lara moaned plaintively and she knew that she'd climax swiftly at this rate. The woman had quickly learnt what Lara liked and responded to. She had soon got the full measure of her prisoner and knew how to make her come to order. With a few weeks of girdle training, she'd conditioned Lara to obligingly come for her as often as it pleased her. Mixed with the pleasure that the girdle offered was the pain of the whip and the heady combination had reduced Lara to a devoted slavegirl who craved attention as often as it was offered.

'Are we feeling rather aroused?' the woman asked, tauntingly.

Before Lara could respond the hard leather of the whip licked viciously against the bare skin of her back making her jerk violently and cry out in alarm.

'Too hard...hurts... please...' Lara begged.

The woman laughed scornfully and gave the whip another expert flick of her wrist. The coil of black leather snaked through the air and cut across Lara's thighs making her writhe and twist as she dangled helplessly by her outstretched arms.

'Can't take anymore...stop it...let me go...'

The whip hissed through the air and sliced high across Lara's back, burning a line like fire across her skin just below her shoulder blades.

'It's not too hard darling,' the woman stepped close behind her and used the handle of the whip to lift her trembling chin.

Lara shivered apprehensively as she felt the woman's other hand stroke down her bare body.

'A few little red lines that fade... no, that's not too hard, believe me. So, how are we feeling?'

Lara squirmed as the woman traced the edge of the latex girdle with one fingertip. Her nails were long and sharply curved and Lara caught her breath nervously as she felt them tracing a line across her skin.

'Now, what next I wonder?'

As the woman spoke she held out the little black control box for Lara to see and with her thumb she flicked the switch to another setting and then pressed her thumb over the button. The phallus embedded in Lara's pussy began vibrating and Lara sighed with pleasure.

'Does that feel good? A little deeper perhaps? A little more vigorous?'

The phallus thickened and the vibrations became more forceful. Lara moaned and closing her eyes, let the delicious sensations wash through her. Just as her fevered panting told the woman that she was about to climax, the phallus in her anus enlarged a little more and the sensation triggered her orgasm.

'Good girl... good girl.'

'Stop... stop...uhhh...please...'

The phallus was still vibrating powerfully and with her pussy aching from her climax it was too much for Lara to bear.

'Oh dear, is that a little too intense for you? Poor Lara.'

With the handle of the whip Kristina lightly tapped the weights dangling from the clamps fastened to Lara's nipples. Lara gave a fevered groan then shook her head vigorously in objection as the phallus in her rectum expanded. With a choked cry Lara dragged down against the cords holding her arms as another climax washed over her exhausted body.

* * *

'Let me explain what results I expect General Kazunga.'

As the Emerald Tiger spoke he stroked the tethered girl's breasts gathering their fullness into his palms and gently squeezing them. The girl watched him silent and wide-eyed.

'The man who has made a mockery of me has his main safari camp in the Amaran valley. You will encircle it under cover of darkness.'

As he spoke the Emerald Tiger slipped a noose of fine cord around one of the girl's generous breasts. She looked at it with an alarmed expression, her breathing quickening now. The General glanced at the girl. It was the blonde American his Monarch had held prisoner for a year or so now. Though still young and a slim little thing, there was no way she could even try to object to what was happening to her. She hung upside, bound, her limbs hog-tied. A broad leather padded gag smothered her mouth and rendered her silent. Only with her wide, pleading eyes could she demonstrate her distress.

'Encircle his camp, General,' the Emerald Tiger instructed, tightening the noose around the breast. The dangling girl began struggling, the ropes swaying as her body writhed, the leather cuffs that bound her ankles and wrists creaking as she twisted.

'Trap his men there and make them try to fight their way out: that way their casualties will be far worse than yours.'

The General nodded his agreement, struggling to divert his gaze from the spectacle of the struggling girl.

'The more trapped his men feel and the longer they are surrounded the more desperate to break free they'll become.'

As the man spoke he bound the cord repeatedly around the girl's breast, drawing it tighter with each turn, so that it was soon a ripe cone of trapped crimson flesh that bulged below the binding. Tears were running down the girl's cheeks and she was shaking her head frantically. Through the heavy gag her pleading could just be heard.

'Send another force of your men to his harbour on the lakeside. Surround it in the same way from the land-ward side.'

As he spoke the Emerald Tiger dealt with the girl's other

breast in a similar fashion.

'Once his men there are cut off, they'll use his boats to try to escape and get help. Then we use the new missiles that we're fitting to the helicopters and we'll pick them off.'

The Emerald Tiger smiled and delicately holding the little clamp between his finger and thumb he squeezed it open and admired its serrated jaws.

'Pick them off one by one.'

As he repeated the sentence he fastened a clamp over first one of the girl's nipples and then the other.

The General stared at the girl as he was handed a small plastic box with a simple switch. He gazed at the fine wires that trailed from the box to the clamps that were fastened around the girl's nipples. The girl looked imploringly at him and shook her head begging him not to respond to the other man's instruction.

'Go on General, she'll enjoy it. It's nothing she can't bear.'

General Kazunga did as he was told, secretly more than happy to watch the girl suffer. The second he twisted the switch she jerked and writhed, twisting frantically against the ropes that held her suspended. She didn't faint though and plainly the electric charge was just enough to make her squirm but no more.

'Now General, switch it off and feel her sex.'

He did as he was instructed and his fingers found her soaking.

'She is addicted to sexual torment. She worships the whip and is a slave to suffering. What's more my dear General, deal effectively with our enemy and she is yours.'

'Your Majesty is too kind.'

'One last thing. The three girls that I recently bought and had stolen from me. Bring them back to me and I will give you an estate in the south. You will deserve such a reward. I had planned to give the estate to our Foreign Secretary but I have just received the tragic news that he has been involved in a fatal accident.'

'A traffic accident, your Majesty?'

'I have no idea,' the Emerald Tiger shrugged ambivalently, 'I did not specify what sort of accident it was to be.'

The two men looked at the girl as she dangled helplessly before them. The General lifted his hand to his nostrils and inhaled the pungent aroma of the girl's musky arousal.

'I will look forward to dealing with your enemies and returning to collect my reward, your Highness.'

The General gave a low bow, turned and left the room. The Emerald Tiger gestured to his two eunuchs who had been waiting in the wings to step forwards.

'Untie her and hold her down over the bench. I need to use her. Remove the clamps from her breasts but don't bother untying the cords.'

A moment later and the girl was held face down over the bench by the two eunuchs. The Emerald Tiger glanced at her as she struggled; perhaps having her bound breasts pressed down against the bench was hurting her. Well, she wouldn't be like it for long and she was young and resilient.

'Spread your legs for me girl.'

The girl did as she was told. The Emerald Tiger smiled, drew his engorged cock from his robes and guided it into the girl's sex. She was delightfully wet but regrettably not as tight as he would have liked. There was, he reflected, nothing as satisfying as forcing his cock into the tight pussy of an objecting girl who wasn't quite ready to accommodate him. Well, he'd use the girl now and then leave her for a while. Once she was asleep, he would return with his eunuchs and take her by surprise. The thought of this brought him quickly to a satisfying orgasm and suddenly all his problems and worries and seemed to melt away.

CHAPTER TWELVE

The six men sat facing the campfire, the bright orange flames leaping high into the night sky and illuminating their faces. Beyond the lights of their camp the darkness was impenetrable. The men were eating and drinking and laughing at each other's stories. Occasionally one of them would glance over his shoulder to look at the girl. She stood watching them from below a tree. Her arms were bound tightly behind her back with rope and a she wore a halter and bridle. The bar of the bridle forced her mouth open a little and gave her the appearance of snarling. The leather straps of the bridle were snug against the cheeks of her pretty face and from a steel ring on the top of the bridle there extended a fine rope which was bound around one of the lower branches of the tree a few feet above her head. The girl's sleek body was glossy with perspiration, which glistened in the firelight. Her boots and bikini lay discarded on the other side of the camp.

The hunt had taken longer than they'd anticipated. Annabella had given them a good run for their money and after capturing her late in the afternoon they elected to spend the night out in the bush: a suitably fitting end to the day's strenuous activity. After all, they could cope for a night without their creature comforts and tomorrow the hot baths and clean sheets of a comfortable bed would be all the more welcome after a night of roughing it with their native levies. The safari park's owner had applauded their decision and congratulated them on entering so well into the spirit of the adventure. He would return the next morning by helicopter to collect them and their trophy.

Their trophy, they all agreed, had been well earned. The girl had managed to hide and evade them for nearly a whole day. In the end they had brought in the natives to help them search for her. It was late in the afternoon by the time the girl had been forced to break cover. Sprinting like a gazelle she had been brought down by a lucky shot. The man had her in his sights for only a few seconds before she'd run into a stand of trees. His dart had hit her left thigh. Once cornered, as she was still conscious enough to lash out with her nails at the first man who approached her, they had let the natives net her. A lasso had then been fastened around one of her ankles and with the rope fed over a tree branch she'd been hauled upside down. Still hissing and spitting, they had then bound her arms behind her back and fitted the halter and bridle.

Now, she stood sullenly watching them while they finished their supper. After they had eaten and drunk all they wanted they would then take it in turns to enjoy the girl, though first they unanimously agreed, she deserved a good whipping for causing them so much hard work.

They had been told that there had been another girl released into the park yesterday as well. Had they caught the first one quickly they could have gone on and hunted the second. She was slim and long legged, she'd out-run them if they weren't clever, the man in charge had warned them with a wry smile. Well, it was too dark now for hunting and the girl would have to stay out in the bush for the night. She would have no worries fending for herself, there were no wild animals anymore. There hadn't been for years. They could go after her tomorrow if they felt like it. Meantime she could enjoy a brief taste of freedom.

* * *

Pippa decided that under cover of darkness was her best chance of escape. She had heard the commotion of the hunt for Annabella and had glimpsed two of the hunters in the distance late in the afternoon. Then an hour or two later there had been a solitary rifle shot. Not long after that she heard the chanting of some natives; they sounded jubilant and she guessed that Annabella had been caught. Dusk had come quickly and Pippa was faced with a choice: find somewhere to sleep for the night or use the hours of darkness to try to escape. She opted for the latter, telling herself that it was a sensible decision. Within a few hours she was bitterly regretting not having chosen to curl up for the night in some undergrowth.

The crack commandos of the Emerald Tiger had landed on the park's shore under cover of darkness the night before. During the day they had laid up concealed in undergrowth and used binoculars to watch the day's activity. Tomorrow the main attacks would begin by which time they would already have infiltrated the enemy territory and would be wreaking havoc with their lines of communications. Tonight though they would take the camp of the six wealthy foreigners. They were under orders to bring back all the girls they could unharmed but to kill the men if they resisted them. If they surrendered then the Emerald Tiger would try to ransom them to their families. Failing that he would feed them to his pet alligators.

Pippa imagined she was walking silently but the men encircling her demonstrated far more stealth than she would have imagined possible. The first she knew that she was not alone was when a hand clamped across her mouth. In the palm of the hand was a broad piece of adhesive tape of extreme stickiness and when the hand was removed a second later, Pippa found that the tape had effectively sealed her mouth.

A black hood was whisked expertly over her head from behind the moment the hand was withdrawn from her mouth and a drawstring pulled snugly around her neck. Plunged into a sense-muffling darkness blacker than the night itself, Pippa struggled helplessly against the numerous pairs of hands that dragged her off her feet and quickly subdued her. Pinned face down on the ground, the skimpy bikini she'd been given to wear was torn from her and half a dozen pairs of hands pulled her arms and legs widely apart.

As the commander of the unit of commandos took his turn first to enjoy her, Pippa relaxed, whoever's hands she'd fallen into no longer concerned her, if this was all they wanted, she didn't mind. As the man shafted her, Pippa obligingly writhed and twisted as she guessed would have been expected from

227

any normal nineteen year old girl who'd just been ambushed by a handful of men. After several of the men had taken their turns with her, she'd climaxed several times herself and her pussy was aching a little more than just pleasurably. These men were very big and rather hard on her, she thought and she could do with a rest. As perhaps the fourth or fifth men rammed his cock into her Pippa shook her head more vigorously and groaned through the tape that sealed her mouth so effectively. If she had known then just how many men there were in the commando unit, she might have objected with more determination whilst she still had some strength left.

* * *

Lara felt the engorged cock slide deeper into her mouth as she sucked greedily. She was on her knees, her ankles and calves bound together by leather belts. Her arms were drawn outstretched to either side of her, ropes bound around her wrists held by two of the group of men who encircled her. She was uncertain quite how many of them there were because she'd been blindfolded.

She had been woken without warning. One minute she was blissfully asleep then the next she was being blindfolded. Of course she had struggled but there were at least four men holding her down so she had no chance. Still, she had struggled because she liked to. It goaded the men and heightened her pleasure. Once blindfolded they dragged her from her bed and took her to what they referred to as the games room.

Quite how long she had been held, she couldn't be sure. The days and nights had passed in a daze, a continuous round of sex games where she was always the toy that was played with. She'd spent several days on the boat and most of her time then had been with Kristina. They had landed at a small harbour and Lara vaguely remembered a bumpy LandRover journey of half a day or more. She had been blindfolded for the whole trip, so when they arrived at their destination, she had really no idea where it was. She had heard that Annabella and Pippa had been released into the park for the hunters. That had sounded so ominous that Lara had bent over backwards to please her new Master and be spared a similar fate. In truth she had spent more time bent over facing forwards so that she might please the man and thankfully he had seemed well pleased by how she devoted herself to pleasuring him.

Now, she sucked dutifully on the cock; blindfolded and not knowing the man who stood over her made it easier to focus on the task in hand; or rather in mouth. The organ was not that long but it was thick and hot and copious amounts of pre-come fluid were dribbling from its swollen tip as she bathed it with long licks of her tongue. The man sighed appreciatively and his fingers tightened their grasp on her tousled hair. Lara knew he was close to coming. Practice had taught her to gauge the signs so finely that she could tell, almost always, just exactly how much longer the man would last before he erupted. This one was now very close. She could make him come within half a minute if she wanted; if she sucked in the way that brought them to climax most effectively. It was amusing though to delay things. They usually enjoyed that and when they finally shot their load it always seemed to be more intense: at any rate their groans of satisfaction were invariably more vociferous.

The shaft in her mouth began to throb and the man groaned deeply, heralding his orgasm. Lara stopped sucking so voraciously and contented herself with merely licking the broad head of the cock. The man sighed and pulled on her hair encouraging her to resume sucking him. Lara furled her lips around the cock head and almost immediately she sensed the man tensing and his shaft pushed upwards. A second later and his semen splashed into her throat. Dutifully she sucked and then licked him dry.

'Your turn, which way do you want her?'

'Get her against the bench, I'll give her a caning to soften up those thighs then we'll have them spread and I'll take her from behind.'

'From behind or up her behind?'

'Now that's a good idea, let's see if she likes that.'

Lara made no objection as they dragged her across to the bench and her stomach was jammed up against the wooden table edge. Her arms were drawn outstretched and someone placed a hand against her back and encouraged her to bend across the table. As the cool wood pressed against her breasts there came the stinging blow of a cane against her left thigh.

'Oww!'

The men laughed. The cane snapped down against her right thigh.

Thwack!

'Oww!' Lara jerked against the hands that held her wrists and pulled her arms. She knew how disappointed they would be if she didn't struggle. Of course the cane hurt but the level of pain it produced was something that she was now so familiar with she was almost used to it. More than that, if she admitted it to herself, the pain brought with it pleasure for her. It was now so intertwined with sexual attention from her tormentors that she craved the taste of punishment as she knew what else would be coming to her.

Thwack!

The cane struck her left thigh again but close under the curve of her buttock.

'Spread your legs darling and the punishment will stop. It's time for you to enjoy a cock up that tight little arse of yours. You'd like that wouldn't you?'

Lara kept her legs close together and was quickly rewarded with another stinging blow from the cane.

Thwack!

'Oww! Stop it! Let me go!' she protested, knowing just the pleading words that they liked to hear.

Thwack!

'I can't bear anymore! Please, you're hurting me!' Lara shook her head and assumed her most pathetic, pleading tone of voice.

Thwack!

Thwack!

She gave a howl of protest and wriggling her bum, spread her legs obligingly wide then she remained motionless; bent face down across the bench, murmuring plaintively. Swiftly a thumb pushed its way into her anus.

'No... please... not that way...' she simpered, wriggling a bit now and pulling weakly against the men who held her wrists.

The thumb was withdrawn and two fingers forced into her in its place. When the fingers twisted inside her, Lara shook her head and tried to pull away.

'If she's going to struggle we may as well strap her!'

'This isn't fair! Let me go!' Lara protested, secretly delighted that they were now going to strap her down. Ever since MacKennan had given Lara her first taste of being bound and rendered utterly helpless, she'd relished the heady feeling. Of course it had taken time for her to reconcile how good it made her feel but now there was no denying it.

The straps were broad leather belts. The men fastened one around each of her thighs and these were drawn apart so her thighs were held spread and pinned to the table legs. Another strap was drawn tightly down over the small of her back just above the curves of her rump. Fastened to the bench it held her firmly down but just for good measure another strap was stretched across just below her shoulder blades and it too was drawn tight so her chest was kept pressed firmly against the bench. Lara's arms were then drawn behind her back and her wrist cuffs clipped onto rings on the belt below her shoulder blades. Now quite helpless, the men took their time, tormenting her and revelling in her pleading and the spectacle of her struggling futilely against the sturdy straps.

For maybe ten minutes Lara was subjected to more stinging blows from the cane. Almost all were directed against her rump, which was left throbbing and acutely tender. Throughout the punishment Lara sobbed and cried and pleaded with the

231

men but they ignored her protests just as she knew they would. Satisfied that she was rendered into the condition they wanted: her body washed with pain and her energy all spent in futile struggling, the men moved onto stage two of her punishment.

'Right then Lara, ready for something else now?'

'Please, no more... leave me alone...' Lara begged, her mind racing at the thought of what lay in store for her.

Hands caressed her aching rump and drew apart the soft globes of her arse. Lara gave a plaintive sigh as something hard and bluntly pointed was pushed against the exposed crater of her anus.

'No...don't...please...stop...'

She could feel the device, she guessed it was a vibrator or butt plug, being pushed into her rectum and for a moment there was that instinctive fear of being helpless as her body was invaded. What if they pushed it too far or it really was too much for her to bear? She struggled against the straps that held her pinned down.

'No! Uhh... stop...it...please!'

The butt plug was driven remorselessly into her: it was very long but she'd experienced worse, or better if she were to admit how it affected her. She sighed, tossing her head from side to side as the sensation of having her rear filled got more and more intense. Then she realised with a sudden shock that the device buried inside her was growing warmer and then hotter.

'That's enough! Really, please, stop it!' she begged, not knowing whether she meant what she was saying or not. Her feelings were too confused now, perhaps a part of her really did want them to stop the torture but the hard truth was that she secretly revelled now in her role as submissive sex slave.

'Something the matter Lara?' asked a taunting voice.

Lara writhed and twisted against the straps, imagining how she must look to the men standing around her. Naked, tethered, her slender body slick with sweat, she struggled helplessly. Though she knew it would be impossible she tried to expel

232

the device with her rectum muscles but it had a flared end and she quickly recognised the fact that she was completely reliant on a helping hand to extricate it. Her own hands were bound and the men watching her were content to leave it in her a while longer and force her to suffer the giddy heat a few more minutes.

'That should have warmed the bitch up nicely.'

Lara groaned as the butt plug was abruptly withdrawn from her aching rear.

'She'll be very sensitive there now, so go gently on her.'

There was a rush of laughter and the next thing Lara experienced was the sensation of a cock being driven up inside her.

'Please stop!'

Lara jerked her arms and legs frantically as the thick cock was almost completely withdrawn from her acutely tender body and then rammed mercilessly back into her. Her protest was loud enough and seemed sufficiently genuine to provoke a response but it was not what she might have hoped. Hands grasped her hair and drew her head back and a hard rubber ball was jammed into her mouth forcing her jaws wide. Gurgling an objection and shaking her head as best she could Lara felt a leather strap being buckled tight against her cheeks. The cock in her rear passage withdrew and this time when it was driven back into her all Lara could manage in objection was a muffled groan through the gag. To her shame though, her complete helplessness had served to heighten her arousal, either that or the sensation of being sodomized was responsible, but whatever the cause, before the man using her had ejaculated Lara herself came and her tensing body was enough to arouse suspicions.

'I reckon the bitch has just come.'

The cock withdrew from her rectum and fingers slid into the slick folds of her sex. Lara shuddered in the afterglow of her climax.

'She's obviously enjoying herself. I'm sure she won't object if we all take a turn.'

Hands drew apart the globes of her rump again and the cock was driven back into her tender rear passage. Lara had too little energy left to struggle much now and after the man had finished with her and another took his turn she lay passively whilst she was used, her body pleasantly washed with feelings of pain and pleasure in equal measure. By the time the second man had finished with her Lara was utterly exhausted and her tethered body was now aching so much she would have begged them to let her alone if only she could have spoken. The gag though kept her silenced and to her utter dismay a third man took up position behind her spread and tethered legs. Lara was resigning herself to more torment when she heard the door to the room open and a breathless female voice blurt out news so startling that for a second there was a stunned silence.

'Enemy attack! It must be troops of the Emerald Tiger. Your guards can't hold them. They outnumber us and are out gunning us!'

The terror stricken voice was that of Kristina and the voice that answered was that of the safari park's owner.

'Okay gentlemen, everyone for himself.'

There was a rush of exiting feet and then a second's silence before the man spoke again.

'Kristina, untie the girl and bring her to the heli-pad. She's too valuable to leave behind and I wouldn't give the Emerald Tiger the satisfaction of recovering her.'

Lara's poor arms and legs were aching so much after her ordeal that it was all she could do to stumble after Kristina who dragged her hurriedly along the corridors and then up a flight of stairs. She hadn't bothered, or didn't dare waste time binding Lara's hands and trusted her prisoner to follow her. With warnings about what would happen to her if she fell into the hands of the Emerald Tiger fresh in her mind though, Lara was more than willing to follow the other woman. When they flung themselves through a door and out onto the roof, the cold night air against Lara's naked skin felt like she'd been subjected to an icy bath and her dazed senses cleared quickly as she took in the sight around her. Flashes of gunfire lit up the night sky and there was the orange glow of fire where buildings were already ablaze. The sound of gunfire was all around but then it was drowned out as the helicopter's jet engine roared into life. The two girls sprinted for the sanctuary it offered and tumbled gratefully inside even as the machine's skis lifted off from the yellow circle marked on the floodlit roof. Lara grabbed the door handle and dragged the door closed as the helicopter swung away from the roof and suddenly there was a gaping blackness below them. Copying the woman sat on the leather seat next to her, Lara pulled her safety belt around her bare stomach and clipped it securely in place. She looked out of the window and saw only darkness. Already the powerful jet helicopter had whisked them to safety. She glanced down at the safety belt strap tight against her bare skin. It was a familiar feeling and deeply comforting now.

Cintinued in '*Darkest Dreams*'.

Silver Moon

Enslaving Anna
Giselle Lorimer

www.silvermoon.co.uk

ADULT FICTION

Anna is one of the most unforgettable of Silver Moon heroines. From the moment she reports for work at Sinclair Precision Components; pure, innocent and trusting her employers recognise that she has hidden depths and set about bringing them to light.

She rapidly finds herself in the hands of a centuries old slave dealing concern and is ruthlessly trained for a life of sexual servitude.

Giselle Lorimer's first book for Silver Moon vividly traces the progression of the sweet natured Anna from innocence to total subjugation with a concentrated eroticism we have seldom published before. Giselle brings her own understanding of female submissiveness to bear with devastating effect and the final acts of submission rank very high in Silver Moon's firmament.

Silver Moon

ADULT FICTION

BOUND to PLEASE

Giselle Lorimer

Charlotte is the classic 'rich bitch', a self-obsessed flirt who is concerned only with her own pleasure. She indulges herself once too often and is seen masturbating. Suddenly finding herself in the hands of dominant and cruel men, Charlotte is catapulted into a series of trials and tribulations which have only one thing in common: each one involves more humiliation than the last. And each time she is convinced that she has reached rock bottom, her masters dream up something else, until she at last comes to realise that her destiny really does lie in being Bound to Please. And there is nothing she can do about it.

Giselle Lorimer's first book for Silver Moon: 'Enslaving Anna' marked a brilliant debut and signalled the arrival of a major new female talent in the genre. 'Bound to Please' is an assured and highly erotic follow-up recounting the lovely heroine's step-by-step descent into complete subjugation.

Ultimate Slaves

Denise La Croix

ADULT FICTION
Silver Moon

Kerry Smith's job interview turns swiftly into a nightmare as the beautiful youngster is abducted and sold by the sinister Salim.

Enslaved by a man she initially knows only as The Master, she and her friend Amber undergo many frightening rituals to slake the lusts of his guests. But when they escape things get much worse and they find themselves on the island Taransay. There a top secret laboratory is pursuing depraved goals and Kerry and Amber find themselves at risk of becoming helpless slaves' to the depraved lusts of anyone their masters want them to serve.

Curiosity may have killed the cat but for Sarah it leads to a life changing experience. When she decides to try on a piece of fetish clothing her boyfriend brings home for a photo shoot, her punishment launches them both onto a bizarre career path. Performing for ever more demanding audiences, Sarah sinks deeper and deeper into the role of submissive.

But once she is taken away to train for a mysterious club and from then on there is no turning back…